T0204637

hearts lie

Theresa Brisko

Theresa Brisko

TJB Creative, LLC

HEARTS LIE
Theresa Brisko
TJB Creative, LLC

TJB Creative, LLC, St. Louis, MO
Copyright ©2016 Theresa Brisko
All rights reserved.

Contact requests can be made to TJBCreativeLLC@gmail.com

Editor: Lisbeth Tanz, www.fuzzydogllc.com
Cover graphic design: Elyse Rudin
Cover and Interior design: Davis Creative, DavisCreative.com

ISBN: 9781732583207 (Paperback)
ISBN: 9781732583214 (eBook)

Library of Congress Cataloging-in-Publication Data
Library of Congress Control Number: 2018909467
Author Theresa Brisko
Book Title: Hearts Lie
ISBN: 9781732583207
Library of Congress subject headings:
       1. Fic019000 Fiction/Literary 2. Fic027430 Fiction/Romance/Workplace
       3. Fic042040 Fiction/Christian/Romance

Publication year 2018

Chapter 1

Lille France 1981

Tracy leaned against the rough bark of the ancient oak tree, closed her eyes, and smiled. A light wind had kicked up and rustled the leaves above her in the late summer sun. She breathed in deeply, marveling at the strong scent of the nearby rose bushes. *I don't think I've ever been anywhere that smelled this amazing.* She felt her body relax in the warmth of the day.

"Hey, you're not falling asleep on me, are you?" Ryan teased.

Tracy's eyes popped open. "No, never!" Then she added with a hint of mock sarcasm, "I was waiting *patiently* for you to respond. Have you forgotten the sentence? I said, 'La jeune fille entra dans la chambre et salua son pere avec un bisous.'"

Ryan sat up, adjusting the book that lay between them on the blanket.

"I know." He continued, "The young girl entered the room and greeted her father with a kiss." He looked over to gauge her response.

"Correct!" she said with a satisfied grin.

Ryan leaned forward, his face inches from hers. "I much prefer cette magnifique jeune fille devrait me donner bisous, however."

Tracy's cheeks flushed at his request that she give him kisses. *Is this really happening to me?* she wondered. He moved closer, touching his nose to hers. She laughed and playfully pushed him back.

1

"We have work to do, mon amour."

"Yes ma'am," he murmured as he leaned forward again to nuzzle her neck.

Sighing, Tracy pushed the book aside. Ryan pulled away slightly, his eyes searching her face. She traced the bridge of his nose with her finger, pausing as she touched his lips. The breeze ruffled his unruly sandy blond hair. "I just can't resist you," she whispered as their lips touched. Ryan pulled her close and gently eased her down to the softness of the blanket and the cushioning ground underneath.

"You are so beautiful," he said, his voice thick with emotion. Their gaze was locked, each knowing, feeling the other's thoughts.

For a time, the only sounds were the water flowing lazily in the nearby river, the birds chattering endlessly in the surrounding trees, and the murmurs young lovers make when lost in each other.

Content in Ryan's arms, Tracy broke the silence. "I wish this summer could go on forever." She turned to look into Ryan's eyes.

Ryan stroked her cheek. "Don't worry. We'll find a way to close the distance between New York and California when we get back to the States."

Just then, a Frisbee landed on the edge of their blanket and broke the tension that was developing. Within seconds a young boy, maybe six years old, came running to retrieve the errant disk. "Je suis désolé," said the boy apologetically. He bowed his head quickly and off he went. Tracy and Ryan both laughed. "He sure came out of nowhere," Ryan said.

Tracy eased up on her elbow and gazed over Ryan's body at the children playing. "I guess life can be unpredictable sometimes," she said almost to herself.

Ryan rubbed her cheek with his finger. "Well, what I don't want to leave to chance is how to contact you when we leave France," he said. "I just wish you would give me your phone number or address, so I can get in touch with you."

"Not right now," she said a bit too emphatically. "I'm just a little unsure and confused about how our relationship might affect my role as your tutor. I don't believe I'm breaking any rules because I'm a student here just the same as you are, but I really need this internship to finish my MBA. I never expected this to happen."

"Me either," Ryan echoed with a smile.

Tracy said, "I have your personal information in the student profile database. I'll call you just as soon as I get back. I leave the day after you. It won't be long. I promise."

"Tracy," he whispered softly, "not hearing your voice for even one day will be too long."

She leaned over and kissed him playfully. "I'm just glad you're over eighteen, so I'm not exactly robbing the cradle."

"Oh right," he said, "you're *really* old. Heck, when I'm twenty-five, and you're, what, thirty-two, seven years won't mean anything."

She chuckled. "I needed that. You sound so confident." She paused and then forged ahead, her eyes shifting from his to the ground. "I guess I'm also worried that when we leave Lille soon, you'll get busy with school and soccer and forget all about me. I'm sure UCLA is a busy place, like NYU but with a lot of young, tanned coeds who will be making moves on the hot, second-year soccer star, Ryan Kupford. How can I expect to compete against them from almost 3,000 miles away?"

3

Tracy's voice became more anxious as her thoughts became words. "I have no money to travel, student loans to begin paying off and it's a tough economy, so who knows what will happen." She searched Ryan's eyes for answers.

"Shh, hush," he said as he moved his finger to her lips. "Tracy, baby, I'm here for you always."

Tracy's mood lightened with his words of assurance, and she smiled.

Ryan sat up on the blanket and cupped Tracy's face in his hands. He looked intently into her big, warm brown eyes and confessed, "I love you Tracy, my Lily of France."

With tears of joy welling in her eyes, she responded, "I love you, Ryan, always and forever with all my heart." They embraced, sharing a long, passionate kiss.

Ryan fell fast asleep as he lay next to her on the soft blanket in the cool shade of the tree. He was physically exhausted from a long day of soccer practice under the hot sun of a cloudless sky. Tracy stayed awake though she dared not move for fear of waking Ryan from much-needed rest.

Tracy reminisced about the events that led to her being with Ryan on this glorious afternoon.

Their time together as a couple was quite brief, just the last month of the summer session. Early on, Ryan was one of the thirty or so members of the US soccer teams at the Universite Catholique de Lille this summer that she was assigned to tutor. The goal was to help the players learn basic French language and the local customs, so they could communicate and maximize their experience in Lille. Tracy felt honored to have been selected for this opportunity by the committee of NYU professors. Their decision was

4

based on her understanding of French culture, command of the language and overall high standing at the university.

Tracy thought back to the first few sessions with the players. She chuckled to herself as she remembered how clinical they were! Everyone seemed to be on his best behavior and just getting to know one another. During the ensuing weeks, she could feel the camaraderie among the players increase as they got more familiar with each other and individual personalities were exposed. The mood was lighter, and even her interactions with the players became friendlier. Although she was their tutor, she was also a student, albeit slightly older, finishing her master's degree. Most of these guys were second or third-year undergraduates in their late teens or early twenties.

As time passed, she couldn't help but notice Ryan, since he was usually the center of attention among his peers. He had an easygoing personality, an infectious smile and a laugh that filled the room. It seemed he always had a joke or story to share, which amped up the energy level of the group. Initially, Tracy was concerned that a student like that might prove to be disruptive in class, especially since she understood these guys were here to play soccer, or "football" as it's called all over the world, except the United States. Their real reason for being in France was to learn new skills from the European camp instructors. The hope was that, once the players were back at college, they might be remembered and noticed by the professional league scouts who frequented both the practice sessions and the evening scrimmages. Thankfully, Tracy's early concerns about Ryan were unfounded. Once class started, he was quiet except to offer an answer to a question or read a passage when asked. He seemed genuinely interested in the coursework.

Several weeks into the program, Ryan had approached Tracy after class one day. "Miss Ward, May I speak with you for a minute?"

"Of course, Ryan and call me Tracy, please."

"I'm really enjoying your class," he began, "though I'm struggling a bit with the language, especially conjugating verbs and choosing the proper tenses." He continued, "I'm wondering if you would consider helping me outside the classroom, maybe once or twice a week for an hour?"

Tracy was thrilled to see this desire in one of her charges and said, "I'm happy to help you, Ryan. Someday the knowledge you gain here might help you in your work or enable you to communicate more effectively with some of the international players since many Europeans speak at least conversational French."

They agreed to meet on Tuesday afternoons when the team had free time before late evening games and on Friday evenings since there were no scheduled games or practices. When the weather cooperated, they held their sessions in the garden near Tracy's cottage on the expansive grounds of the convent associated with the Universite. When the forecast called for chilly or rainy weather, they met at the school, easily finding an unoccupied room to hold their session during the summer lull.

Tracy had marveled at how quickly Ryan made progress with his language skills, catching up with most and even surpassing others in his class. Looking back, she recalled fondly how easily dialog seemed to flow between them. Some days their allotted hour came and went, and the conversation spilled over into more personal subjects. Tracy was a bit cautious in sharing, as she felt she should perhaps maintain a level of professional distance from Ryan.

She learned he was a sophomore engineering student struggling to balance the rigorous coursework with the demands of an NCAA Division I soccer program. Ryan admitted, "I'm considering changing my major to sports marketing or communications. That's what most of the jocks do."

Tracy had no desire to be judgmental about his educational choices, but she could see that he was very bright and maybe just needed to apply himself a bit more. From the sound of it, he spent most of his time hanging out with friends when he wasn't involved with soccer activities.

She offered, "I can't imagine the pressures you face as a college athlete, which leads me to wonder why you chose engineering in the first place."

"I'm good at math, and my Dad and I have always worked on cars in our free time."

Tracy pushed him a bit, "So do you like the coursework?"

"Mostly I do." Then he confessed, "It just seems like I have to study a lot more than I did in high school."

Tracy nodded. "I found that out too. College was a lot harder! But I decided my career goals were my number one priority, so I chose to focus my time and energy on my studies."

"Well, *soccer* is my number one priority." Then he added a bit sheepishly, "But I could probably put a little more effort into studying," Placing his elbows on the table between them, he leaned forward and asked, "How did you choose your major, Tracy?"

She chuckled and said, "Well, I've been hooked on making money since I was about ten years old. It all started innocently enough. I had my eye on a shiny green bicycle that my parents could not afford. It was gorgeous, complete with a banana seat and yellow and green plastic streamers hanging from the giant U-shaped handlebars! That winter, we had a lot of snow, so I took advantage of that and shoveled my neighbors' sidewalks and driveways to earn enough money to buy my bike. The next spring, I rode my bike out of the store."

Ryan laughed and said as he pretended to ride a bicycle, "I can just see you on that bike riding down the sidewalk, probably with pigtails flying in the wind!"

Tracy smiled, then turned more serious adding, "Eventually I realized that investment banking was the business for me, so I pursued finance."

Talking about her favorite subject now she continued excitedly, "The work of buying, selling, merging, and recapitalizing companies can be beneficial to owners, shareholders, employees and even customers of affected organizations. Productivity gains achieved by eliminating redundancies after an acquisition or merger can yield improved profits to reinvest in the business. The company might choose to pursue new product development or invest in machinery, equipment, or other infrastructure to grow and serve markets and customers more effectively and efficiently. Profits generated can also be used to fund further acquisitions or pay dividends to investors or owners. Cash flow is the lifeblood of business, and there are many ways to increase cash flow. A business can reduce inventory, extend their payables cycle, increase prices, and decrease expenses just to name a few. Then there's the business of underwriting a company to go from privately held to publicly traded stocks. That presents tremendous opportunities for companies and owners to realize huge inflows of capital to accelerate growth plans or monetize years of investment."

"Wow, you're really passionate about your field, Tracy!" exclaimed Ryan.

"Yes, I can't wait to put my education to work. And Ryan, there's tremendous opportunity to make personal money in this business. I'm excited about the possibility of living in a nice loft, wearing stylish clothes, eating at fine restaurants, and taking exotic vacations all over the world. Professionally my goal is to make partner before I'm forty. I've also thought about devoting time and money to developing a charitable foundation someday. I have time to fine-tune the mission, but I'm passionate about empowering young girls."

Ryan confessed that he was amazed by her focus and drive. "Until now, I've only experienced that kind of commitment and ambition in sports. I've never really thought about how that energy and passion might be transferred to a career."

As the weeks went on and their talks progressed, Ryan expressed his interest in the business and admiration for Tracy's understanding of finance and economics.

She recalled his comment one recent afternoon, "When I get back to UCLA I'm going to cut back on the partying and focus on two things, soccer and studying. Well, three things, figuring out how we can be together." Tracy smiled as her heart warmed with this recollection.

She was still lost in her thoughts when she felt Ryan stirring. As he stretched out his long, lean body, he yawned loudly. Turning his face toward Tracy, he exclaimed, "I'm as hungry as a bear coming out of hibernation! I'm officially starving!"

"Well, you're in luck. I packed a snack of cheese, bread and fresh salami for us. And grapes for dessert."

"That sounds fantastic though I've got other thoughts about dessert," he said as he grinned and winked at her.

"Hmm," Tracy mused thoughtfully. "Let's eat, and we can figure out dessert later." She smiled and shook her head at him.

After their appetites had been satiated, Ryan stood up, pulled a soccer ball from his bag and, almost instinctively began to juggle it from foot to foot.

Not pausing in his foot-work he said, "Hey Tracy." "I was just thinking; I haven't ever seen you juggle a soccer ball."

"No, you haven't. I'm sure I would end up on my backside if I tried!"

"Aw, c'mon. Here, watch me, then you try," said Ryan. He started by juggling the ball on his right foot a few times, and then switched to his left foot and then back to his right. For several moments, he switched back forth from foot to foot. His skills were showing when, without letting the ball ever touch the ground, he did the same movements using his thighs. He popped the ball hard enough to bump the ball with the top of his head before it landed precisely back on his right foot.

"That is amazing!" said Tracy clapping her hands.

Ryan handed her the ball, and she acquiesced, "Okay, I'll give it a try." She managed to drop it gently on her right foot after which it went straight to the ground. She tried it a couple more times with the same result. She persevered for a minute or so before admitting, "Clearly, I should stick to volleyball!"

"I have to admit that until recently I didn't think soccer was much more than a bunch of kids being in top physical condition running hard the whole game and developing excellent coordination skills."

Ryan laughed. "Yeah, it can look like that. So, have you changed your mind?"

"Oh yes," Tracy said nodding. "I've really enjoyed learning about the strategy of the game from you. Watching your matches has made me realize there's a lot more thinking by the players on the field as well. It amazes me to see you pass the ball to a spot where I don't see anyone, then miraculously one of your teammates arrives at exactly the same time as the ball. Timing that precise requires thoughtfulness, skill and must take a lot of practice."

"Merci beaucoup Mademoiselle Ward," said Ryan as he took a bow and kissed her hand.

Tracy blushed as she pulled him close to share a long kiss.

"You played volleyball in high school, didn't you?" asked Ryan as he held her in his arms.

"Yes, I sure did!" Tracy said as she stepped back. She added, "We won the District championship during my junior year and made it to the state semi-final. Watching you guys makes me think back to the many hours of practice my teammates, and I endured. Some people think volleyball is simple, just jump and hit the ball, but it's physically and mentally challenging. We almost endlessly repeated drills, ran sprints, performed vertical jump exercises and strength and conditioning routines. There were also set plays and configurations to memorize."

"I feel your pain!" exclaimed Ryan.

Tracy continued, "We were so fortunate to have one of the most experienced and knowledgeable coaches in Janet Daley. She was gifted both in sharing her wisdom as well as in motivating us. I loved the sense of teamwork and the competitive nature of the game. Early on, I struggled a bit with harsh criticism from Coach. "In fact," Tracy added, "it was Coach Daley who helped me recognize that my tendency to be a perfectionist was holding me back from improving. Sometimes I would give up if I didn't get it exactly right. Once I embraced failing as a learning tool, I was more willing to try new techniques, and it made me a better player."

"No question, it benefits you and the team," said Ryan. "It's also a great life lesson."

Tracy nodded. "Absolutely! You're right that it goes beyond the court, Ryan. During one of my internships, I proactively asked my manager to give me feedback on my work. I made it clear that I welcomed tough criticism to help me improve my skills and increase my knowledge. He seemed a bit surprised and told me that some of the interns weren't willing to accept hard input, which limited their growth. He said, and I quote, 'Tracy, if you want to become the smartest person in the room, you need to be open to criticism.'"

In the distance, the sound of church bells could be heard. Ryan and Tracy listened to the hollow clanging sound made by the huge metal bells which finished their serenade by announcing the time with one long strike for each hour passed.

"Wow, six o'clock already," exclaimed Ryan. "I've got to get back to the apartment for the team dinner."

"I wish we could stay here all night," Tracy said wistfully. "But I too must hurry off to dinner with the Sisters, or they might send out the local gendarme to search for me!"

Tracy gathered up the blanket and picnic basket. As she secured the basket on the ledge at the back of the bicycle, Ryan came up behind her and wrapped his arms around her. He nuzzled his face into the back of her neck. "See you later tonight my love," he murmured.

Tracy leaned back into his body though she dared not turn around or they might both be late for dinner.

"I'll be waiting for you."

Chapter 2

Brussels, Belgium

It was Tracy and Ryan's last Friday in France and a rare day with no soccer or school-related activities. They made plans to take the early morning train to nearby Brussels and explore the Belgian capital. They were greeted by a bustling city with a mix of ancient structures and somewhat surprising, a good number of newer high-rise buildings. They promised themselves that today would be a day to walk the avenues and people watch along the way. Frankly, they were a bit burned out on touring old churches, museums, and even medieval castles. They were happy to stroll around the city in the shade afforded by the tall buildings as it was a typical sunny, warm and humid late summer day.

By midafternoon, they found themselves drawn to an expansive green space on Rue Royale, near the Northern Quarter financial district. It appeared they were in the Botanical Garden of Brussels. Tracy was a bit confused since she recalled that the National Botanic Garden was outside the city area. "I'll clear up our confusion," she said as she pulled out her trusty guidebook.

"Ah ha," she exclaimed to Ryan after thumbing through a few pages of the book. "These are the grounds of the *original* botanical garden. The book says that 'in 1938, most of the botanical resources,' I guess they mean the plants, flowers and shrubs, 'were relocated to a new site in Meise,' which is north of the city."

"Well this is still a beautiful garden," said Ryan. "Hey, that looks interesting. Let's check it out," he suggested as he pointed at a large, two-story round building encircled with huge windows. They entered Le Botanique, an old greenhouse whose first floor had been converted into an entertainment venue at some point in its history. Because there were no concerts scheduled today, they walked freely around the interior and explored at their leisure.

Steps and a sign for the Witloof Bar pointing upstairs caught their eye. Curious, they followed some well-dressed patrons up to the second floor. Tracy and Ryan both gasped as they eyed the view from the semi-open expanse. While the building wasn't tall, it still allowed for a birds-eye perspective of the former botanical gardens.

They started looking for a place to sit when they realized the space was reserved for a private event. They made their way back to the stairs. Just as they were about to leave, something caught Tracy's eye. She grabbed Ryan's arm and whispered, "Wait a minute." They lingered at the top of the steps watching the group.

"It looks like they're celebrating something," Ryan offered. Tracy nodded. Cigars were then passed around; it was obviously a joyous event. The man sitting at the head of the table pushed his chair back noisily, stood up, raised his glass, and proposed a toast to their recent accomplishment.

"Bon travail Messieurs! C'est magnifique!" he stated. He was wearing a charcoal gray three-piece suit, a crisp white shirt with a maroon, blue, and gold striped tie and matching pocket square. As he lifted his glass, one of his large gold cufflinks was exposed and sparkled in the sunlight.

16

Cheers for each man went up as he called out individuals and round after round of backslapping, handshaking and glass clinking ensued.

She explained, "Sounds like he's the head of a regional bank. He's congratulating his colleagues on beating out a larger, more widely known European bank with their acquisition of a regional institution." She continued, "I recognize the name of their competitor. This would seem to be quite a David versus Goliath win for them."

"They sure are a well-dressed bunch," said Ryan. "Their suits look really expensive."

Tracy nodded. "Yes, I imagine they are worth a pretty penny." After spotting another flash of sunlight off the cufflink, she nudged Ryan's arm and said, "Did you see the cufflinks on the guy giving the speech?"

"Holy cow!" exclaimed Ryan. "Do you think they're solid gold?"

"I wouldn't be surprised," Tracy agreed, but she was focused on something else more interesting—and distressing—to her. All the attendees were men. They were laughing jovially, dressed in traditional and expensive business attire. She leaned over, again whispering, "Look at that Ryan! Can you believe there is not one woman in that group? It drives me crazy to see that!"

Ryan looked more closely at the group and said, "Yeah, you're right. Honestly, I didn't notice there weren't any women with them until you mentioned it." He turned to face Tracy and found her looking at him with a quizzical expression on her face. His face flushed with embarrassment and he stammered, "I'm sorry, Tracy. I, I'm not attuned to that issue the way you are. I'll try to be from now on, though," he said taking her hand and searching her eyes.

They turned their attention back to the group and watched a moment longer, then Tracy said, "We should probably get going." She took one last look as they began their quiet descent. She imagined someday being part of a similar gathering wearing a smart, well-tailored business suit. Maybe even being the person giving the speech.

As they emerged into the sunlit garden, Tracy still felt uneasy about what they'd just witnessed. It struck her as odd but notable that what she perceived as glaringly obvious and unacceptable seemed normal to Ryan. She wondered to herself, *Is Ryan an aberration or is he representative of most men?*

She thought for a second about telling Ryan that she did have a position waiting for her after graduation, but she held back. She was superstitious about telling anyone outside her immediate family in case the job fell through. Besides, it would be an exciting surprise to share with him when they got back to the States.

Ryan caught her smiling at her thoughts. "What are you smiling about, Beautiful?" he teased.

She smiled wider. "Nothing in particular. Just the future and endless possibilities."

Chapter 3

Tracy's Cottage

As he had many nights before, Ryan snuck over to Tracy's cottage. It was his final night in Lille. He couldn't see her earlier because of the full day of activities the coaches had planned for the players. It ended with a dinner banquet that lasted until almost 11:00 PM.

Ryan rapped softly on the door and called her name in a whisper, "Tracy, it's me."

Tracy opened the door to let him in and took a quick look around outside to be sure no one saw him enter the cottage. Thankfully, the waning sliver of the moon gave off just a hint of light, and most of the stars were shrouded by wispy, passing clouds.

She closed the door behind her and turned into Ryan's open arms. She held back the tears she felt welling in her eyes as she commanded herself to let this final night in Lille be a completely happy memory.

They kissed passionately, exploring each other in the darkened room with only a small candle creating faint, dancing shadows on the walls.

"Mmmm, you taste delicious Tracy. You're so soft and warm; your hair smells amazing!" he said as sniffed in loudly.

"And you taste like red wine. But it tastes good," she assured him and placed another kiss on his waiting lips.

"We're legal age to drink here you know," Ryan chided. "And now that we're finished with the program the coaches even ordered it for our banquet tonight." Then he produced a half full bottle of red wine saying, "Compliments of my buddies. One of them had on a baggy jacket and smuggled this out for us."

"Nice…and thoughtful of your buddies! Besides, my cupboards are pretty much bare at this point," she said while gesturing toward the empty metal canners rack on the kitchen wall. She retrieved two small juice glasses from the kitchen cabinet, and Ryan poured the wine.

Ryan spoke first proclaiming a toast to Tracy. "To you Tracy, my lovely Lily of France."

Tracy felt her cheeks flush as her body began to pulse with desire for this amazing man standing inches from her. "And to you Ryan, thank you for opening my heart to a whole new world."

They clinked their glasses together and took a sip of the wine.

Within moments, the glasses and wine were forgotten as they began to kiss and gently caress each other. What little clothing each had worn was discarded on the floor. Running his hands over her body, Ryan moaned, "You are so beautiful." Tracy's body responded to his every touch, and she held him tightly as he carried her to the bed. They began making love slowly at first. Soon, urgency and desire swept over them both. Passion ruled the night more than once. Exhausted, and with their bodies finally sated, they succumbed to sleep.

Tracy felt Ryan awake with a start. His body leaned on hers as he peered over her to check the time. She knew he had to go. The cover of darkness always shrouded him as he left her cottage. Even on this last night, he made sure to protect her privacy. She usually slept through his departures knowing she would see him the next day, but this night was different. It was their last goodbye in this beautiful, magical place. Knowing he couldn't see her in the darkness, she squeezed her eyes tight to stop the flow of tears that threatened to fall. Through some effort, she managed to keep her breathing slow and long, as if she was asleep.

The bed creaked as he sat up. After a soft yawn, he stood, and then made his way to where their clothes lay on the floor. Tracy heard him sigh as he dressed. It took all her strength to not leap from the bed and hold him again. Instead, she balled up the sheet in her fists and stayed still and silent.

Ryan walked back to the bed, leaned down, and kissed her on the head. She wanted to cry out when he whispered, "I will miss you Tracy, my Lily of France, my love." She continued her charade instead. The next thing she heard was the door opening and then closing with a click of the latch. She sat up and pulled the sheet to her mouth. For minutes she dared not count, she rocked back and forth and sobbed.

Chapter 4

Tracy's cottage

Tracy had slept fitfully after Ryan left. When she finally awoke again, it was to a bright, sunny day. She lingered in bed, moving her hand back and forth across the space where, just hours before, Ryan had lain beside her. She mused, *Where is he now? Maybe already at the airport for their early morning flight back to the US. I wonder if he's thinking about me? I miss him already*, she thought. *What lies ahead for us?* She felt her heart pounding in her chest, and her pulse quickened. *When I'm with him or think about him, my heart just won't lie still. I feel so alive.*

Her small travel alarm clock blared its shrill "good morning!" She leaned over to turn it off. She was tempted to snuggle back into bed and take refuge under the soft duvet, but she knew she had a few papers to review before she was to leave the next day.

Plus, she was to have a final breakfast with Sister Agnes, her landlord, overseer of the French class curriculum and her friend. She smiled thinking how wonderful and surprising it was that they had become quite close over the summer.

She looked around the cottage that had been her home for the past three months. Who knew something so meagerly furnished could feel so warm and inviting? She checked the clock again and decided it was time to get out of bed.

She walked a few steps over to the small bathroom. It had all the necessities, a tiny shower, pedestal sink, and toilet. She looked up into the mirrored door of the vanity cabinet. A hairline crack had spread down one side, and the mirror was permanently cloudy and smudged from age, making her reflection a bit distorted. She yawned and rubbed her eyes, trying to improve the focus in the mirror. *I feel about as hazy as I look in this mirror.* She reached up and pulled the small door open to reveal three shelves that were barely deep enough to hold her basic toiletries. She rummaged around looking for her facial soap. As she searched, three items fell out into the sink. *Darn it! I will not miss this cabinet!*

Tracy turned on the cold water on the old faucet, and the water sputtered a bit and then flowed into her open hands. She splashed her face with the cool water, brushed her teeth and thought about how fond she had grown of Sister Agnes these pasts few months. It seemed that Sister enjoyed chatting with Tracy as well. Tracy was raised Catholic and still held to many of the Church's beliefs, although she found it difficult to reconcile certain doctrines with issues facing a more complicated and connected world. When she and Sister Agnes had talked about some of these topics the wise, elderly nun would typically nudge Tracy to read and contemplate a specific verse from the Bible rather than offer an opinion. She had reminded Tracy that a well-worn copy sat on a shelf in Tracy's cottage and counseled Tracy to consider that many of life's difficult problems could be solved by reading the Bible and praying for the Lord to give answers. "Remember though, Tracy," Sister Agnes had said, "the answers may not be what we expect. Sometimes we might even find them distasteful, but Jesus assures us that He has a path for each of us that leads to everlasting life with Him. We believe that to be our goal with all our heart. Our choices and actions during our life will lead us there."

Tracy found it difficult to grasp the depth of faith demonstrated by the Sisters and at this point in her life chalked it up to the realization that her calling was not to be a woman of the cloth. She did find, however, that seeking Bible passages more often and listening to the readings during the morning masses she occasionally attended, provoked worthwhile contemplation, and yielded valuable insights.

Tracy chose to wear a simple peasant style skirt with a teal and yellow flower pattern. She topped it off with a rust colored three-quarter length sleeved cotton shirt. She looked at the three pairs of shoes she had brought for the summer and picked the tan ballet flats, leaving behind her brown sandals and well-worn white tennis shoes.

Chapter 5

The Convent

Tracy headed out for the short walk through the tree-lined path that led to the main convent building. She had given herself extra time to stroll slowly because she wanted to soak in every detail of the beautiful grounds. She stopped at the wooden bench nestled in the hydrangea bushes not far from her cottage. She sat down and breathed in the delicate scent from the few remaining blooms on the shrubs. *I think this was my favorite spot of all to sit and read,* she thought. *It's so peaceful and quiet out here.* Although a two-lane road was barely fifty yards away, the leafy bushes created an impressive sound barrier. She ran her hand across the slats of the bench. The surface of the wood was worn so smooth that there was no fear of getting a splinter.

She got up after a few minutes and continued up the path toward the three-story gray stone convent. She could see the arched roof of the chapel area to the right side of the building. The convent roof and the chapel were both covered with nondescript faded black shingles.

Tracy stopped briefly to pray in the small stone grotto carved into a quiet corner of the flower garden. She knelt to pray in front of the statue of Mother Mary, quietly reciting the "Hail Mary" in French. Her heart was bursting with gratitude as she worshiped in this sacred space. She finished her prayer and as she rose, felt a pang of Catholic guilt. According to the learned doctrine, sex outside of marriage was forbidden. *It seems archaic,* she thought as she physically shook her head in disagreement. *Sometimes I don't know what to believe. I'm trying to be a good and decent human being!*

Tracy entered through the back door of the convent that opened into the dining room. It was a large space, furnished simply, with a long wooden table and bench seating rather than chairs. Across the room along the wall stood an old wood hutch, painted light blue with tiny white flowers. Normally it held a hodgepodge of plates, glasses, serving bowls, platters, pitchers, and utensils. Right now, it sat mostly empty since the table had already been set for breakfast by whichever two nuns were assigned the task for the month. Each bench seated three to four nuns and there were four benches dotted along each side of the table. Tracy took her assigned seat at the far end, next to Sister Agnes who sat at the head of the table.

The nuns were a punctual group and spent little time making small talk during their meals. At exactly 7:30, the single church bell in the chapel gave one deep ring. In less than a minute, twenty-four nuns were seated at the table. They greeted each other in a cheerful chorus of "Bonjour! Bonjour!" They prayed the Hail Mary in unison with their heads bowed and holding hands to form a circle around the table. After the prayer, plates of steaming pancakes were passed. The nuns were a frugal bunch, as each ate only one or two pancakes and stretched the morning orange juice by first filling their glass half full of water. Tracy ate her breakfast and silently committed the scene to her memory. She took a deep breath. The faint scent of herbs wafted from the kitchen and filled her nose. She recalled the many jars of jams, marmalades and dried herbs that filled the shelves in the kitchen. All from the gardens on the convent grounds lovingly tended by the nuns.

Breakfast was over in less than fifteen minutes. Each nun deposited her dish, glass, and silverware into the sink and then went off to her daily jobs and chores. Two nuns worked together to wash, rinse, and dry all the tableware. Sister Agnes invited Tracy to join her in her small office.

Tracy spoke only in French when in the company of the nuns. However, Sister Agnes would sometimes speak words or full sentences in English when she was alone with Tracy. She explained that it was good for her to practice her English language skills, although she expected Tracy to answer in French.

"Please, sit down Tracy," Sister Agnes said motioning to a chair. "I would like you to tell me about your summer experience, and then we can go over the student's papers that you have for me."

"Merci et pour vous," said Tracy, thanking the nun as she presented Sister Agnes with a box of jasmine tea wrapped in a simple ivory lace bow.

"Thank you, Tracy," said Sister Agnes with her arms outstretched to offer a warm embrace.

"De rien," said Tracy as she accepted her hug.

"Shall we share a pot of tea today, Tracy?"

"Oui, merci beaucoup," said Tracy accepting the invitation with gratitude.

Sister Agnes untied the bow and took one tea bag from the box. "I will keep the beautiful bow as a fond memory of our friendship," Sister Agnes said as she tucked it carefully into a nearby drawer.

She motioned for Tracy to sit down on the lone chair in her office across from her desk. It was a simple blond wood chair, typical of a teacher's chair. This one looked like it might be of similar age to the century-old convent, though it was still quite sturdy. It was likely still in service due to the handiwork of the groundskeeper who played double duty as the handyman around the convent.

Sister Agnes poured water from a glass pitcher into an electric pot she kept on top of her two-drawer black metal file cabinet. Once the water was boiling, she poured it into a stoneware teapot with a single tea bag ready to steep and set the teapot onto a doily on her desk.

One teabag! Tracy thought to herself. She marveled at this automatic and humble display of frugality. The nuns seemed to waste nothing and use every item to its fullest utility.

Satisfied the tea was ready, Sister poured the hot yellow liquid into two mismatched small china cups. She fetched the electric pot and refilled the teapot with the remaining hot water.

Sister sat down in her well-worn black leather chair which creaked even under her petite frame as she settled into the seat.

Each woman took a small sip. "This is delicious, Tracy." Sister closed her eyes and inhaled deeply. "Such a lovely fragrance," she almost whispered.

"Oui," said Tracy, nodding in agreement.

They sat in comfortable silence as each woman savored the subtle flavor of the jasmine tea. Tracy watched Sister Agnes. She seemed lost in her experience of this delicacy. While they had enjoyed tea in Sister's office before, it had always been regular black tea. Noting the look of enjoyment on Sister's face today left Tracy feeling happy she had chosen a gift that was an unexpected joy.

Tracy broke the silence, still speaking in French, "First, Sister Agnes, I want to thank you for all that you and the other Sisters have done for me this summer. It's been hard being far from home for three months, but you made me feel comfortable. I'm grateful for your generous invitation to take meals with the Sisters, and it's been very special to join in your early morning masses. I also appreciated having the privacy of the cottage."

"You're welcome Tracy. We have thoroughly enjoyed your company as well. Please tell me what you have enjoyed most about your experiences."

"I've come to love the city of Lille and its citizens and I feel that some of Lille is now part of me forever. I've learned so much from my business school classes at the Universite and increased my global knowledge through the lectures given by some of the most successful European business leaders. I've also earned a tidy sum of money tutoring the U.S. men's college soccer players, which will go toward paying for my final semester of classes."

Sister Agnes nodded and smiled.

Tracy continued excitedly, "It's been such fun to travel around the region during my free time. I loved taking the train for short trips to Paris and Belgium, exploring the history of Ghent and Bruges, strolling through the churches and museums, and lingering over espresso with a good book. And riding my bicycle along the beautiful Deûle River that runs through Lille will live in my memory forever. Thank you for the use of the bicycle Sister Agnes!"

"Oh, Tracy," said Sister Agnes with a broad smile, "I'm so glad you have enjoyed your time here. The energy of youth is a

31

beautiful gift from God!" she added, crossing her hands together over her heart.

Sister looked at Tracy as if to perhaps, commit her features to memory. She then leaned forward in her chair outstretched her arms and reached for Tracy's hands which were rested on the desk. Tracy responded by extending her arms and allowed the old nun to clasp her hands around hers and looked into Sisters eyes which she noticed were moist as if holding back tears.

Sister Agnes said, "I see a strong spirit in you that reminds me of Jeanne of Flanders, a brave woman who lived and ruled our region long ago. She is beloved to this day."

Tracy blushed at the comparison with such a notable figure and stammered, "Thank you, Sister. I've learned a great deal about her during my time here. I found her history intriguing!" Tracy added wistfully, "It was love that brought Jeanne to Lille, her love for Count Ferrand. And it was her love of the city and its people that compelled her to lead its ten thousand citizens during her husband's imprisonment. I was surprised that even today local people speak fondly of her as a courageous and benevolent leader."

"I'm glad you have taken the time to learn about the rich history of our community, Tracy," the old nun said as she gently released Tracy's hands and settled back in her chair.

Tracy continued, "It's wonderful to see that some of the good Jeanne of Flanders brought to the region under her rule lives on today, as in Countess Hospital's honoring of her memory. Like Jeanne herself, the hospital stands strong and beautiful."

"Oui, mon enfant," Sister Agnes agreed. "The hospital brings help and hope for many sick or injured people who come through her doors. It is one of the most advanced hospitals in the region with modern equipment and highly skilled physicians. And surely the maternity ward has also brought joy with the cries of babies born within its walls. Her mission has continued for over seven hundred years."

"I have also thought about how hard it must have been for the Countess to rule for so many years, especially as a woman," said Tracy. "That knowledge inspires me to model Jeanne's courage as I prepare to finish my business degree and enter the male-dominated investment banking business of Wall Street. I've seen how rough things can get when the competition of the deal gears up. Many men in the industry don't think a woman can or even should be in the thick of it all."

"In fact, during my first summer internship, a male intern, Joe and I were invited to sit in on morning briefings. As interns, we listened intently and said virtually nothing. Occasionally, we were assigned a task. I noticed right away that when the partner in charge wanted a file or document retrieved from an associate, he would ask Joe to get it. When he wanted coffee, he would ask me to get it. By the fourth day, I decided I'd had enough, and after the meeting, I asked the partner for a few minutes of his time to talk about an issue that was concerning me. He seemed annoyed but agreed to listen to my concern."

"Oh my, said Sister Agnes, "that seems unfair and biased. What did you say to him?"

Tracy scooted her chair a bit closer to the desk.

"I said, 'Mr. Jones, are you aware that since our first day you have asked Joe to interact with other associates to retrieve files and me to *fetch* coffee?' He just looked at me without saying anything. When he did speak, rather than answer my question, he asked *me* a question."

"He asked, 'What was last year's return on investment ratio of the acquisition target discussed in this morning's meeting?'"

"I answered, '18.5 percent, Mr. Jones.'" He drilled me with his eyes and dismissed me from the meeting with a perfunctory 'thank you for sharing your concern, Ms. Ward.' He didn't even acknowledge that my answer was correct!"

"That sounds dreadful and rude!" exclaimed Sister Agnes.

"There's more. I exited the meeting and spent the rest of the day nervously wondering if my internship was over. I knew I was taking a risk confronting him, but I felt like I had to take a stand early or be viewed as the subservient coffee server rather than a person on par with my male colleague," Tracy stated.

"What did Mr. Jones do?" Sister Agnes asked as she leaned forward in her chair.

"Thankfully, he assigned the coffee task to Joe during the next morning meeting and asked me to retrieve a document from an associate. After that, it seemed like he tried to rotate the tasks between us." Tracy smiled at the memory.

"I'm glad it worked out well for you!" Sister Agnes replied looking relieved.

"Me too, Sister Agnes," said Tracy. "I really needed the internship both for the money and the experience. At the same time, I felt sullied by the situation. We had similar credentials, but Mr. Jones' initial behavior left me wondering if Joe was more accepted simply because he was a man."

"Oui, ma petit chou chou," Sister Agnes cooed with a loving chuckle.

Tracy smiled at the nun's phrase of endearment which translated literally means "my little cabbage."

Sister continued, "You have learned a great deal, and your strength and passion have brought new life to our tranquil convent this summer. I won't pretend to understand all that you speak about in the business world. We are simple nuns here, focused on our educational mission and spreading the word and love of our Lord through work and prayer."

"I have found the Sisters to be kind, wise and educated women, Sister Agnes. I'm sure that your work has helped many students learn and be prepared to contribute to society in valuable ways."

"Thank you, Tracy. It's very nice of you to say that."

"As for me," said Tracy, "I received an outstanding education at New York University and earned top grades. I've had internships with two leading mergers and acquisitions firms, so I've got a good understanding of the real-life business of buying, selling, and merging companies. My participation in sports gave me the backbone to learn from heavy doses of constructive criticism. Now through my experience here, I can see myself calling on Jeanne of Flanders spirit and perhaps seeking prayers from you and the other Sisters to ask the Good Lord to keep His arm around my shoulder and His hand over my mouth if my temper starts to flare in the thick of the battle."

"Of course, my child," said Sister Agnes, "our prayers will be with you. And patience is a virtue to practice always."

And then, with a gleam in her eye, Sister Agnes said, "I think perhaps you have found something else in Lille this summer. These past few weeks you smile more often, your laugh is lighter, and your eyes shine more brightly. I noticed that one of the young men you are tutoring from the US football team seems to be aware of only you when you are in a room together. His gaze rarely leaves you and his interest in his French language studies has grown since his early days here at the school."

Tracy blushed and stammered, "Oh Sister Agnes! Is it so obvious? I have tried so hard to stop myself. It's somewhat awkward because although I'm a student, I'm also a tutor. I'm afraid if my supervisor in the States finds out I might be reprimanded."

"Hush, my dear, do not worry. He is a young man, and you are a beautiful, intelligent and charming young woman.

No one here would interfere with something as beautiful and magical as love between two people."

Then Sister Agnes took Tracy's hands in hers again and offered her advice and blessing to Tracy. "It is best to pray and let matters of the heart take their own course. I wish you happiness, peace, good health and may you know that the love of Jesus is always with you, Tracy."

"Merci beaucoup, Sister Agnes. Your blessing means a great deal to me," Tracy said holding back tears.

Sister Agnes sighed. "Tomorrow you will leave us, Tracy. You will go back to your home in New York City, finish your schooling and make your way in the world. I believe you will achieve your ambitions and make your mark in this business world you wish to enter. I am certain you will do well. However, I shall miss you and our talks. I have grown quite fond of you."

"Oh, Sister Agnes! I shall miss you, too. I am so grateful for everything."

The two women smiled at one another for another moment. Then Sister Agnes said as she poured more tea, "I suppose we must begin reviewing your students' assignments."

They moved quickly through the paperwork. Before Tracy knew it, it was time for her to go as Sister Agnes had other duties to attend to.

Tracy stepped forward to hug Sister Agnes goodbye. "I shall never forget you, Sister."

"Nor I you, Tracy," Sister whispered as she gave an extra squeeze to Tracy.

Tracy walked back through the dining room to the door she'd entered earlier. She turned for one last look and caught Sister Agnes watching her from the office doorway. "Be safe my child." The somber tone startled Tracy. She raised her hand, waved, and stepped out into the sunshine.

Chapter 6

Tracy's cottage

That night Tracy tried to sleep, but it was no use. Her mind was in turmoil. When she arrived in France three months ago her goals were clear: to earn much needed money from her tutoring job, complete the coursework at the Universite to boost her credit hours, gain global business and cultural knowledge and spend any free time exploring the local area, major cities in France and as many of the surrounding European countries as she could. And explore she did! Her university-issued student ID card gave free use of the local transit system and even allowed her to buy discounted train tickets to Paris and nearby cities of Bruges, Ghent, and Brussels. Tracy found overnight stays to be affordable at the many youth hostels across Europe. They were generally clean and safe and great places to make new friends from all over the world.

Tracy tossed and turned in her bed. She tried to pray herself to sleep but remained wide awake. Next, she tried breathing slowly to calm down and clear her mind. No luck. Nothing seemed to work. She got up, ran the kitchen faucet cold for a full minute and drank a glass of water.

She sat down at the small table and stared out the window into the darkness. She thought back to the many times she tooled around town and took day trips exploring the greater Lille area with the sturdy bicycle the Sisters had loaned her for the summer. She remembered her favorite route and clearly saw herself riding along the Canal de Moyenne-Deûle, the Deûle River. A paved path ran alongside the tree-lined river and meandered through the west end of the city. Wide expanses of open space offered ample areas for pickup "football games," flying kites, throwing Frisbees, and meeting local people of all ages. *Oh*, she thought, *What beautiful memories to take with me of this amazing summer experience.*

She got up from the table and walked slowly around the little cottage, touching furniture and surfaces as she passed. She wanted to absorb every detail of her private sanctuary. Hoping she'd tired herself a bit more, she returned to the bed. As she lay down, the full weight of being without Ryan hit her. She said aloud though only she could hear the words, "My dearest Ryan. We've been apart for less than twenty-four hours, and I miss you terribly. My heart and my body ache for you, for your touch." She wrapped the duvet around her, as she felt chilled although the night was warm.

She reprimanded herself, *I must think about the happy times, or I fear I might drown in my sadness!*

Her thoughts turned to the streets of downtown Lille, lined with cafes and restaurants, some no more than pop-up stands serving cappuccino and brightly colored macarons of many flavors. Others truly gourmet, in her mind, perhaps five-star establishments with famous chefs, restaurants that Tracy could only dream of right now on her tiny budget. Still, she loved to linger close by and breathe in the delicious smells of camembert and brie cheeses, and the delicate white fish kissed with truffle oil and spices and then grilled quickly to mouth-watering perfection. Tracy visualized the meal partnered with an array of brightly colored fresh vegetables also drizzled with a touch of olive oil, seasoned with local herbs, and charred on an open fire. *Mmm, I can practically taste it.*

Perhaps most of all, she recalled the aromatic smell of freshly baked bread that seemed to linger over the entire city. She estimated there were dozens of little bakeries, as it seemed that every block announced yet another "boulangerie" or "patisserie" with a window full of delicious treats tempting you to sample their homemade delights. Tracy felt herself laughing aloud and thinking how glad she was to have had a limited budget or she might have gained ten pounds over the summer! Thankfully, she had eaten very well because she could buy a loaf of bread, a hunk of cheese, a bottle of red or white table wine and a bunch of grapes, figs, or other fresh fruits for just a few francs. *Great,* she thought to herself, *now I'm making myself hungry, and there's not a speck of food on the shelves or in the refrigerator!*

More memories of her magical summer came to fill the void that should have held the unknown dreams of restful sleep.

Tracy thought back to one of her favorite activities, people watching! Sometimes she would sit at a café and discreetly gaze at men and women dressed in stylish clothing and hats. Most were older than Tracy, and she wondered how they earned their living to afford their lifestyle. Were they bankers, merchants, industrialists, educators, government workers? She held no illusions about what it would take to succeed—hard work, long hours, weekends buried in research combing through financial sheets and crunching numbers till your fingers hurt from punching a calculator.

Her eyes were now wide open. She looked at her small travel alarm clock and noted the time, 1:00 AM. She sighed loudly. *Nights are long when sleep fails to come.*

She felt a sense of anxiety about what lies ahead for her career. Were her aspirations too high? She had set a goal for herself to be a partner before she turned forty.

Tracy had confidence that she possessed the intelligence and education to succeed. She recognized that she had a lot to learn and was eager to do so. She relished being exposed to new ideas, information, and tools. NYU had just introduced computers in their curriculum to help with analytical calculations and financial modeling. This new world of punch cards was daunting and brought with it computer programming languages called Basic and Fortran. Tracy had committed herself to learning how to use these new tools. She figured, correctly as time would tell, that it would be beneficial to have this cutting-edge knowledge in a competitive job market. She knew that the marquee firms courted Harvard and Yale for most of their fast-track recruits. But some also looked to schools like NYU for those "diamonds in the rough," achievers who had risen to the top of their class at local private or public colleges but for whatever reason hadn't gained or sought admission to Ivy League schools. These students were known for their street smarts as well as book smarts. They also typically had the gritty ambition to do the grueling grunt work necessary to truly learn the business and earn their way to the top. Tracy was proud to count herself among the latter group.

She sat up in bed, hugged her knees to her chest and wondered if she should just get dressed. She shook her head, leaned back on the pillows, and allowed her thoughts to continue their wandering journey.

Only one semester separates me from earning my MBA and starting my career with Fontella & Scharf! She smiled recalling the generous compensation offer they had made to her after finishing her internship last summer. Knowing she had this job waiting for her was one of the reasons she could take this summer work in France. In fact, Michael Fontella, one of the founding partners of the firm, personally encouraged her to take the summer abroad program. She remembered him saying that the international travel and study would be a worthwhile cultural experience for her.

Just as Tracy felt her body relax, her thoughts turned again to Ryan. She still wondered how this could have possibly happened and even felt somewhat disappointed in herself that she let it go this far. She had not been looking to fall in love or even indulge in a summer fling. Until now, her education consumed her, and she was content to socialize with other like-minded students in her minimal free time.

Tracy acknowledged that she enjoyed the companionship of a man. She had dated in the past, even had one steady relationship and enjoyed the hugs and kisses, the feeling of being treated specially with gifts of flowers and kindnesses, but she also felt it was unfair to any man to make serious commitments she couldn't possibly keep right now.

That led her straight to the obvious question, *how in the world did I allow myself to fall so completely and hopelessly in love with Ryan?* Her eyes closed but she wasn't sleeping. In her mind, she saw a bolt of lightning and simultaneously heard a loud clap of thunder just before a drenching rain began to fall. With that flash of memory, she was carried back to the afternoon where everything changed. She even remembered feeling the earth rumble as she and Ryan sprang up from the garden bench where they were studying to take cover in her nearby cottage.

"Wow, that storm blew in quick!" Ryan said, shaking his head and arms to dispel the raindrops that covered him.

"It sure did," Tracy agreed as she pushed back her wet hair.

Ryan hesitated just inside the door and looked around. "So, this is where you live?"

"Yes, my cozy little cottage. Rather spartan, but sure beats sleeping in the convent with the nuns!" she replied with a laugh.

"Yeah, that would be creepy. I'm mean I'm sure the nuns are nice but..." Ryan's voice trailed off.

"Oh, no apology necessary. You're right. Most of the Sisters are delightful, and I take meals with them almost every day, but sleeping among them would seem odd. I'm thankful the Mother Superior had this old groundskeeper residence cleaned up for me. It suits my needs perfectly!"

"The entire space is maybe 350 square feet, but a lot is tucked into this room, like my kitchenette here in the corner." Then she pointed to a door. "That leads to my tiny but functional bathroom." She skipped the white wrought iron daybed that was covered with a white duvet nestled into the far corner of the room. Instead, she pointed at the windows above the bed and said, "Those windows are a godsend. I'm always amazed at how they seem to capture even the slightest of breezes. It would be stifling in here without them!" She motioned to the table and chairs near the kitchenette. "We can sit here."

Ryan's large frame dwarfed the simple metal chair. "The cushions are nice," he said. "I'm pretty sure these chairs wouldn't be nearly as comfortable without them," he added.

"Thank you! I picked them up at a local thrift store. They looked practically brand new, and you're right—it sure beats sitting on the metal seat and back! I especially liked the deep red color. I think it brightens an otherwise drab space."

Ryan nodded as he looked over the space again. "That's for sure. There's only that one picture on the wall," he said as he pointed toward a picture of Jesus, depicted traditionally, with gold flames and a cross sprouting from His flaming red heart.

The pounding rain had turned to a gentle patter. A light breeze floated in through the open kitchen window near the table. A simple glass vase, almost a bowl, sat on the table. In it was a beautifully preserved spray of white lily of the valley with bright green leaves and stems.

Ryan breathed in deeply. "It smells fantastic in here! Is it from those flowers?" he asked gesturing toward the vase.

Tracy took in a deep breath and confessed, "Actually I think it's the roses. I'm so used to it I hardly notice it anymore."

"Oh, that's it. They're right outside those windows over there, near the bed," said Ryan nodding. "I've never smelled anything like them before."

"I hadn't either, so I learned all about them from the groundskeeper. I think I would like to plant them in my own garden someday. They're called Triomphe de Lille."

Ryan nodded, then leaned in, so his face was just inches from hers and said, "And your hair smells fantastic too." Her eyes were locked on his as she felt him ease her hair behind her ear. He began to gently stroke her cheek, which she didn't stop. She didn't want to; it felt like he should be doing that. She held his gaze for what seemed like an eternity and then he leaned in and softly kissed her. He pulled back slightly, and she gave him a shy grin. Then she leaned in and kissed him back. Hours later, they were cuddled together naked and spent under the soft white feather duvet. Even with few words spoken, it seemed that both were comfortable with what had just happened. They were young, single, and maybe falling in love.

Tracy was jarred back to the present. She shook her head to clear away the memory. The longer she thought about her relationship with Ryan, the more she found herself questioning her rational thinking skills. *Could it be that I'm not as tough as I think I am? I gave away my virginity years ago, but it seems like I'm in a place with Ryan that I've never been before. I think he's captured my heart and I'm not even sure how it happened.*

She had allowed herself to be caught up in her emotions and her physical desires. Her heart, which normally seemed to lie still now stirred at the mere thought of Ryan. His voice and the feel of his touch made her heart beat rapidly and jump with excitement. These feelings were new to her and scared her almost as much as they delighted her.

It was no use. Tracy couldn't sleep, and now she couldn't stop thinking about Ryan. She stared at the ceiling in the darkness. Maybe she was blowing off steam built up over all the years of hard work and sacrifice. Maybe it was the environment, the beauty, history, and romanticism of Lille, indeed all of Europe she experienced that had touched her soul more deeply than she realized.

Tracy thought back over the last four weeks and about how they tried to spend as much time together as possible without compromising their responsibilities- Ryan to his soccer schedule and Tracy to her tutoring and coursework. Amazingly, she felt like she had completed her homework and the final ten pages of her paper more quickly and effectively than ever. She chuckled inwardly that she herself could be a specimen in a study of "Impacts on Motivation," one of her human resource management classes. Tracy was still keenly focused on her longer-term goals of graduation and starting her job, but short term, she couldn't resist spending all available free time with Ryan. She felt drawn to him like a powerful magnet to steel.

Tracy had begun showing up in the makeshift grandstands to watch Ryan's soccer games, usually with a book in tote that she hoped to read, but perhaps more as cover with the goal of not drawing attention to her recent attendance. Of course, she found it impossible to keep her eyes off Ryan. She admired his athletic prowess and sharp soccer skills. He was lightning quick and seemed to have a skill for sending the ball to the exact spot a teammate would be to receive it. He also displayed the courage and ability to shoot and was one of the top scorers. Based on her observations, the European scouts also noticed Ryan's talents. Sometimes she saw them huddled together talking, pointing discreetly in Ryan's direction, and making copious notes on their ever-present clipboards. She was happy for him since she knew he loved this sport that to her seemed more like marginally controlled chaos.

After their session that afternoon Tracy had said to Ryan "I noticed a few of the scouts seemed to be pointing at you and chatting among themselves. Is there a chance you might play for a European team?"

Ryan said, "It's a long shot, and I'm too young right now. The big money today is in Europe, but there aren't many US guys playing over here. Maybe as our skill level goes up, we'll get more opportunities." He continued, "I'm hoping to finish my degree and land a spot on one of the US North American Soccer League teams. Professional soccer is still new back home but trying to gain a foothold with fans."

Tracy said, "I didn't even know that league existed until you told me about it!" She continued, "To me, *football* is American football. Period. I must say though I'm intrigued at just how consumed all of Europe seems to be with soccer. Fans here are fiercely supportive of their hometown teams, and it's crazy that near riots can break out at the pubs and taverns if the local team is defeated or the crowd feels that the referees botched a significant call!"

Ryan laughed and said, "Yeah, these folks take their football very seriously." He continued, "I grew up cheering for my hometown team, the San Diego Sockers but most of us would take a spot on any one of the twenty or so NASL teams." Then, he winked at Tracy and added, "Now I'm going to work my butt off to sign a contract with the NY Cosmo team after I graduate so we can be together!"

Tracy had looked deeply into Ryan's eyes and pulled him close to her. She said, "That would make me very happy, but it will be hard to wait three years for us to be together."

Ryan said, "Yes it will really hard to be apart, but we'll find ways to see each other. I promise."

Tracy remembered breaking the tenseness that had come over them saying, "Yeah, living in New York presents its' own spirited rivalries. In fact, some friendships, family relations, and even job opportunities can be decided by the answer to the question, 'Mets or Yankees, Jets or Giants'?"

Tracy had waxed nostalgic and gave Ryan a glimpse at her family life saying, "Sunday at my house in the fall is a ritual of early Mass at our church down the block, family breakfast at home and watching football all afternoon."

"Sounds like a nice, relaxing day to me," Ryan answered.

"Hey Ryan," Tracy had said, "I was just thinking that since both New York football teams finished at the bottom of their respective divisions last season, maybe the fans *would* turn to soccer in bigger numbers."

"That would be great!" Then he added, "And I'll be the star of the team!"

She chuckled softly to herself envisioning him as a professional soccer player and her somewhere in the stands watching him play just like she did this summer.

"Tick, tock, tick, tock"… the sound made by the large, nondescript, institutional style clock on the wall, normally muted during the day by the sounds of birds chirping, bees buzzing, garden equipment and engines humming was now loud and rhythmic. It broke her idyllic vision. The thin red arm announced every second, "Tick, tock, tick, tock"…while the black hands read 2:10 against the white background.

Wide awake, Tracy continued her summer history tour, savoring thoughts of those final days in Lille. Once the soccer schedule slowed and the scouts left, Ryan and Tracy spent more time together. Tracy took Ryan biking on the paths along the Deûle River and introduced him to her favorite people watching spots near the cafes and restaurants.

They relished their carefree days together. The week before last they hopped the train and visited the nearby medieval city of Ghent, where they toured centuries-old castles, churches, and museums. Tracy laughed as she thought about how they snuggled together on the train and each took turns reading out loud about the amazing sights they were about to see. Their first stop was St. Bavo, where they stood in awe of the magnificent twelve-paneled fifteenth century Ghent Altarpiece, also known as The Adoration of the Mystic Lamb. The brochure gave them an overview of this artwork created by the Dutch van Eyck brothers.

In person, the 11'x15' size was almost overwhelming, yet the intricate details and emotions depicted could give even non-believers reason to pause and admire the work. Tracy recalled their tour guide explaining the detailed and incredible history of the artwork, saying, "The Ghent Altarpiece has been moved many times since its creation in the early 1400s and was almost destroyed during periods of iconoclasm. Some of the panels were even sold, then some damaged by fire and even hidden in a salt mine during World War II. Thankfully, the artwork was saved from destruction by The Allies just as the Nazi regime was in its final days of defeat. Eventually, all panels were returned to St. Bavo's except for one panel, The Just Judges, stolen in 1934 which has never been recovered."

Tracy and Ryan learned that the replacement panel they were looking at was commissioned as part of an overall restoration of the entire piece around 1945.

Scattered all over Europe were structures that dated back centuries. Tracy and Ryan sometimes found it exhausting and confusing as they listened to a guide explain the history of a church or an area and the many hands it had fallen into through wars and famines and natural disasters. They agreed that it was very different in the United States, where a one-hundred-year-old building is considered historic. Tracy giggled when Ryan added, "Heck in

California hardly anything is that old except the giant redwoods, maybe an occasional mission or fort and coincidentally some of the grapes in the vineyards that were imported from France."

Sleep continued to evade her. The clock that was now counting down her final hours in Lille read 3:20.

Tracy got back out of bed and opened her purse for the hundredth time to be sure she had her passport, plane ticket, and the Citroen car keys. Snapping the purse closed, she crawled back into bed and stared at the ceiling. She had noticed the Universite Catholique de Lille identification card still in her wallet and tucked right behind it was her used train ticket to Paris from the weekend she and Ryan had slipped away to experience The City of Light.

After spending several hours touring The Louvre, they realized they were famished. They headed northwest along the Rue Saint Honore and happened upon the famed Ritz Hotel on Place Vendome in the central city. Having lost some of its luster over the years, the hotel was now undergoing major renovations. It was hardly recognizable behind all the scaffolding, and plastic sheeting draped over the walls. Tracy and Ryan weren't sure if a hotel reservation was needed to get in, so they slipped in through a construction entrance while the doorman was helping guests with their luggage.

They walked through a tarped tunnel for about thirty feet and found themselves in a hallway just off the main lobby.

"Well Tracy, let's pretend we own the place," Ryan said offering his arm to her.

Tracy smiled and gave him a slight nod of her head. She hooked her arm in his, and together they strolled leisurely through the hotel.

As they passed the lobby bar, the same idea seemed to hit them both. Tracy said, "Darling, shall we sit a spell and enjoy a bottle of bubbly?"

"Mais oui, Mademoiselle," said Ryan.

Tracy laughed hearing Ryan say "Yes, my dear" in French. She quipped, "Pretty soon the student might become the teacher!"

The Little Bar was nearly empty, so they had their pick of seating options. Ryan chose a cozy loveseat in a quiet corner and ordered a half bottle of the least expensive champagne as well as ham and cheese croissant sandwiches.

The waiter delivered the bottle to their table and presented it to Ryan for his inspection.

Ryan said, "Oui, merci beaucoup." The waiter smiled at the young couple and asked in English, "Honeymoon"?

Clearly, he recognized they were Americans, and Tracy blushed at his inquiring if they were on their honeymoon.

"Nous sommes des etudiants en vacances," Tracy responded in perfect French, smiling as she explained to the waiter that they were students on vacation.

"Excusez-moi," said the waiter as he bowed to Tracy. He then uncorked the bottle, eliciting the universal "pop" sound. He deftly filled the delicate, crystal flutes.

"C'est bon, merci," said Tracy, assuring the waiter that she wasn't at all offended by his question.

"Amusez-vous bien!" he replied, offering his parting wish that they should enjoy themselves.

Ryan turned his attention to Tracy and declared a toast, "Viva la France et la plus belle fille du monde!"

Tracy smiled at Ryan's declaration of her as the most beautiful girl in the world. She accepted his compliment, and they lightly touched their glasses together.

They sealed the toast with a sip of the delicious beverage and a kiss. Tracy recalled how she enjoyed the crisp, tingling feeling the chilled champagne made in her mouth.

Perhaps it was the champagne, but Tracy's heart felt like it might burst with joy as she slowly sipped the sparkling wine nestled next to Ryan in the most beautiful of settings. There was no talk of autumn or the road ahead to break the beautiful, magical moment.

Tracy opened her eyes again and found herself back to present time on this final, waning night in Lille. She blinked, thinking about that moment in the hotel. *I think that's when I fell completely in love with him,* she mused. *Well, if it's true that love conquers all, I believe it will be so for Ryan and me.*

Her balled fists rubbed her eyes. Her mind was not going to stop. It was after 4:00 AM and much too late for sleep.

I have so many things to do when I get back to New York, she thought. Her mind fed her a steady stream of thoughts, which only served to increase her anxiety. *I need to finish the semester and earn a passing grade on my final paper to graduate. Then I start my job at Fontella & Scharf. Gosh, I need to buy some new clothes and shoes! I've got to look the part of an aspiring young executive. This is what I've been working for my whole life. My dream is becoming a reality!* She smiled. Her life was falling into place.

Chapter 7

Tracy's cottage

Tracy watched the darkness turn to bright daylight on her final morning in Lille. Unfortunately, she was physically exhausted and emotionally drained after a night of tossing and turning. The birds were their usual chirpy selves, and the bees were busy buzzing around the roses, seeking their breakfast of nourishing nectar. She heard the distant sound of the groundskeeper's lawnmower, already in action somewhere on the convent's expansive estate. Life was going on as normal in Lille.

"Get a grip Tracy," she muttered as she did a final check on her belongings to be sure she hadn't left anything behind.

She loaded up the tiny blue and white Citroen for the short ride to the Lille airport. The groundskeeper had graciously loaned it to her for the early morning flight so she wouldn't have to worry about hiring a taxi. The town was so safe that he instructed her to simply leave the keys under the driver's side mat and he would retrieve the car from the parking lot later in the day.

She turned to take one last look at the convent and the beautiful grounds. She slowly breathed in the sweet but smooth scent of the Triomphe de Lille roses for the final time. Her eyes lingered on the little cottage, *her* cottage now. She wanted to drink in every detail and commit this beautiful sight to her memory. This is where she found true love. She found Ryan here. A flame had been lit in her heart, and she committed herself to do everything possible to keep it burning strong and true. She believed that Ryan would do the same.

She was about to get into the car when she heard Sister Agnes calling her name. She looked up the path toward the convent and saw Sister Agnes and Sister Maria walking quickly toward her.

"I'm glad we caught you before you left for the airport Tracy," said Sister Agnes. "We wanted to say goodbye and good luck to you."

"Sister Agnes asked Father to speed up morning Mass, so we could catch you," Sister Maria exclaimed.

All three women laughed and stood looking at each other for a moment.

Tracy moved toward Sister Agnes and gave her a warm embrace. "Thank you again for everything Sister Agnes, goodbye."

"You're welcome, Tracy. Safe travels and God bless you all the days of your life," said Sister Agnes.

"Goodbye Tracy," said Sister Maria.

"Goodbye Sister Maria," echoed Tracy.

Tracy got into the tiny Citroen and familiarized herself with the simple dashboard.

Okay, really need to leave now, she admonished herself, *that plane won't wait for me. Maybe someday when I have my own plane it will, but not this one.* And then she laughed. She gave a last wave to the nuns as they stood by to see her off.

She turned the key and was thankful that her father had insisted she learn to drive a car with manual transmission "just in case." That knowledge was coming in handy now as she maneuvered the car south of the city toward the regional airport.

Try as she might to remain positive, dark thoughts kept swirling in her head. She was sad to be leaving Lille and still conflicted about the future of her budding romance with Ryan. More doubts crept into her mind. Was their relationship strong enough to survive the distance between Los Angeles and New York? How will they even afford to pay for long distance phone calls?

Maybe letters can keep our relationship moving forward, Tracy thought. Surely, I've read about couples who sustained their love, even deepened it over time, through writing to each other. Soldiers and their loved ones separated for months, even years, have kept love burning in their hearts through extremely difficult and stressful conditions.

But, Tracy thought sadly, *will Ryan even make time to write to me? He seemed sincere and mature beyond his age, but will his love stay true when he gets wrapped up in all that college offers? Will my feelings for Ryan be as strong after I get back to New York and immerse myself in my studies and then my work? I must be crazy to think that this relationship has any chance of succeeding.*

She turned to drive south on Av. Jean-Jaures toward the airport. Unbidden, the tears she had been fighting began to trickle down her cheeks. She wiped them away with the back of her hand and blinked to see the road clearly. *Maybe my worry stems from my own college experience. Ryan has a long road in front of him. He'll have a grueling schedule of practices, workouts, travel, and all that goes along with being a standout athlete in a top-ranked NCAA Division I sports program, including all those admiring and eager California girls.* Her nose had begun to run, and she sniffed noisily.

Is his love for me strong enough to survive all these obstacles and the temptation that no doubt will come along with the territory? She felt lost in this worrisome thought. At a stop sign, she squeezed her eyes shut and willed the tears to stop. When she opened her eyes, it was as if he was standing in front of her. She could see him vividly in her mind.

His broad, genuine smile, his deep blue eyes, and tanned skin. She could hear his voice and the promise he made to her on their last night together when he professed his love and desire to be with her forever. The vision drove away her worries, and she felt happy and peaceful. *We are two halves that complement and complete each other.* She believed with all her heart that he loved her. His voice filled her inner ears, "Tracy, I'm here for you always."

A tiny "beep" from behind her washed his image away. She was still at the stop sign! She waved her hand in apology to the driver behind her and sped up, her thoughts drifting back to Ryan.

She smiled as a warm glow enveloped her body. She could feel the strength of Ryan's commitment and knew that they were meant to be together. Tracy glanced at her watch as she approached a green light at the intersection of Boulevard de Strasbourg, just at the city limits. *I'm right on time.*

As she entered the intersection, she gasped as she spotted a delivery truck coming at her from the right. She tried to swerve to avoid a broadside hit, but her small Citroen was not a nimble car. The truck slammed into the passenger side. Her body was pushed to the left, and her head hit the driver's side window—hard. Her ears were filled with the sound of bending metal and breaking glass. The smell of burning rubber assaulted her nose. Someone was screaming. *Is that me?*

She tried to maintain control of the car, but her unfamiliarity with it and the manual transmission plus her exhaustion left her powerless. She skidded into the opposite lane, where another car approached. Seconds before impact, Tracy saw a look of horror on the opposing driver's face as he vainly tried to avoid hitting her. She knew it was too late. She closed her eyes and braced her body. The accident seemed as if it were happening in slow motion as she felt the front of the car push in. Her body, already battered from the first impact, flailed helplessly in the driver's seat. Her head snapped forward and hit the steering wheel. Windshield glass rained down on her, and there was something else. *Pain. Oh God.* "No! Ryan!" she screamed. Suddenly, silence. She couldn't open her eyes. *Stay awake,* she commanded. *Stay*.... Her head slumped forward. The world went dark.

Chapter 8

UCLA, Los Angeles, California 1985

"Hey, Ryan! Wait up!" Ryan turned to see Paul, his best friend, running to catch up with him after practice.

"You in a hurry to get somewhere?" Paul asked as he caught his breath.

Ryan laughed. "No, I'm sure I've got something to study, but it can wait if you want to grab a beer."

Paul, never one to turn down libations, readily agreed. "Sure."

They walked a few short blocks off campus to a nearby pub. Once they were settled on their bar stools, talk turned to the future and, of course, soccer.

"I can't believe the season's almost over," said Paul as he hunched over his bottle.

"I can't believe our soccer career at UCLA is almost over!" Ryan replied. "Five years of hard work and coming so close in the Cup Quarterfinals last year. Losing that has made me so hungry for this year's opportunity to win the first ever championship for the Bruins. And for us. We're hitting on all cylinders right now, and we're in top physical shape. Plus, most of us have played together for the last four or five years. I'm telling you, buddy, this is our year!"

"I think so too Ryan," said Paul. I've heard the guys say they want to win it for the seniors, especially for you. Ryan, you inspire us with your dogged work ethic and the way you give it your all.

You're smart out there, *and* you're a team player. Maybe mostly though, no one wants to catch your wrath if we fall short." Paul laughed and winked at Ryan.

Ryan feigned surprise. "Me?" he joked.

He accepted his earned reputation as a fierce, though fair, competitor who demanded that his teammates give their all, too. In appreciation for his inspiring efforts, the team had chosen Ryan as captain at the start of the school year.

They each took a drink, careful to ration the delicious liquid since they limited their drinking during the playing season.

After a brief silence, Paul turned to Ryan and asked, "Have you decided if you're going to graduate at winter semester?"

Ryan sighed. "I'm still not sure. I've got the credits for my engineering degree, and I'm sure I can get a job. I could take other classes, or I could stick around and start my master's degree. Coach said he would put me on the payroll as an assistant, so I'd get free tuition and a salary. My agent said he's had a couple calls from European teams, but we both know that's a long shot, so I'm not getting my hopes up."

"Man, I'm glad I've got another semester to think it over," said Paul turned back to his beer. "Here's to my being a slow learner!" he said as he raised his bottle in a mock toast.

Their bottles made a satisfying clink.

Shaking his head in disbelief, Ryan said, "I thought I had it all planned out until the professional league folded last year. Then there was talk that some of the team owners and executives might get things going again. I was ready to start looking for an apartment in Chicago when my agent told me they were interested in me."

"Yeah, I remember that," Paul said. "Didn't you say they thought you might be the next Pele?!"

"Okay, you got me there, dude," Ryan laughed. "It's pretty heady thinking about playing pro. But, the U.S. league's not coming back anytime soon. At least, that's what my agent is hearing, so we all need a Plan B."

Paul raised his hands to set the record straight. "Whoa, Ryan. You have the talent to play anywhere. And when your head's in the game, you're unbeatable. Since you're staring into space, I'll take a risk and ask you where your head is right now. Hmm?" Paul poked Ryan in the arm.

"I'm just thinking about how lucky I've been to be part of this team and the whole experience." Paul pretended to wipe sweat off his brow. "Whew, I am happy to hear you say that, my man! A few years ago, I thought we were going to lose you to a ghost from New York."

Ryan didn't say anything at first. Then he exhaled, put his chin on his hand and stared at the bar.

"Yeah," he said as he sat up and shook his head. "I was pretty messed up when she never called or wrote to me after we got so close in France. Those first months after I got back were not the best of my life," he admitted. Paul nodded but stayed silent.

"Oh man, I just remembered...." Ryan began. He rolled his eyes at Paul and asked, "Do you remember going to the library with me and copying pages from the New York phone book?" Ryan shook his head again and uttered a soft chuckle.

Paul bellowed, "Heck yes, I do! I think you alone supported the pay phone right outside the library. Who knew there could be that many people with the same last name in one city, even if it was New York. What was her name?"

Ryan hesitated. It had been a long time since he'd said her name aloud.

"Ward. Tracy Ward," he answered as he stared into his half-empty beer bottle.

"Yeah, that was it. I'm not sure how I could forget. She was *all* you talked about for months!"

They both fell silent as they nursed their beers. Still staring at his bottle, Ryan admitted, "I still think about her sometimes. Maybe it's my ego, but I just couldn't believe she dropped me like that. Remember we even read through obituaries in the New York newspapers at the library? I mean I'm glad we never saw her name, but it's just weird. She didn't seem like the kind of chick who would just duck out." Ryan shrugged his shoulders. "I guess I didn't really know her."

"She was more than a few years older than us," said Paul. "Maybe she just realized it wasn't going to work. I remember you said she wanted to get a job on Wall Street. Those are tough SOB's. I was in New York City once and saw that statue of the big bull with the giant horns looking like it's snorting and charging. Maybe she was more interested in taking those Wall Street dudes by their balls than figuring out how to keep a long-distance relationship going."

"Ha, that's a vision. Yeah, I know that's probably what happened, but I used to think about the things we said to each other in France and the way she looked at me and well you know… other stuff. I remember though, she said she was afraid of getting in trouble because she was tutoring us along with taking classes. Maybe she just decided our relationship wasn't worth risking her graduation or the money they paid her that summer."

"Or maybe she wasn't as innocent as she seemed," said Paul with a raised eyebrow.

"Yeah, well whatever the reason, it's long over," said Ryan as he stood up and tossed the empty beer bottle into the nearby metal waste can. It landed with a loud thud. "If we're going to win this championship, I need to head back to my room and get some sleep. See you tomorrow Paul. And thanks for everything."

"I've got your back buddy," said Paul. "Like I told you then, there are plenty of fish in the ocean, and you've caught a few good ones since then." Paul winked at Ryan.

Ryan chuckled, puffed out his chest and said, "You bet I have."

It was a short walk to Ryan's dorm. He felt exhaustion sinking in as he walked down the hall to his single room, closed the door and looked in the mirror. Talking to himself aloud he wondered, "Why then do I sometimes feel more like the lone survivor of a shipwreck with no desire for all the fish around me? I see her face in my mind, and it's like drinking the fresh water I need to survive."

He brushed his teeth, thought about taking a shower and then decided to just change into a fresh tee shirt and shorts. He tossed his practice uniform onto a pile of dirty clothes.

He turned out the lights, collapsed onto his bed and fell sound asleep as his head hit the pillow.

Chapter 9

UCLA was favored to go all the way, and it was up to them to prove their worth. They let only one game slip in the regular season and bested other competitors to make it to the final round of the National Championship. Ryan was one of the team's top scorers and a force to be reckoned with on defense in the midfield. He was quick, strong and his knack for getting the ball to exactly where his teammates were going to be paid off, as he led the team in assists.

Physically, he was a specimen to behold. He stood six feet tall and was one hundred seventy-five pounds of muscle with quick reflexes and sprint speed worthy of a track and field star. His trim waist belied the size and strength of his upper body, which helped him win and keep many a ball against smaller, weaker competitors. He was as smart a player as he was physical and seemed to be able to see the field and execute their game plan in a way that gave him the ability to control the pace and direction of play.

Somehow, he also managed to earn just enough credits for an engineering degree. On a whim, he took some finance classes and was surprised at how exciting he found them to be. He was thankful that his athletic scholarship would enable him to graduate without any school loans.

His college career was ending, but at the moment Ryan was only focused on winning the National Championship for UCLA and his teammates. He simply would not let himself be distracted by the future right now.

The final game against American University was brutal. At the end of regulation time, it was a scoreless tie. In what became the longest overtime game in NCAA history, Ryan intercepted a pass in their own zone and laced the ball up the field through traffic to Paul's waiting foot. Paul executed a quick pass to the fresh legs of a young sophomore who landed a perfectly timed shot against an off-balance keeper. The winning goal was theirs! When the final three whistles were blown, it was official. They did it! They were the NCAA National Championship winners.

Overjoyed and completely spent, Ryan and his teammates converged into a giant pile of humanity at the center of the field. All the work, the sacrifice, the pain, and the commitment paid off for them. The heavily weighted West Coast crowd cheered wildly for the first ever Bruins National title. The celebration lasted well into the night and continued when they returned to campus, where they were greeted and feted like warriors returning victorious from battle.

Amid all the hoopla and chaos, Ryan and Paul found a quiet spot to take a few minutes and let it all sink in.

Paul was still jumping with excitement as he said, "We actually did it! I knew we had what it would take to win it all, but there was a part of me that just wouldn't let me see this moment. Does that make any sense?"

"You bet it does," Ryan said nodding. "I let myself visualize set plays, critical passes, even a winning goal, but maybe it's just superstition or something because I never let myself think about what this celebration would be like. It's almost overwhelming now that it really happened."

Paul turned serious. "Coach said the European scouts were really impressed with you out there. And they should be. You were awesome Ryan. Your leadership made the difference. When most guys, including me, seemed like they were running out of gas, we saw you dig deep and put it into overdrive. You made all the difference, and here we are." Paul swept his arms wide as if to show how large the win was. "Maybe you will be headed overseas."

"Thanks, Paul," said Ryan. "I just wanted this win for us. I'm not sure what the future holds for me, but it will work out."

"You'll figure it out, man. You always do."

In the following weeks, Ryan came to discover how his playing would pay off for him. "*Football*" was going to be his career, at least for now. He was picked up by the English Premier League, signing a lucrative contract with the Stoke City team located in Stoke-on-Trent, smack in the middle of the UK.

Chapter 10

New York, New York

Two thousand miles away in a sports bar, a group of young investment bankers from Fontella & Scharf had gathered to watch the NCAA Championship soccer match. They had snagged a table in front of the lone television, much to the chagrin of latecomers.

As Mike, a junior banker, walked up to where everyone was huddled, John said a bit sarcastically, "Well look at you in your Penn State sweater."

"I'm just happy I found it," said Mike. He struck a pose with his hands on his hips and added, "And bonus, it still fits! They may not be in the final this year, but we've been there."

"Well, you're not the only one decked out in college gear. I see a few UCLA shirts and caps around the bar," said John as he looked around the room.

Some of the patrons had no allegiance to either school, and some cheered for American University just because it was an east coast school. Many seemed to care little about which team would win. They simply enjoyed a competitive sporting event.

The group was largely male, not unusual at a Wall Street hangout, but there were a couple of women among them. Only one was an investment banker, however. She approached the table, holding the hand of her husband, Bill.

"TRACY!" the group responded enthusiastically when they spotted her. Tracy's beaming face was their answer. She loved her colleagues, loved her work and, of course, loved her new husband of only one month.

John spoke to Bill first. "Hey, Bill. How's married life?"

Bill grinned and winked, pulling Tracy close. "It couldn't be better, John," he replied.

John turned to Tracy, "So are you used to your new last name yet? Honestly, I was shocked you changed it given that you're such a feminist and all."

Tracy rolled her eyes. John could be a bit of a pill at times.

Tracy smiled sweetly and answered, "Yes, I'm getting used to it." She turned away from John to look at the TV, shutting down any further questions from him.

A roar erupted from several patrons as UCLA almost scored.

"Hey Tracy," Bill said pointing to the television, "Do you think any of the players you tutored in France are on the UCLA team?"

"I suppose it's possible, although I'm afraid I wouldn't remember or recognize them if they materialized right in front of me," she answered.

Another co-worker leaned forward, listening to the conversation. "Tracy," Marco asked with a hint of hesitation, "Why wouldn't you recognize or remember them?" He held up his hands, "If I'm impertinent, I'm sorry."

Tracy smiled. "It's okay, Marco. You're new, and I try not to make a big deal about it. The short version is that I tutored in France over the summer before I completed my MBA. As I was driving to the airport, I was involved in a horrific accident, which left me with a form of amnesia, compliments of a sizable gash on my head, a slightly different nose, and a broken arm, now fully functional," she responded gently while flexing her arm.

"Oh, my!" Marco exclaimed. "That's awful. I'm glad you healed so well."

"Thank you. I was lucky the truck driver who hit me wasn't hurt badly and pulled me from the car before it caught fire. Also, the hospital in Lille, France was advanced in trauma treatment and happened to have one of the world's top plastic surgeons on staff. They nursed me back to life, sewed me up and made me presentable again. All my physical wounds have healed. The only thing missing is my memory of that summer or even a couple of months leading up to it."

Marco looked dumbfounded. "So, you don't remember *anything?* Isn't that weird?"

"Nope. Nothing. And yes, it feels odd to not remember a chunk of my life. In a way, that summer program was to be my graduation trip, a time to relax a bit even though I was tutoring and taking a class. I do remember looking so forward to going. I sent my parents some postcards during my summer in Lille, but I didn't learn any details about my travels from them because all I ever wrote was 'Having a great time. Thanks for helping me make my dreams come true.' My camera and all the rolls of film I planned to develop when I got home burned in the wreckage."

She sighed and continued, "Whatever experiences I had in Lille are buried in Lille, at least for now and quite possibly, forever. All it took was one careless delivery driver who admitted he was looking over his route papers and didn't see the red light or my car as he approached the intersection. Thank God, he looked up in time and hit the brakes, or I might not be here right now. I was in a medically induced coma for several weeks to help my brain heal. As soon as the doctors cleared me for travel, my parents, who had traveled to Lille to stay with me, arranged a medical flight back to New York where I finished my recovery at home. Most of my long-term memories came flooding back quickly, especially as I was exposed to family, friends, and familiar surroundings. I was lucky that I didn't develop anterograde amnesia, which blocks the ability to form new memories. With nothing else to do while recovering, I finished my final coursework mainly from home."

"That's incredible. Your guardian angel was sure with you that day," Marco said as he took her hand. "You are very brave. You tell your story so matter-of-factly. I can't imagine any of that experience was easy. But I'm curious. Do you ever wonder how your life might have been like if...?"

Tracy pulled her hand back and shook her head. "No, there would be no point. In fact, I don't think my life would be any different, especially," she said looking over at Bill, "since I met this guy." She winked at Bill who was grinning from ear-to-ear.

Another roar from the crowd took their attention back to the television. The game was fierce and had moved into overtime.

Tracy looked intently at the players on the small screen. Marco's question had jarred her more than she let on to him or Bill. And she had lied. She did wonder if her life would have somehow been different. She squinted, trying to see the players' faces more clearly, but nothing seemed to register with any familiarity. Her thoughts raced. *Should I know any of those men? I guess it's possible that I tutored one or more of them. I knew I'd be working with players from West Coast teams because that information was in my course paperwork.* Her gaze shifted from the TV to Bill. He was fully engaged in the game. She smiled at his intensity. *Well, according to my religious beliefs, everything happens for a reason,* she reminded herself.

The noise in the bar had reached a crescendo. UCLA had scored in overtime! The UCLA alumni bought a round of drinks for everyone in the bar, putting even the American University fans into a better mood.

Bill downed his drink and leaned over to whisper in Tracy's ear, "Wanna get outta here?"

She nodded. They said their goodbyes and headed out into a blustery December evening.

"Shall I hail a cab?" Bill asked.

"No, let's walk. It's not that far, and I need to clear my head from the booze and the overheated warmth of the bar," Tracy answered looping her arm through his.

"I am the luckiest guy in the world to have you on my arm, Mrs. Knapp." Bill smiled at her as they waited for the light to change.

"Bill, I can't imagine my life without you anymore. These past two years have been the best years of my life."

"Like I said, lucky me," Bill concluded. "I still think about the first time we sparred against one another. I think I was a bit blinded by your intelligence; your dark, piercing brown eyes; your amazing sense of humor and quick wit balanced with your ability to connect with people deeply and honestly. Blinded until I realized we were about to get our client's pocket picked by your shrewd M&A team."

Tracy raised her eyebrows and said, "Hold on buster, that's not a fair assessment of the situation! My team was completely within bounds to make that deal an asset only sale."

"Yeah sure," said Bill, "but not at the original offered price. Our client would have been left holding some big pension

liabilities and potential environmental costs among other residual issues."

"Hey, everyone knows you get what you negotiate," Tracy
quipped. "Besides, it all worked out, and each of our clients was
happy with the outcome of the deal, and both companies are
thriving!"

Bill squeezed Tracy's arm, "And I got the best part of the
deal...YOU!"

"Yes, you did," Tracy agreed. She smiled broadly. "And I do
appreciate your compliments."

They stepped into a doorway to watch holiday decorations
being hung in a store window and escape the wind for a moment.
Bill put his arm around Tracy and asked, "Does it still bother you
that some of my colleagues were rude and talked over you when
you tried to speak up during the meetings?"

"Yes, and I know I should let that go," she answered. "But it's
so darn frustrating! It's still happening."

The store clerk spotted them watching. She smiled and waved.
They waved back.

"Tracy, I understand where you're coming from—as much as
I can as a man. It's unfair, but there are still plenty of old-school
types that just can't seem to reconcile a woman's femininity with
high intellectual capacity or the competitive spirit necessary to
make it in investment banking. Things are changing but not at a
fast pace."

"Not fast enough for me, at least," Tracy said shaking her
head.

"And your understanding of that, Mr. Knapp, is one of your
traits that drew me to you," she said poking him in the chest.

They stepped back onto the sidewalk to continue their journey home and were both taken aback by the sudden burst of wind. She put her arm through his again. "So, I don't blow away," Tracy said only half-jokingly.

Bill chuckled a bit to himself and stole a glance at her to see the wind whipping her hair around her face. She seemed lost in thought. He guided them around a Salvation Army bell-ringer, still thinking about their conversation. Tracy had shared many stories about work problems that stemmed from obvious sexist actions by colleagues, superiors or even clients, and almost always male. In addition to talking right over her, almost worse was the silence that typically ensued when she offered an idea or possible solution to an issue. Adding insult to injury, sometimes a male staffer would offer up the same concept a little while later, and a chorus of men would chime in that the solution was brilliant. Bill winced thinking about how that must feel—to be completely discounted as a professional in your own field.

He was impressed how Tracy coped with her colleagues. She had decided that in most cases her best bet was to say nothing, believing that if she said anything she wouldn't be viewed as a team player. "Silence is golden," she once said to him, "especially if they choose my solution because it confirms that I'm learning. It's not always about the recognition. I do believe, though, that it will come one day." Through his own professional experience, he admitted that her way was probably necessary, but he wondered and even worried a bit, about how that additional and unnecessary stress might affect a person, even someone as strong as his amazing wife.

He realized they had stopped and Tracy was talking to him.

"Bill? Helloooo, are you in there? Do you have your keys handy, my love? We're home."

Chapter 11

Chicago 1986

"Excuse me, Michael and Tracy," said Holly, their administrative colleague. "Your car to the airport is downstairs."

"Thank you, Holly," said Michael. "It's game time Tracy, I'll meet you at the elevator in a few minutes."

Tracy put the client presentation folders into her briefcase and took a last look at the conference table to be sure she had all the necessary paperwork for the meeting in Chicago that evening.

As they got into the car, their driver said, "We should arrive at LaGuardia in less than thirty minutes, Mr. Fontella. Not much traffic at this time of day."

"Thank you, Tom," said Michael.

Turning to Tracy, Michael said, "Jack Benson and I go back a long way, though I know better than to count on relationships to close a deal. Generally, it will get you to the table and maybe a wink or a nudge in the right direction, but it's just business, and they're going to battle for the best deal. I believe you and your team have thoroughly covered the bases, Tracy, so we should be in a good position to land it."

"Thank you, Michael. Everyone worked hard on this proposal. And many long nights, said Tracy."

"I remember those days Tracy," Michael waxed nostalgically. He looked out the window at skyscraper after skyscraper as the driver weaved his way north toward the airport. "Hours and hours of research, digging for details, looking for nuggets to differentiate and demonstrate our value to the client. It is a lot of work, a lot of hours and requires sacrifices. The all-nighters subside as responsibilities increase but being ready to work, travel or just be available for the business at a moment's notice and at any hour will always be necessary. If a person has a family, it's critical to have their support."

"I'm fortunate that Bill understands and supports my career Michael," said Tracy.

"Good for you Tracy and good for us," responded Michael with a wink.

The car pulled up to their designated airline entry door, and Tom retrieved their overnight carry-on bags from the trunk. "Have a safe flight Mr. Fontella," said Tom. "You too Ms. Knapp."

"Thank you, Tom," said Tracy. *I think that's the first time I didn't have to remind Tom my name*, thought Tracy to herself. *Progress on another front! Yes!*

They settled into their first-class accommodations and ordered water as their pre-flight drink.

As was his custom, Michael was asleep before they were wheels up. He was a high energy executive and made it clear that his body responded well to even short midday naps when needed. Tonight's dinner and negotiations might well run late, so Tracy took his cue, pulled down her window shade and retrieved her sleep mask from her briefcase. She was out within minutes as well.

Upon arrival at Chicago's O'Hare airport, they made their way to the arrivals exit door and quickly found their waiting limousine, a black stretch that could probably hold six people although it was exclusively hired for them.

"Excellent," said Michael looking at his watch. "At this time of the day, we should get to the downtown dinner club by 5:30 PM, right on time."

"Yes, sir," said their driver. "No problems reported on the inbound Kennedy today."

Turning to Tracy, Michael resumed chatting about his relationship with the CEO of the firm they were wooing. "Jack is a boating enthusiast, sailboats to be specific. He and I have spent many weekends cruising his 36-foot Hunter out of Newport, Rhode Island, where he docks for the summer."

Michael closed his eyes for a minute and seemed lost in his thoughts.

"I love the feel of the breeze blowing and cruising out on the open water." He opened his eyes and turned to Tracy, "Do you and Bill like to boat, Tracy?"

"We enjoy bicycle riding, mostly around Central Park, which is near our apartment," Tracy responded. "It's also very convenient with our work schedules being as they are."

"Here we are sir," said their driver as he pulled up in front of the private club. The driver retrieved their bags from the trunk and opened the curbside car door. "Would you like me to bring your bags inside?"

Michael looked over at Tracy who shook her head. Michael said, "No, thank you. We'll manage from here."

Michael motioned for Tracy to go ahead of him and a doorman was holding the door open however as she approached he pointed to a sign above the entrance that read, "Men only, woman enter through side door."

While Tracy didn't blame the man for doing his job, she made a split-second decision to ignore the instruction and walked straight through the forbidden door. Outwardly she remained calm and composed however inside she could feel her heart beating fast. She wondered if the club's social police would arrive blowing whistles to mark the flagrant foul and then escort her back out the door.

Waiting inside the lobby was their host, Jack Benson. His eyes darted around the lobby as if to ensure no one else had seen her act of defiance.

"Hello Jack," said Michael loudly, diffusing the situation by extending his arm to shake hands.

"Hello Michael," responded Jack as he accepted the handshake.

"Jack, please meet Tracy Knapp, Senior Manager and one of the firm's rising stars."

"Hello Ms. Knapp," said Jack. "That's quite a compliment coming from Michael. I hear he's a tough master."

"Very good to meet you also, Mr. Benson," said Tracy extending her arm to shake Jack's hand. "And please call me Tracy."

"All right Tracy and first names here also."

A porter came over and handed keys to Tracy and Michael. "I'll take your luggage to your rooms," he said.

"Thank you," said Michael.

"Let's head up to our private dining room on the 15th floor and have a cocktail," said Jack. "I'd like to chat about a few things before the other board members arrive."

"That sounds great Jack," said Michael.

Jack motioned for Tracy to go before him however she was unfamiliar with the layout of the building. "Please, lead the way, Jack," Tracy said.

Jack walked down the hallway, and they boarded the elevator. Tracy's inner anxiety had calmed, but for a fleeting moment, she had felt a kinship with the famed civil rights activist Rosa Parks. While she knew she wouldn't face termination of her employment for her act of social defiance as did Ms. Parks, Tracy resented the stress that resulted from standing up against yet another humiliating and discriminatory situation. And maybe worst of all was that neither of these two educated, professional men acknowledged or even seemed concerned that the separate entryway was demeaning and hurtful. *This crap just needs to end now*, she thought to herself. As the elevator doors opened, she pushed the stressful thoughts out of her mind and regained her focus on the mission at hand.

The meetings and dinner went smoothly, and Tracy and Michael were victorious. Another IPO win for Fontella and Scharf. She slept soundly that night and woke refreshed at 5:00 AM. She showered and dressed quickly to meet Michael in the lobby at 5:45. Their limo arrived right on time and traffic was light at this early hour.

"Great work yesterday Tracy," Michael said as they rode to the airport for their return trip. "You really showed Jack and his board how our plans will unlock value for their company by raising much-needed capital to fuel their growth strategies."

"Thank you, Michael. It was a great team effort that allowed me to present our proposal so effectively. Thank you also for your leadership. Your strong relationship with Jack was critical in getting us to the game, and Jack's comments over cocktails helped me stress the most critical issues during the presentation to the full board."

"You're welcome, Tracy. Our business is built on trust and the impeccable reputation of our firm. Relationships are beneficial, especially when times get tough. I'm glad to see you networking with leaders at social and business functions as well as through charitable work. I was pleased that you accepted the board role at Bellevue Hospital."

"Thank you again, Michael, for informing me about the board role and supporting me through the selection process."

"My pleasure Tracy. I was happy that you embraced working with a hospital board after your personal experience. I'm confident you will contribute to making Bellevue an even better hospital in the years to come, and it's good for our firm."

"I will do my best, Michael. And yes, I was very fortunate to receive great care in France, so I'm thrilled to support improvements to the healthcare system in our great city."

"You're on your way, Tracy. I also want to apologize for the uncomfortable situation made by that sign at the club entrance. I've been there before and can't say I ever noticed it."

"Thank you, Michael." She felt like she wanted to say a lot more but chose to say nothing. *I must remain positive that things will get better and stay committed to driving change, but how many battles can a person fight before you just burst or throw in the towel?*

Chapter 12

Europe Spring 1988

"Hey Ryan, have you made plans for the offseason?" asked Micky O'Hara as the Stoke City team bus barreled down the highway to their next game in Leicester City.

"I'm staying on your side of the pond this year," answered Ryan. "My folks and younger sister are coming for a week, so I'll be playing tour guide. But I'm glad they'll be here, it's been almost a year since I've seen my family."

"Hey bloke, we're your family too," Micky said as he jokingly punched Ryan in the arm.

"My apologies, brother," Ryan said bowing his head to Micky. "That is the truth. I've been fortunate to find a home here with you guys and our fans."

"Actually, I think we all just get a charge out of your accent!" said Micky laughing.

"Ah, the truth finally comes out!" exclaimed Ryan. They both laughed heartily. "After that, I'm going to take a couple weeks and roam around Europe. I've got some open invitations to visit people, and at least one of those is on a boat docked in Monaco."

"There are no "boats" docked in Monaco, my friend. Only some of the most luxurious yachts in the world. Enjoy yourself, Ryan. You've had a great season, and we're solidly in the middle of the pack this year."

"Thanks, Micky. Your expert defensive skills helped us midfielders do our jobs. I'm just happy to be part of the team and want to keep playing as long as I can contribute, and these legs hold up!" said Ryan as he patted the black elastic brace surrounding his right knee.

"How is that knee of yours Ryan?"

"It's as good as it can be for now. The doctor said it's a partially torn ACL, so it's a little jiggly but no surgery unless it tears completely. And that my friend could be the end of my career or at least a long and tough rehab so let's hope it stays where it is. Unfortunately, it won't repair itself either although the doc said the surrounding muscles might strengthen up a bit, which would help. The good news is there's no pain."

"Ryan, you wouldn't let on if you *were* playing with pain, but glad to hear you say that. Let's win one today!"

"You bet!" echoed Ryan.

Chapter 13

"It is with great pleasure I introduce to you our newest partner—one of the youngest at thirty-nine and the first woman—Tracy Knapp," Michael Fontella said with a flourish.

The thunderous applause from her colleagues made Tracy's smile all the wider. She had so worked hard to earn full partner status; it had been her goal since day one at Fontella & Scharf. As her colleagues congratulated her, she was struck by how sincere they all were, both men and women, of her accomplishment.

"No one deserves this more, Tracy," Marco enthused as he shook her hand. "I feel privileged to be on your team," he added.

"Thank you, Marco. I couldn't have done it without all of you." She meant it.

A pop was heard from the corner of the room as Michael opened the first bottle of champagne. Once everyone had a glass in hand, Michael raised his and said, "Tracy, today is a special day. Not just because you're the first female partner, or because you earned partnership at a young age, but because you're YOU. I knew from the moment I met you that you had the fortitude, guts, and intellect to succeed in this business. That you've climbed the ranks in such spectacular fashion is not a surprise to me or anyone else in this room. Congratulations, you've earned it!"

Cheers of "Here, here!" were heard as glasses were clinked around the room.

A few minutes more of cheer and champagne passed and then it was time to go back to work.

As Tracy opened the door to her office, she was pleasantly surprised to see a dozen yellow roses waiting for her. She opened the attached card to read:

My Dearest Tracy, Today marks the crowning achievement of all your hard work and dedication at F&S. The girls and I are so proud of what you've accomplished. We love you to the moon and back. Bill, Nicole, and Jean

Tracy closed her eyes and held the card to her chest. Almost 15 years in the making, what amazing times I've experienced! She sniffed the roses and made her way to her chair. She smiled at the pictures of her family on her desk and then twirled around to look at the Manhattan skyline.

Maybe it's the champagne she thought. *I don't feel like working right this minute.* She leaned forward in her chair to look down toward the street sixty-five stories below. The floor-to-ceiling windows in her new office gave her an impressive view. *I made partner before forty. I did it!* She sat smiling at the vastness of the city when suddenly she raised her hand to her head. *What? What did I just hear?* She looked around her office. *I heard my voice... but a younger me...'I'm going to make partner before I'm 40.' Who was I talking to? Where did I say that?* The unexpected memory unsettled her. She looked at her hands. They were shaking. *Oh, my God. Could this be a forgotten memory returned? After all this time?*

She sat with her eyes closed, trying to recall the voice she'd heard and the circumstances, but it was gone. She thought about what her doctors had said. The possibility existed that she could regain some or all her memories from that summer, but when that might happen, if ever, was anybody's guess. They said she might recall a memory by seeing something or experiencing a triggering event. *Maybe this was a triggering event,* she mused, or *maybe I've just had too much champagne*, she thought feeling more under control again.

Tracy turned to face her desk again. She reached out her hand and gently traced the frame of a photo of her daughters with her fingers. *I never knew I could love two little people so much. We are so blessed. Thank you, Lord Jesus.*

Chapter 14

Commuter train to NYC

Time had passed quickly as Tracy's career picked up steam. In addition to her education, she really had the instincts, drive, and people skills needed to be a successful investment banker. Her firm continued to place more trust in her, and her responsibilities grew. As a result, she made her clients, her company, her teammates, and herself a whole lot of money.

Her election to partner earned her a place on the management board of the company.

At times, she admitted to herself that hers was a crazy lifestyle with a full-time live-in nanny to support a busy, two-career couple and almost any free time devoted to the girls. Occasionally she had taken the girls and their nanny, Karla, with her on business trips. Even at a young age, they seemed as comfortable sleeping in a hotel room in Vienna as they were in their own beds in rural Rye, NY where Tracy, Bill, and their young family had settled.

Physically the girls were quite different from each other. Jean was blond with green eyes while Nicole had light brown hair and bright blue eyes. Both displayed the athleticism of their parents, well mostly their father who had played basketball for Yale. Already the girls were swimming and playing tennis. On weekends, they occasionally headed into the city to enjoy Central Park. Most weekends from summer through fall, they rode bicycles along the winding roads in The Hamptons, where Bill and Tracy had purchased a weekend home to enjoy the clean, fresh country air and the beautiful beaches.

Tracy knew that she and Bill worked long and hard, and sometimes the stress of it all seemed to be building higher and higher. Their schedules were packed with work, family, and charitable organization commitments. There was little alone time for the two of them, but then she figured that's the way it was for most families now. Sometimes, she missed the simplicity of the days when it was just the two of them.

One morning, they were having a quick cup of coffee and fruit before heading out to go their separate ways. Tracy looked up from the *Wall Street Journal* and said, "Hey, do I know you?"

Bill put down the financial magazine he was reading and looked wistfully at her, saying, "Hmm I hope so because you're the most beautiful woman I've ever laid eyes on and you're sitting in my kitchen."

"Well Bill Knapp," sighed Tracy as she looked longingly into his eyes. "There was a time when that look and those words would be enough to make me call the office and say I'd be a couple hours late. Today, however, I have a huge meeting with a very important client that demands my participation."

"I understand," said Bill clearly disappointed. "I don't like it, but I understand. Go ahead and leave me hungry. I'll have to be satisfied with memories of the days we lounged around watching movies, reading books and jetting off to exciting places to celebrate our victories, well, usually your victories. Those were the days."

"Yes, my darling," said Tracy. "Many fond memories and hopefully many more to come."

Tracy gave Bill a quick kiss and headed out the door issuing a reminder, "I'm staying in the city tonight since I have a client dinner and early morning meeting tomorrow. See you Friday. Love you."

"I love you too Tracy." He watched her walk out the door and then went back to reading his magazine as he sipped his coffee.

Tracy drove to the nearby train station, parked in her assigned spot, boarded the 5:50 AM and settled in for the just under one-hour ride to Grand Central Terminal in NYC. Tracy normally used the time to catch up on her business reading of financial newspapers, magazines, and reports. Today, she let her mind wander as she stared out the window into the still-dark sky. She thought about how things had changed for women at her firm and in business since she entered the workforce as an intern almost two decades ago. Fontella and Scharf now had more women in leadership than any similar firm in New York. With that said the actual number of women compared to men was still a small fraction. Some things were slow to change, and broad acceptance of sharp, high achieving women was one of them.

Over the years Tracy dealt with many clients, almost exclusively male, who initially seemed to question having a female on the team but usually warmed once they got to know her and saw how she contributed to the process.

Internal colleagues sometimes proved to be more problematic since the situation demanded regular interaction. Some individuals simply seemed uncomfortable, and a few were still downright dismissive. She admitted it was a fine line when you worked in an environment that by nature required criticism, but you got a feel for some of the offenders over time. Navigating these situations necessitated a ridiculous amount of mental effort, especially if the individual was in leadership. She felt huge pressure to earn their support and get results, personally and for her fledgling team. She was a woman leader in a man's world. The safe route would have been to simply build a team from the readily available talent pool of white males and forge ahead. But Tracy felt that she and the firm would achieve greater success tapping into a much larger population of eligible workers. She also wanted to be a catalyst for more women to enter the business and level the playing field as quickly as possible.

Tracy was proud to have built the most diverse team in the company with women, minorities and what some of the other partners referred to as simply "eclectic" folks, as well as being in the top ranks of achievement. Tracy simply saw each associate as the brilliant, eager, hard-working contributor they were and felt privileged to have assembled and lead this esteemed group.

As a young manager, the issue of her perceived "crusade for women" had been raised by a superior in those words during an annual performance review. To her credit, she patiently listened to this perhaps well-meaning, yet clearly misguided leader and smiled through a perfunctory "Thank you for sharing your constructive criticism."

Tracy chuckled to herself as she remembered that evening at home with Bill when she unloaded the day's events on him. They were about three-quarters of the way through a bottle of their favorite cabernet when Bill shared his perceptions of how women were treated in his office.

Bill said, "Some of the guys absolutely hate being one-upped by a woman regardless of the circumstances." While he admitted that he didn't personally feel that way, he hadn't challenged and certainly never admonished male colleagues for this behavior.

"The double standards still abound, Tracy," Bill had said. "I've heard guys describe a female who's a tough negotiator as a *bitch*, despite her success and some guys think, erroneously I might add, that surely she must lack a caring heart and can't possibly possess the feelings of a 'real' woman."

Tracy had listened quietly, commanding herself not to shoot the messenger. She knew these were not Bill's feelings or actions.

"Heck, Tracy," Bill continued, "I've overheard colleagues, men and even some women, snipe that a woman so focused on her career surely wouldn't be interested in or capable of being a great wife and loving mother. And if she's physically appealing, she might have it even tougher if jealousy enters the picture. It seems odd because guys don't generally fear other guys that are good looking. It's unfair, but some of these old stereotypes are deep set and permeate all levels of organizations."

While Tracy didn't like to hear this or admit the existence of these archaic and hurtful prejudices, she knew all this was real, and it added unnecessarily to the workload and stress experienced by many women, who were striving to support their families and contribute to their organizations.

Tongue in cheek, Bill offered that being married to her was far more effective than taking diversity training classes offered by his firm's human resource department. Over time, he became more aware of these tendencies and more vocal about calling folks out when confronted with these situations. He told her what bothered him most was that many of these guys either already had families of their own or wanted to be husbands and fathers. They were a tough, sharp-minded bunch, and many believed they were fair-minded executives. He shook his head as he rhetorically asked, "Don't they see the irony, the hypocrisy in their thoughts and actions?"

Lastly, he told Tracy that he had begun to proactively support women in group meetings and suggest including them in social events. He was surprised when several women personally expressed their appreciation to him. He was also surprised that some of his male colleagues chided him for taking a *feminist* stance and noticed that sometimes *he* was being excluded as his buddies headed out to lunch or the local bar after work.

Tracy realized how hard this must have been for Bill, but then she already knew she had fallen in love with and married a man of high integrity and strong moral character.

Real change, she thought to herself, *came from the top leaders, and some either turned a blind or perpetuated the culture through their own actions.*

Tracy's train slowed as it approached the Mount Vernon East station. As the train regained speed, she noted the disparity between the muted colors of fall foliage in the light mist to the mostly gray and glass structures looming in the distance and sighed.

Tracy thought back to the day she told Michael that she was pregnant and that she intended to continue her managerial role on the team. Since she was the first high ranking woman in the firm to bear a child, she wasn't sure what to expect. She remembered the conversation as if it happened yesterday.

"I have happy news for the Knapp family, Michael. I'm pregnant."

"That is wonderful Tracy. I'm very happy for you and Bill," said Michael, himself a father of three. Then silence.

Tracy offered, "If all goes well, I should be back to work in about six weeks. Bill and I intend to hire a live-in nanny to care for our baby. I've formulated a plan to cover my work responsibilities, and my peers have agreed to oversee my team's projects during my absence. I'll also make myself accessible as needed during my absence."

"Thank you, Tracy," said Michael. "That sounds like a winning plan." Then he added, "Do you recall when Jim Donohue had that unfortunate heart attack last year?"

"Yes, that was a difficult time for him," said Tracy.

Michael said, "What I remember is that you and the other leaders rallied to help him while he recovered, which ended up keeping him out of the office for two months."

"Of course, Michael. It was the right thing to do. We wanted to ensure that his clients were taken care of properly so Jim could focus his efforts on his rehabilitation program."

"I was very proud of the team's efforts. I'll expect the same from each during your time away," said Michael. "And don't hesitate to call on me for help."

"Thank you, Michael," said Tracy.

"Life happens," said Michael.

Things ran smoothly while she was on leave and Michael even came to her house to visit a few weeks after Nicole was born.

Tracy felt fortunate to have relatively uncomplicated pregnancies and deliveries. As time went on and Jean was born less than two years later, she was also very thankful to have two healthy children with no more than typical health issues thus far.

A light drizzle had begun to fall on the gray October morning. Tracy sipped her coffee as she continued reminiscing about how she and Bill got to where they were today.

They found Karla with the help of an east coast nanny agency a few weeks after Nicole's birth. She was loving, good natured and experienced. She had a special fondness and the personality to care for babies and young children. Karla had served her last family for eight years until a recent job transfer took them to the West Coast and she decided to remain in NY where she had family and friends.

Tracy thought about the early years of their growing family when she and Bill both had morning commutes to the city and similarly long work days. Occasional instances of walking the house at wee hours comforting a sick child were gladly Bill or Tracy's responsibility. Karla was happy to take over in the rare case when both had out of town travel scheduled, or needed an uninterrupted night's sleep in advance of a critical meeting. Bill and Tracy considered themselves very lucky, and Tracy said many a prayer of thanksgiving for their good fortune.

Even with all the home bases covered, Tracy sometimes wondered if she was doing the right thing for their family and for herself. Perhaps, only another mother can truly understand the mixed feelings and emotional conflict of leaving your baby to go back to work. Maybe it is the biological shift of hormones, the physical changes that a woman's body and mind experiences during that time, but, mostly, she thought, it was simply the power of love that stirred your heart and made you look at some things differently when graced with the gift of a child.

Realizing the demands of their chosen professions and the needs of their growing family, Bill and Tracy had decided last year that one of them needed to move to a role that required less travel, more predictable hours and perhaps a bit less stress overall. After a few long, late night discussions, they agreed that Bill had the best opportunity to make a career change. He put out a few feelers and quickly landed a senior financial role at a solid regional bank that was trying to grow its commercial lending business.

It turned out to be the perfect fit for Bill and for their family. The job offered significant responsibility, excellent compensation, albeit less than his prior role, and best of all, predictable hours that had Bill home in time for dinner almost every night.

The train pulled into the terminal right on time, and Tracy hailed a cab as she left the station. "St. Peter's Church, 22 Barclay Street, in the Financial District, please," Tracy instructed the driver as she entered the car. The car weaved through the light early morning traffic and pulled up in front of the oldest Catholic church in New York City just in time for morning Mass.

Tracy paid the driver in cash. "Have a nice day," she said to the cabbie as she stepped out of the vehicle.

"You too, Miss and thank you," he responded.

Tracy opened the front door of the church and walked up the main aisle as quietly as her heeled shoes would allow. She slipped into her usual pew about halfway toward the altar, lowered the kneeler, took a cleansing breath, and tried to calm her mind as she prayed. Within minutes the church bells rang, and the congregation rose to begin the Mass. Thirty minutes later the priest gave his final words of encouragement to "Go forth and share the good news of the Lord". The group of maybe twenty-five people responded in unison, "Thanks be to God." After leaving the church, she walked a few short blocks to her office to begin her workday.

Chapter 15

Cornerstone Bank of New York, Rye office

Back at the house, Bill lingered over his breakfast. He too was reminiscing about their life journey and how his path veered from what he thought would be a long career in investment banking. Sometimes he missed the adrenaline rush of closing a big deal and the crazy hoopla that typically ensued. With the client satisfied, the partners hosted celebrations at some of New York's finest steakhouses or trendiest cigar bars. They were served the best champagne and cigars were smoked luxuriously, some of the guys even used $100 bills as torch lighters! He shook his head and smiled at the memory. *Yeah, those were heady and fun times*, he thought.

In some ways, it reminded Bill of how he felt during college when he played basketball at Yale University. Sure, it was an Ivy League program, and he and his teammates were selected as much or more for their brains as their ball skills, but competition was competition. They worked just as hard as the guys at The University of Kansas, Indiana, or any other top NCAA program. As competitors, they knew what it felt like to win, lose, practice, learn plays, strategy and watch film until you just about collapsed from exhaustion. Most importantly, they knew what it took to be successful, to be focused on your game and to work as a team to achieve goals and objectives.

Bill felt fortunate to have had these experiences and to have leveraged it all in his work as a moderately successful investment banker. He recognized that, like most people, some of his best personality traits could, in their extreme, be manifested as weaknesses. Bill was highly analytical, methodical, and extremely patient. These are great qualities in an analyst, but as he took on more leadership work, some of his colleagues felt opportunities were missed when Bill took too much time to make decisions. He realized and accepted that maybe he lacked the lightning reflexes that were instrumental during rapid fire, heated negotiations.

Thinking back, he realized that sinking free throws rather than pressured outside jump shots was his strong suit. It's not that free throws were easy, especially late in the game when the score was close, and you were the away team with the opponent's "sixth man" waving and screaming to try and distract the shooter. Bill was simply able to block all that out, focus on the mechanics, and routinely registered a free throw percentage of ninety percent or higher. It earned him the moniker "Cool hand Bill" which carried through into his professional and personal life. In many respects, Bill seemed almost unflappable. He was calm under pressure as he pondered highly charged situations. He thoroughly analyzed the facts and considered possible alternatives to arrive at the best solution to a problem. In his new role, he had ample opportunity to review financial reports, analyze debt scenarios and gather critical information in a comfortable timeline.

Being completely honest, Bill admitted that he lacked the killer instinct sometimes necessary to be a highly successful investment banker. Sure, everyone knows there's a win/win element that makes for a successful deal, but the fact of the matter was that it's your job to make the best deal for *your* client. Period. If the other side misses something, it's their loss and your gain. And if you miss something, well, it can be your head on a platter and your job with it. He admitted that Tracy was experiencing more success at it than he and her earnings now far surpassed his.

The rational side of his brain knew that meant she should be the one to stick with it, and he was comfortable with her success.

After the girls were born, something inside of him changed. He realized he found great enjoyment in watching them grow and helping them in ways big and small. It was all those reasons that made it the right decision for him to move to a different track.

He put his empty coffee cup in the dishwasher, grabbed a banana off the counter, picked up his briefcase and headed out the garage door to his shiny black sedan to make the 10-minute drive to his office.

It began to rain as Bill parked his car. As he opened his door, he pushed out the umbrella he always kept in his car. It opened with a satisfying pop. Once in his office, he dropped the umbrella out of the way by the door, put his briefcase on the credenza, turned on his computer, grabbed his coffee mug and headed to the office lunchroom.

He looked up as he poured a cup of the steaming black liquid.

"Good morning Jamie," he said to one of his colleagues.

"Good morning Bill," responded Jamie. "Good day to work in an office with rain moving in."

"Sure is," said Bill. "On the bright side, a good rain always cleans up the streets and sidewalks."

Jaime laughed and said, "You always see the bright side, Bill."

Bill took a hesitant sip of his still-to-hot-to-drink coffee, walked back over to his office, and settled into his chair. His calendar was light today, and he allowed himself to continue reminiscing. He looked at their wedding picture prominently placed on the corner of his desk. He believed their love was heart to heart, soul to soul. Just thinking about Tracy made him smile and count his blessings.

For his part, he was making a positive contribution to his employer, his family and in a larger way to other families of working men and women. He believed his support of his families' choices and his wife's career would eventually help his own daughters when they entered the workforce in whatever profession they pursued. More than ever, he felt committed to being a positive force in leveling the playing field for all workers. Integrity, skills, knowledge, education, accomplishments, drive, commitment, and results should be used to decide who gets promoted, lands the prime roles, and earns the most money. Sex, religion, the color of your skin or any other secular criteria should not inhibit anyone's opportunity to get on the playing field, contribute and succeed.

The bottom line for Bill was that he couldn't be happier. Some days he worked out of this nearby Rye branch of the bank and even on days he went to the main office downtown he took the 5:15 PM train home. This meant he arrived in time to enjoy dinner with his beautiful daughters, now five and seven. He loved to hear about their school activities and was usually able to adjust his schedule to take part in special school events and parties. He also used vacation days for some of their school holidays and day trips to museums, parks, the zoo, and other places the girls would ask to visit. Bill made sure to inform Tracy of these events, and if her schedule allowed, he would find a way to fit in a family lunch in the city. The girls loved being with their mom, and she would make them feel very special when they visited her office.

She let them sit at her desk, type on her computer, and write on her stationery. Bill kept the office visits brief knowing that everyone was busy, but he understood that it helped Tracy to have this time with her daughters. There were many late nights at the office and extended out of town business trips that kept her from her family for days at a time.

Bill smiled as he looked at the picture of his family on the back of his credenza. *Time to get back to work* he said to himself as he answered his ringing phone.

Bill's work day flew by and in a flash, he was back home pulling his car into the garage. As he opened the car door, he heard happy voices greeting him from the mudroom entrance.

"Daddy's home, Daddy's home!" the girls exclaimed in unison.

"Hello ladies," Bill said. He set down his briefcase and scooped up both girls in his arms, giving each a kiss on their forehead.

"Hello Karla, something smells delicious," said Bill taking a deep whiff.

"Hello Bill," said Karla. "Grilled chicken, green beans, and homemade mashed potatoes tonight. Oh, and a big salad."

"That sounds great. I'm starving!" he said.

"We're hungry too," Nicole volunteered, answering for her younger sister, too.

"These girls are on another growth spurt," laughed Karla. "They had a snack less than two hours ago."

"Yes Daddy, don't you think I'm taller today than yesterday?" asked little Jean.

She stood tall as Bill put his flat hand on top of her head. "Looks like you've grown an inch overnight," said Bill. Nicole stole a glance at her father and gave him a wink, making sure he knew she was in on the exaggeration. Bill smiled at her and winked back.

"Now off to wash your hands before dinner," he instructed.

They were back in a flash and sat down at their usual places for dinner. Karla's routine was to set everything on the table and then let the family enjoy dinner together while taking hers to her suite upstairs. This arrangement suited everyone's needs. Bill and Tracy were able to spend private, quality time with their children over dinner and Karla was happy to have time to relax after a busy day of performing her childcare and household duties.

Bill and Tracy insisted on no talking while chewing food to avoid the possibility of choking on food, so there was little chit-chat as they ate their salads.

Bill cleared the salad plates and loaded each plate with the main meal.

"Daddy, may I please have the barbeque sauce?" asked Nicole.

"Here you go."

"Nicole, will you put some on my plate too?" asked Jean.

"Sure," answered Nicole.

The girls liked their mashed potatoes buttered. Bill took his chicken without the sauce and left the potatoes naked. *Got to cut the calories somewhere*, he thought to himself.

"Is Mommy coming home tonight?" Nicole asked.

"She'll be home tomorrow in time for Friday night pizza!" he responded, smiling.

"Oh good!" said Jean. "And we usually watch a movie on Friday," she added excitedly, "so we need to pick a movie, Nicole."

"I chose the movie last week, so it's your turn if you want to pick it, Jean."

"Sure!" exclaimed Jean.

As they finished their food, Bill started the conversation.

"So, what's the most fun thing each of you did today at school?" asked Bill.

"Recess outside," blurted Jean. "We got to play on the new playground."

"That sounds like fun," said Bill. "What's your favorite piece of equipment?"

"The swings," said Jean excitedly. "They go really high when you kick your legs up!"

Bill laughed as he imagined his adventurous little girl with a big smile on her face, pumping her legs to drive the swing high in the air.

"How about you Nicole?" asked Bill.

"Art class was really fun today," said Nicole. "We're creating our own cartoons. We had to think of a story and write it down. Next, we're going to draw pictures to tell the story."

"That's very interesting," said Bill. "Would you like to tell us about your cartoon?"

"Sure!" exclaimed Nicole. "My story is about a girl who finds a magic wand that has the power to make animals talk. She brings the neighborhood dogs and cats together for a party and all the kids are amazed when they hear the animals talking to each other."

"That sounds like a fun story," said Bill. "I can't wait to see it when you're finished."

"Teacher said it'll be ready to show our parents at the next parent-teacher conferences."

When dinner was over, each girl took her plate, cup, and utensils to the sink for Bill to load into the dishwasher. Bill finished clearing the serving dishes.

The girls sat at the kitchen table with their homework while they waited for Bill to finish.

"Okay, ladies, let's look over your homework assignments so Dad can refresh himself on what kids are learning in school these days," said Bill. The girls typically finished their homework under Karla's guidance, so the goal of this cursory check was to ensure the work had been done and that they understood the subject matter.

"Jean, would you please read this paragraph for me?" asked Bill as he picked up a textbook.

"Sure Daddy." Jean placed her finger under the first word then slowly moved it along as she read each word aloud.

"Excellent, Jean," said Bill.

"Your turn Nicole. Looks like you're making great progress with learning your multiplication tables.

"How about writing down multiples of eight through times twelve?" asked Bill.

Nicole took a blank sheet of paper and methodically and correctly wrote out the answers. She presented the completed work to Bill.

"He looked over her work and said, "One hundred percent young lady, well done."

With homework checked, it was time for the girls to get cleaned up before bed. As Bill ushered them toward the staircase he asked, "Would you like to continue that chess game we have going before you head to bed?"

"Yes Daddy," they chimed in unison.

In a flash, they ran up the stairs and the sounds of the girls running through the hall giggling and chatting filled the house. Doors banged shut as they ran from bedroom to bathroom. 'That's a lot of energy,' he said to himself as he finished loading the dishwasher. He took a last look around the kitchen for any errant cups or dishes. Satisfied all had been captured, he shut the door and pressed the start button.

The girls were back downstairs in a flash smelling as amazing as only a freshly washed child can smell. They all settled in on the cream-colored soft leather sofa in the family room, near the gas fireplace Bill had turned on to get the room nice and warm after the girl's showers.

Jean stretched her feet toward the flames. "The fireplace makes the room feel nice and warm Daddy."

"Daddy, will you finish brushing the tangles out of our hair?" asked Nicole as she handed the hairbrush to him.

"I'd be happy to help," said Bill taking the brush and gently running it through each girl's hair. He was confident they could do this on their own but enjoyed having Dad brush their hair. Truth be told, Bill was quite sure he enjoyed it more than they did.

"Thank you, Daddy," said each girl as he gave them a kiss on the head to indicate he was finished.

The girls moved from the couch to floor so they could see the chess board. "Okay, let's look at where this game stands," said Bill. They surveyed the board.

The chess board was made of marble and the color of the squares alternated between coral and creamy white. The chess pieces were cast pewter shapes of traditional animal and human figures. While the animals were silver, the human figures were dressed in the Old English style of clothing and painted with bright accents of red, white and black.

The session was more of a chess lesson than a game as Bill guided them through various chess strategies. He felt strongly that chess helped build their thinking skills, taught them how to focus intently and slowed them down before bed. Besides, it was enjoyable time with his daughters.

When the lesson was over, it was up to bed. Each girl had her own room although the bedtime ritual started out in one or the other's room. Tonight, rather than choosing a traditional book from the numerous titles on the shelves, they decided Dad should make up a story. They loved that his stories always seemed to center around two young girls although he never used their names. The girls always seemed to have exciting, though sometimes scary adventures. On this night, Bill weaved a tale about how the girls wandered into an enchanted school.

He said, "The chalk began writing scary messages on the wall, and the books began opening to chant evil spells that turned many of the students into wild animals and insects. Rumble, bumble the dictionary said to one little boy and just like that he turned into a bumble bee!"

"Bzzz!" teased Bill as he pretended to sting each girl by tenderly poking their arms and tummies.

They tried to wiggle away and giggled with delight.

The story ended as the brave and heroic young girls commandeered erasers to wipe out the messages and used strong rubber bands to close the books and break the spells, bringing the children back to normal.

"Hurrah!" the girls cheered. "The evil spirits are defeated!"

Bill was about to dole out goodnight kisses, when Nicole piped up, "Daddy, we need to say our prayers." "Yes, we can't go to sleep without saying our prayers," echoed Jean.

With hands folded they recited, "Now I lay me down to sleep. I pray the Lord my soul to keep. And if I die before I wake, I pray the Lord my soul to take. God bless Mommy and Daddy, our grandmas and grandpas, our cousins, all our relatives and friends and everyone in the whole world. Amen."

"I love you girls," he said as he gave each a hug and good-night kiss on her forehead.

"Love you too Daddy," said each of the girls.

Nicole scooted off to her room across the hall from Jean's. Bill looked lovingly at each of his little girls before he turned off their bedroom lights and closed their doors.

Chapter 16

The Knapp home gymnasium

Bill headed down to their fully equipped gym and indoor half basketball court in the soundproofed basement. He turned up the volume of the home intercom speaker on the wall just in case one of the girls might awaken and call for him. *Treadmill tonight*, he said to himself as he ramped up the machine to 5.5 mph. He picked up the remote and clicked to the nightly financial news station on the TV facing the treadmill. While the news stories played in the background, he thought about what life might be like if he had also stayed in investment banking. The business could be extremely unpredictable, so the need to drop everything at a moment's notice and work on a deal came with the territory. The new phrase, 24/7/365, aptly conveyed that people were working somewhere at all times and on all days as holidays and work hours differed from country to country. More powerful computers and new forms of communications gave the means to transact business without regard to a clock and at ever-increasing speeds.

China was just beginning to awaken from its long commercial slumber, and while the countries direction under communism was unclear, the potential for disruption was daunting. With the hope of climbing out of desperate personal financial conditions, many Chinese people seemed willing to work long hours and days on end with few breaks for relatively little money. In some cases, it was literally the difference between life and death from famine or disease with limited health care available, especially in remote areas. In today's global world, you had to be smarter, quicker, more creative, and more available to your clients and your employer to get the job done and beat the competition.

The alarm on the treadmill sounded as it hit 30 minutes. The machine slowed automatically through its' four-minute cooldown period. After that, Bill grabbed a basketball and headed over to the half court. "Got to stay in shape," he said aloud and added, as he began bouncing the ball, "sitting at a desk all day is a killer." He put himself through a pace of layups, outside jump shots, and free throws. He made twenty consecutive free throws, pumped his fist in the air and exclaimed "Yes! You've still got it, old boy!"

He took off his shoes, socks, and sweat-drenched shirt. He grabbed a towel and headed into the steam sauna. He set the timer for 15 minutes and sat down on the bench.

He closed his eyes and felt his pores open as the steam rolled across his body. *I am a lucky man*, he thought to himself. Then he considered that the only way this could be better was if Tracy were seated there with him. Memories of the two of them making love in this very room came to mind, and it brought a big smile to his face. "When was that?" he wondered. It had to be a couple years ago. How much he missed those days! He was pressed to remember the last time they shared a truly passionate kiss, the kind that literally took your breath away. They were still having sex, occasionally, though it was of the twenty minutes from foreplay to completion variety. While physically satisfying, it sometimes left him longing for the days they used to linger in bed for hours, naked bodies touching, maybe reading a good novel or watching a classic movie. Sex then was more spontaneous, now it was pretty much planned around the nighttime ritual of getting the girls to bed and hoping that the other partner was still awake and had enough energy for the act.

Nights like tonight had become more common, with Bill at home while Tracy burned the midnight oil at her office working on another mega deal. He knew she would love to be with her family. He never questioned Tracy's love for their daughters, and he believed she still loved him.

Bill felt like he and Tracy understood each other's professional challenges and found an empathetic ear with each other. Those talks, however, had grown more infrequent as her days at the office grew longer. Their lives had become so busy, maybe too busy. Sometimes, Bill felt like they were drifting apart as a couple. He didn't think Tracy would be unfaithful to him, but then he had to admit to himself that many spouses are surprised when they discover that their life partner has broken their marriage vows. Some of their closest friends, with and without children, split up for largely unknown reasons, politely and simply stated in the court papers as "irreconcilable differences." Perhaps a spouse consumed with serving the children's needs or devoted to community or charitable affairs didn't recognize that their marital relationship needed attention or failed to understand the nature of their spouse's work environment. Some of these tough-skinned executives just assumed that their spouse *couldn't* understand the stress and so the chance to talk things over was missed entirely. As a result, the lines of communication became frayed, and some eventually were left broken.

With more women working and kids headed off to daycare or in the hands of hopefully capable nannies, both spouses should be able to better appreciate the others work and family stress although, some may be simply too tired to provide the emotional support sought from their spouse. Sometimes the "I'm sorry to hear that honey" or "That's wonderful dear and, by the way, will you unload the dishwasher while we're talking?" just failed to meet the admittedly selfish needs of the spouse who just experienced some great failure or success in their work and longed to share it.

Maybe that's where "the other woman" or in the case of a working woman, "the other man" entered the picture. Someone who just seemed to listen and care about what you had to say, what you were feeling and likely made time to be more available to you, without the strings of commitment and endless chores that faced them at home.

Bill arched his back, then stretched out his arms and legs to avoid cramping up in the 110-degree heat and humidity of the steam room. He took a long drink from his water bottle.

The buzz of the timer interrupted his thoughts. Bill left the steam sauna feeling cleansed and headed into the shower. He turned the temperature control to 78 degrees. If felt like he was being sprayed with ice water! He steadied himself by holding onto the temperature dial. As he felt his pores close, he also let the water wash away his stress along with the unwelcome thoughts. His shower finished, he took a thick towel from the warming rack and soaked up all the water from his body. He put on a fresh pair of boxer shorts and a clean white tee shirt. He grabbed another bottle of water from the refrigerator, turned off the intercom speaker and headed straight to bed. He was exhausted.

Chapter 17

The Park Helmsley Hotel Suite

Tracy arrived at her familiar "home away from home" around 9:30 PM that evening after her client dinner. "I'm exhausted," she said to no one. She kicked off her high heels and stood uncertainly for a moment. She inhaled deeply and said, "I need to, no correction, I *get* to hit the treadmill for at least half an hour," to distract her mind from the comfortable bed just feet away. She considered calling Bill but realized that meant she would likely be skipping her workout. *I'll see him tomorrow.* She looked in the mirror at the floral pattern scarf she was wearing, tied in a fancy knot well below her open neck collared shirt and said aloud, "Gosh, I'm glad the bow tie died." She chuckled as she undressed, hanged her suit in the closet and changed into the clean workout out clothes folded on the bedroom bureau. *Mmm, they smell fresh. Thank goodness for the housekeeping staff who take great care of me.*

She rode the elevator to the hotel spa floor. The fitness center, pool, dry sauna, and steam rooms were thankfully open 24 hours. Tonight, Tracy shared the main space with two other guests, both men. One appeared to be about ten years her junior and the other probably near 70. The younger man was using the exercise machines, and the older man occupied one of four treadmills. Tracy filled her water bottle and grabbed a small, clean towel from the rack before heading over to an open treadmill. No words were spoken, and no one made any attempt at eye contact which was fine with her.

Facing the treadmills was a television on the wall that was blaring a West Coast pro basketball game. It held no interest for Tracy, and she thought about asking if the older gentleman would mind changing to a late evening business program but refrained since he seemed interested in the game.

Oh well, I should just clear my mind anyway. She chose the manual program, set the incline to 2 percent and ramped the speed to 4.5 mph. She felt that a light jog would be best tonight. She had only one glass of wine, a tuna steak, and grilled vegetables for dinner but worried her body might revolt if she tried to push too hard.

Tracy stared at the beige wall and thought about what was going on at her house about now. The girls were likely sound asleep in their beds, and Bill might be exercising in their home gym. A huge plus for their family was that Bill hardly ever brought work home in his new job. Knowing the girls were safe, secure, and loved by their caregiver and that Bill was home for dinner almost every night was comforting to her. This also helped her stay focused on her work. The needs of her clients, her colleagues and the firm were important priorities and largely consumed her waking hours. She carved out time for her charitable work with the Bellevue Hospital Board and fit in a few five-mile runs each week, in an attempt to keep her mind and body toned and fit for the grueling physical and mental stress she felt. Beyond that, she committed her free time to Bill and the girls.

Tracy was thankful to have access to one of the firm's suites at The Park Helmsley. She kept a small wardrobe and a cache of personal necessities for times she might be called out of town unexpectedly or just decided to stay overnight in New York. Occasionally she and Bill scheduled date nights in the city. They typically enjoyed an intimate dinner at one of many amazing restaurants and, weather permitting, would walk and talk for hours knowing the girls were in good hands at home. During these rare evenings, they reconnected with each other though, admittedly, the conversations largely centered on their daughters' needs and activities. Schoolwork, report cards, piano and dance lessons were all in the mix. Recently, the girls had begun playing tennis, and both took to the sport like fish to water.

Feeling good, she pushed the treadmill up a few notches to 5.0.

Tracy thought about how she admired Bill for his kindness, intelligence, and relaxed personality. Of course, she also enjoyed his 6'2" athletic physique and his irresistible dimples that appeared during a true smile. Bill had a perennial boyish look with sandy blond hair and bright blue eyes. He took his career seriously yet never seemed to be consumed by it. His move to the bank seemed almost effortless. They both found it interesting that his openly stated desire for a more normal work schedule to support his young families' needs was greeted with respect and even admiration from his colleagues and the bank's owner. They considered him somewhat of a Renaissance man and showcased him in internal communications and recruiting materials as evidence of a family-friendly work culture. Tracy and Bill both saw some level of hypocrisy in this because they had seen women sidetracked or stalled in their careers when they voiced similar desires as if women were perceived as somehow less reliable or committed to their work.

On the other hand, women like Tracy, who had families and chose to commit themselves to their careers, still seemed to be largely viewed by men, and even some women, as an oddity. It was hard enough just to be a female in this business or almost any business for that matter. A few industries such as healthcare, food products, and retail, seemed to be opening to women, but many others were almost devoid of females. Manufacturing firms, especially mining and metals companies were a bastion of white males with the rare exception of a senior level female in human resources, mid-level financial or legal positions. When it came down to interacting with the real decision makers, the power holders were almost exclusively men. By now Tracy was accustomed to negotiating mostly with men, but she still held hope that one day women would be accepted into these roles and that seeing them at the table would be routine.

She thought about how she had changed over the last fifteen years since she embarked on her career. As hard as she tried to maintain her feminine qualities, she knew that in some ways she had adopted a rougher, tougher persona. Early in her career, Tracy was uncomfortable with comments from some of her colleagues and clients about her "beautiful hair." A few dared to touch her hair saying they just couldn't resist. While she felt her personal space had been violated, she didn't make a case out of it because she felt it wasn't worth the battle. She simply chopped off her long brown tresses with the desire to fit in and avoid distraction. It worked. No more hair issues. Once the girls came along, it was also easier to style in the few minutes she devoted to personal care among her endless list of to-do items. In the last year, however, she decided to grow it a bit longer again. She liked the look, and it felt more natural to her. So far, the few compliments she had received on her new look seemed genuine. Maybe more importantly, she now held a position of greater power and influence which changed the way men communicated with her. The whole aspect was ridiculous and simply added to women's stress in the workplace.

Her thoughts turned to the current business environment.

The M&A climate was favorable. Interest rates had come down from sky-high levels of the early 80s and capital for investment was readily available. All in all, this made for a steady flow of work though Tracy worried a bit about what would happen if business slowed, and there wasn't enough work for everyone. Would the firm stand by her? It wasn't a purely selfish thought that drove her concern. She was a full partner and had already amassed quite a fortune by most standards that could support her family for a long time. Additionally, Bill was secure in his job and each had marketable skills and contacts.

Tracy's concern was also for her team. Though unspoken or even unrecognized by some, working for a woman came with some degree of risk. Outright sexism or acts of discrimination seemed to be waning, but situations still occurred that left her feeling undertones of unfairness. Plum assignments seemed to be doled out to teams headed by a male partner while Tracy's team mostly generated their own work or were given more delicate or complicated projects. On the rare occasion that she questioned an assignment, she was usually told that the client felt more "chemistry" with the chosen person. Tracy accepted the insight yet wondered privately if the client simply preferred to interact with a man. *Chemistry my ass*, she had thought many times. I think you mean *anatomy,* but no one's going to push that button and risk alienating the client.

Overall though, her staff seemed content that the benefits outweighed any downsides. They were a diverse group by legal definition as well as attitude and seemed to complement each other's knowledge and skill sets. They combined their efforts to provide a comprehensive package for their clients and achieved desired results. Tracy was in a good place professionally and personally, but her driven nature always seemed to keep her striving for more.

She felt her left foot miss a step and thankfully jumped to land on the right rail while she pulled the "stop" cord. That was close, she thought, as the machine came to a halt.

"You okay there?" asked the man on the other treadmill.

"Yes, thank you," responded Tracy. "I guess I'm more tired than I thought."

She inserted the cord back into the machine, pressed the speed button until it flashed 3.0 and walked at that pace for about four minutes focusing on her feet. When her time was up, she picked up her room key and the towel that had been hanging on the handrail. As she deposited the towel into the bin on her way out the door, she realized she hadn't even broken a sweat. Once back in her room, she changed into her pajamas, crawled under the soft, white feather comforter, and fell sound asleep as soon as her head hit the pillow.

Chapter 18

Europe/Stanford, California/Palo Alto, California

On another continent, Ryan Kupford had continued making his mark, and more than a nice living, thanks to his athletic skills and a shrewd sports agent. What American players lacked in skill compared to European or South American "football" players, was more than compensated for in their work ethic, competitive team spirit, and relentless drive to excel. When Ryan came on board, the other players seemed to step their play up a notch, and the good chemistry was producing solid results for Stoke City. Ryan wasn't exactly a household name, but his team had done well in their division, and most importantly, the owners were pleased that fans filled the stadium for their games.

After six years and at age 28, Ryan's body felt battered from the relentless physical exertion and hits taken over many years. His partially torn ACL was no better or worse at that point, and he decided to invest some of his substantial earnings in furthering his education by earning an MBA from Stanford. He kept himself in shape by volunteering as a strength and conditioning coach for the men's soccer team, and they were thrilled to have him share insights from his collegiate and professional experiences. Truth be told, he felt like he gained more than he gave since the role helped him bridge from the high-octane world of professional soccer to "civilian" life.

After graduation, Ryan landed a finance job with a private, fledgling software company in Palo Alto that went public shortly after he joined. It was a great opportunity to learn how a corporation really functioned. And learn he did. He committed himself to his work and took every opportunity to contribute by accepting assignments. His drive and enthusiasm impressed his superiors. Before long, he was a key member of a team assigned to analyze acquisition targets, and he found himself beginning to interact with investment bankers, some headquartered in New York.

He learned how the successful firms operated and observed how the most effective associates conducted themselves. They asked critical questions, were incredibly knowledgeable and came armed with limitless data about the potential acquisition. He also saw how competitive this business was and realized that excited him. He was hooked and knew that his next job would be at an investment banking firm, likely requiring a move to New York.

When he said the words, "New York investment banking firm," it was like an old wound opened and almost 15 years of suppressed memories came bleeding out. Memories of Tracy. It was Tracy who introduced him to the business of investment banking, though, at the time he never saw himself in the field. Heck, back then all he saw was himself in a UCLA soccer uniform. He remembered how odd he found it that she was over-the-top excited about embarking on her career. Tracy Ward. *Where would she be today?* he wondered. *Did she pursue her dream of investment banking?*

He allowed himself to drift back to that summer. He could almost smell her perfume and the scent of those amazing roses outside her little cottage. Her cottage. The place where they first made love and shared amazing intimate moments. He closed his eyes as he remembered the summer of 1981 in Lille France. The place where he fell completely in love with Tracy Ward, the woman he thought he was destined to be with forever. So long ago, yet the memories seemed fresh, vivid and were painful even now. She would be about 40 he calculated. That age triggered a memory where she had confided some of her dreams and ambitions to him. One of those was to make partner by age 40. He remembered her saying that she had never spoken those dreams aloud for fear of jinxing herself, though she didn't consider herself particularly superstitious. No, what was it she said about luck? "Luck is when opportunity meets preparation" she had said matter-of-factly. He smiled. What an amazing woman! While Tracy was in good physical condition and had played high school volleyball, she wasn't a collegiate athlete. And in Ryan's world at that time competitiveness was strictly related to athletics. It was Tracy who helped him see that even non-athletic people could be competitive, some maybe even more so than athletes. He hadn't really given much thought to that again until he entered the MBA program at Stanford. Clearly, there were men and women in the program who were far from athletic that "had game." Some had developed their competitive streak playing chess or as members of debate, math or science teams or simply drew on their passion for business. He realized then that he needed to up his game intellectually because these folks were unafraid of his physical stature. It was a lesson well learned.

He scolded himself for unlocking these painful memories, but it seemed that he was powerless to stop his mind from drifting back to that magical summer. He felt the warmth of her smile, the electricity of her touch and the heat of their passion night after night in her cottage and a few other private places they had managed to find. He looked down and didn't know whether to laugh, cry or be angry about the bulge growing in his pants.

Ryan made a few calls to former B school associates in search of contacts. Within days, he was fielding calls from recruiters hot to introduce him to potential opportunities because of his valuable tech experience. The interview with Fontella & Scharf came about quickly. The airline tickets to New York along with the job information packet arrived by courier the same afternoon the recruiter called. It was a Friday, and the plan was a full day of interviews the following Monday beginning at 9:30 AM. They had booked him on the red-eye flight Sunday night out of LAX around 11:00 PM, so he'd have to sleep on the plane. He noticed the tickets were first class, so at least the seat and service would be comfortable. *First class! That's a nice touch.* Of course, the fact that they booked him on the red-eye was likely intentional, probably meant to convey that these folks do whatever it takes to get the job done and work all hours necessary. That would be somewhat different from his current company where "9 to 5" was the norm. However, when a critical project came up, Ryan was quick to volunteer. The payoff was that he had learned a lot and had earned the reputation as the CFO's "go to person" to be counted on to get the job done. It also paid handsomely, especially as the stock price continued to rise and his stock options vested. Tech was a good place to be right now, and that was why Fontella & Scharf was interested in him. The recruiter was clear that Ryan had the experience they were looking for to accelerate their growth in the sector.

He was anxious to open the job packet to learn about the role and the firm. He wasn't familiar with Fontella & Scharf, although that wasn't surprising since he only knew a few marquee firms and those he had interacted with. The recruiter assured him it was an up and coming boutique shop with an impeccable reputation and forward-thinking leadership.

Just then his phone rang, and he saw that it was his boss, Mary Johnson, the CFO.

"Hello Mary, what can I do for you?"

"Hi Ryan," said Mary. "I have an opportunity for you and a couple others to help me out with a snag that's developed on the Genesis Project."

The Genesis Project was the code name for an acquisition they were exploring.

Without hesitation, Ryan said, "Sure Mary, how can I help?"

Mary said, "Well the short story is that we have some concerns about the timing of when the company has booked future sales into their revenue stream. We need a small team to dig into the books and get the numbers right before we settle on a valuation. We're at a critical juncture, so it needs to be done right away. You might need to work through the weekend because the project must be completed by Sunday night to meet an important deadline on the offer. Will you help me out and take the lead on this?"

Ryan was conflicted because he wanted to focus on prepping for his job interview, but he was also excited about this project and hated the thought of letting Mary down. She had been a supportive boss and mentor to him.

"Sure Mary," said Ryan. "When do we start?"

"As soon as you can get to Conference Room C," she answered. "The others will be joining momentarily. Thank you, Ryan."

He quickly reviewed the plane ticket to be sure he knew the airline and flight time, and then slipped the interview packet into his briefcase. *Well*, he thought to himself, *If worse comes to worse I can read it on the plane.*

The team of three worked tirelessly on the painstaking and tedious work. By Sunday evening, the office kitchen and over-flowing trashcan contained the remnants of takeout foods, many pots of coffee and cans of caffeinated beverages that fueled them through the weekend. They finished the report, and Ryan emailed it to Mary around 8:00 PM.

Just enough time for a shower and shave before I head to the airport, he reasoned.

Chapter 19

Los Angeles International Airport

Ryan arrived at the gate about ten minutes before they closed the aircraft door.

"Have a nice flight, Mr. Kupford," said the gate agent as he collected his ticket.

Ryan walked down the jetway, boarded the plane and found his seat. He placed his briefcase in the overhead bin and took off his suit jacket. The flight attendant appeared promptly with a hanger in hand to place it carefully in the wardrobe.

"Thank you, Ms. Sanders," said Ryan, noting her nametag.

"May I offer you a cocktail or beverage before takeoff, Mr. Kupford?" she inquired.

Yeah, first-class travel was the way to go, he thought smugly.

He smiled and nodded. "Yes, thank you. I'll have a gin and tonic with two blue cheese olives, please."

The flight attendant returned in a flash with his drink.

Oh, that's good, he mused as the drink went smoothly down his throat.

After the plane reached cruising altitude, the flight attendant returned with another drink saying, "Pardon my boldness, but you look like you could use another one. Rough weekend?"

Ryan chuckled, took the offered drink and said, "Yes, but maybe not what you're thinking. I worked all weekend on a special project for my company."

"Oh, you poor man," she cried. She reached up into the overhead bin and brought down a pillow and a blanket. Ryan didn't want to offend her by refusing her well-intended offer although he had no intention of sleeping.

"Thank you, Ms. Sanders. Will you also hand me my briefcase, please?"

"Good luck," she offered as she handed him his briefcase. She turned on her heel and retreated to the galley.

Ryan reached up and activated his overhead light, illuminating the darkened space. His seatmate gave a loud grunt. Ryan pulled out the information for the interview and began reading about the junior analyst role. Too quickly, he felt his eyelids grow heavy. He tried squinting to keep his eyes focused, but he just couldn't fight the fatigue from a total of about five hours of sleep over the entire weekend. It was no use. He realized he needed sleep more than he needed to prep for this interview. He was glad he had accepted the project work because he learned more about sales revenue annuity streams and the changing GAAP rules on how and when this revenue is accounted for on the financials. After all, this was his current job and a good one at that, so he was glad to have been asked to work on it. And without being cocky, he also knew that Fontella & Scharf wanted him for his knowledge and tech experience, so he held the better hand.

With that settled in his mind, he put the papers back into his briefcase, slid it under the seat in front of him and turned off the overhead light. He moved the seat as far back as it would go, adjusted the pillow to his liking and fell into a deep and restful sleep.

What he didn't see in the packet were the biographies and pictures of the firm's leaders, including the most recently elevated partners, Steven Mack, age 42, MBA Harvard and Tracy Knapp, age 40, MBA New York University, now known as Stern School of Business. Had he seen the pictures he might have been more prepared for what would happen when he walked into the first interview with the partner in charge of the team for which he was interviewing, Fontella & Scharf's newly created Tech Team led by their rising star and his former lover.

Ryan slept soundly and was awakened by the attentive Ms. Sanders shortly before they began their approach into New York.

"I'm sorry to disturb you Mr. Kupford, but we'll be landing shortly. I thought you might want to freshen up and have a bite to eat."

"Yes, thank you," Ryan said with a yawn as he rubbed his eyes. "I can't believe I slept through the whole flight, but I really needed the rest. And yes, I'll take you up on the breakfast and coffee please."

She helped him adjust his seat and gave him a hot towel. He finished his eggs, sausage, toast, fresh fruit, and coffee just as the pilot announced their final descent into LaGuardia. Although he had an aisle seat, he glimpsed the New York skyline as the plane made its way to the waiting runway. *This city is huge! The skyline seems to go on forever from all sides. I love it.*

Chapter 20

New York, New York

After touchdown, he was greeted by a private driver that awaited him in the arrivals area. He settled into the limo, and then phoned his work voicemail. First up was a message from his current girlfriend, Jodi. "Hi, Ryan. Missed you this weekend but understand you had to work. Call me." *Hmmm, he thought to himself, Jodi is a cutie, and I would miss her if I moved to New York, but this is important for me.*

He deleted Jodi's message and cued up the next one. "Hey Ryan, this is Mary. Your report is spot on. Thank you for a job well done. Enjoy your day off." Ryan smiled broadly. No matter what happens on this interview, Ryan knew that he had an excellent career in the making and that knowledge made him even more confident as he took in the sights and sounds of The Big Apple.

The driver drove south on Broadway and slowed enough at just the right time for Ryan to get a good look at the Wall Street Bull, both mighty and fearless in its charging position with nostrils flaring. *Taking this route was no accident*, he thought. Just viewing the iconic statue sent a surge of testosterone through his body. He appreciated the attention to detail this planned detour represented. No doubt this was another signal of the way this firm operated and why they were reportedly fast becoming a top deal-maker where an aggressive guy like him would love to work and learn. *Easy boy*, he thought gripping his knees. *Don't want to seem over anxious, or I'll lose my leverage.*

The driver slowed the car and double-parked right in front of the entrance to the skyscraper where Fontella & Scharf occupied the top ten floors. He stepped out of the car, took a deep, calming breath, pulled his shoulders back, put on his most confident smile and walked into the revolving door. He was greeted warmly by a smartly dressed young male staff member.

"Good morning Mr. Kupford. I'm Jeremy, Ms. Knapp's administrative assistant."

That's different, thought Ryan as he tried to hide his surprise. *A dude office assistant to a female manager. I wish I had read the file. I don't know if this Ms. Knapp is in human resources or operations. Oh well, just follow along, and you'll figure it out.*

"Hello, Jeremy." He reached out to shake Jeremy's extended hand.

"How was your flight?" Jeremy inquired.

"Fine, thank you," Ryan replied. "I appreciate the first class accommodations."

"You're welcome, Mr. Kupford," said Jeremy with a smile. "It's the way we do things around here."

"Please, call me Ryan."

Jeremy nodded and made a mental note of approval that Ryan asked to be addressed by his first name. "Ryan it is. Right this way."

They bypassed the security desk, and Jeremy led the way to a bank of eight elevators. The elevators on their left serviced floors 1 through 30 and the bank on the right, floors 31 through 65. Jeremy chose the bank on the right and pushed the button for the 64th floor when they entered the elevator.

After they exited the elevator, Jeremy led Ryan to a conference room with floor-to-ceiling windows and an unobstructed view of the Statue of Liberty, just to the south.

"Nice view!" Ryan exclaimed.

"Yes, it is," Jeremy said nodding. "We like to think of it as inspiration to do well for our clients and be a shining example of what freedom and capitalism can do for society."

He presented Ryan with a fresh copy of the day's agenda and pointed out the location of the facilities.

"Would you like a quick break before we begin?" asked Jeremy.

"No thanks Jeremy, although I appreciate you sharing the layout," said Ryan.

"The names and titles of all the associates you'll meet are listed on page two," Jeremy offered.

The conference room was a large, comfortable space with a highly polished, dark mahogany elongated oval table set with coffee, water, fruit, and muffins. "May I pour coffee for you Ryan?" Jeremy asked.

"Yes, thank you. Just cream please."

He took a gulp of coffee and was just about to review the file when a voice called out. "Hello, Ryan." He turned and reached out to clasp the hand of Pat Holiday, whose business card introduced her as Senior Manager, Technology Team.

"Glad to meet you, Pat," said Ryan.

"Welcome to Fontella & Scharf," Pat announced. "And right off the top, I must inform you that we'll have to make a few adjustments to the schedule due to an unexpected business opportunity that came up this morning. Please understand that Ms. Knapp is extremely apologetic and disappointed that she won't spend as much time with you as planned. However, she will join us in a few moments to meet you. As you know from the bio's, Ms. Knapp is one of the firm's newest and youngest partners."

At that Ryan felt obligated to confess, "Actually Pat, I didn't read much of what was sent."

He went on to explain, "The file arrived Friday, and I intended to read it and research the firm over the weekend. That was before my CFO called a couple colleagues and me into her office Friday afternoon about a project that needed to be completed by Monday morning. We worked the whole weekend and finished the job late Sunday night. I snagged about five total hours of sleep on an office sofa since Friday and figured I would read the file on the plane. Great intentions but my eyes were closed not long after we were wheels up and the spine on the file has yet to be broken."

Pat listened to Ryan and studied his face as he spoke. She seemed to be weighing what he shared, perhaps considering his truthfulness about the circumstances.

Ryan knew he would be working with, maybe even for Pat if he was offered and accepted a job on the team. He believed honesty was the foundation for building trust between colleagues and simply wanted to clear the air on this important issue.

In the end, Pat nodded and simply stated, "Thank you for your honesty, Ryan. What you wouldn't find in the file anyway, but just coming to light, are the recent successes of our new technology team headed by Ms. Knapp. We're focused on helping companies secure the capital they need to grow as well as providing M&A services. That explains her interest in you. I'm here to tell you that the opportunities to grow, learn, contribute and make serious money are limitless. Also, if you decide you'd like to meet further with

Tracy tomorrow morning and can rearrange your business plans, we'll make overnight accommodations for you and take care of the flight change."

"Thank you, Pat," said Ryan. "Let's see how the day progresses, and I'll let you know."

With a slight softening of her tone, Pat said," Ryan, I'll share with you that Tracy personally vetted your work resume and background. She believes you could contribute immediately to our team. I do too. The real mission today is to introduce you to the colleagues you would be working with, help you get a feel for the culture of the firm and expose you to our environment. This is a fast-paced, high stakes, all in, no holds barred atmosphere where complete, sometimes brutal honesty is required and constructive criticism often borders on hard hits straight to the gut."

Ryan found himself getting even more psyched for the day's events. In just these first minutes, he knew working here would feel more like being part of a competitive sports team than his current financial role where he normally operated independently. He reasoned that the project he worked on this weekend was similar to a typical day at the office around here. As he looked at Pat, he realized by the smile on her face that she already figured that out.

At that point, the name "Tracy" cycled back through his brain, and though he tried not to show any change in his demeanor a thought struck him like a thunderbolt, could it be *his* Tracy? Tracy from so long ago? The Tracy that he had worked so hard to purge from his memory after years of hoping she would come back to him, reach out to him, even just tell him the truth about that summer no matter how much it would have hurt? It's always been the not knowing that he struggled with most. His mind raced through what he had heard and recalled the managing partner's name was Knapp, Tracy Knapp. Okay, must be a coincidence. Surely there would be many women named Tracy working in New York. But then he thought, *how many would be working for New York investment banking firms and be partners, especially newly announced as Pat had indicated*? He tried to quickly do the math in his head. He was now thirty-three years old, so Tracy, his Tracy, would be about 40. Pat had mentioned Tracy Knapp as one of the youngest partners. He had to know. "Pat, you mentioned that Tracy Knapp was one of the firm's youngest partners. How old is she?"

Pat sensed Ryan was holding something back and she countered with a question of her own, "Why do you ask Ryan?"

Answer a question with a question, typical negotiating technique, he thought. *Learn more information and give as little as possible until you know why the other person is asking and only then decide your response. Impressive.*

Before he could answer, Pat smiled and asked, "Are you thinking about breaking the record for the youngest partner if you join the firm?"

That question wasn't a stab in the dark. Pat was aware that Ryan had played professional soccer in Europe and likely learned about his reputation as a fierce, but fair, competitor.

Ryan grinned. He opened his mouth to answer, but before he could get the words out, in strode his ultimate suitor, possible new boss and without question the woman he had fallen in love with 15 years ago in Lille, France. She looked straight at him, offered a warm greeting, and gave a firm handshake. Without so much as a flinch, she introduced herself as if they had never laid eyes on each other before.

"Hello Ryan, I'm Tracy Knapp. It's very nice to meet you."

It took every ounce of strength he could muster to stay calm and composed. He may have appeared solid on the outside, but his mind and his heart were racing. Part of him wanted to reach out and bring her to him, hold her, stroke her still beautiful though somewhat shorter, dark brown hair and pick up where they left off so many years ago. He had found his long-lost love! Another part of him felt a growing rage that wanted to lash out at her and demand answers he felt he deserved after years of silence. But something just didn't seem right. Could anyone be that good of an actor? And if so, for what purpose? The woman in front of him, Tracy Knapp, was in fact, formerly Tracy Ward. At this moment that was about the only thing of which he was certain.

He searched her face and thought she looked a bit different than he recalled. Of course, she would be older, but as his eyes settled on hers, he just knew it was Tracy. She still had the most beautiful, sparkling, brown eyes. He quickly surmised that she had married along the way. And here she was standing right in front of him showing absolutely no sign of acknowledging their past relationship. How could this be? Could she really be that cold and calculating? Was this a test or a sick joke? He was unsure how to respond, so he went with his instincts to play along for now. He accepted her handshake and managed to eke out a robotic, "Nice to meet you, Ms. Knapp, I'm glad to be here."

Pat was about to speak, maybe to restate Ryan's last question, but Tracy, clearly in a hurry and not in the mood for small talk, interrupted.

""Clients first" is not just a sentence in our mission state-ment," Tracy said. "It's a way of life and requires an almost total commitment to the firm. How do you feel about that Ryan?"

"Understood and accepted, Ms. Knapp."

"Well said, Ryan and please call me Tracy. First name basis for everyone in the firm, even the founding partners, is part of our culture to level the playing field. We believe associates must feel free to interact and challenge each other as we figure out the best solutions to problems and develop breakthrough strategies that maximize our client's and our firm's successes."

"Makes sense to me, Tracy," Ryan responded in a more confident tone as he tried to regain his composure.

Tracy continued, "Pat will guide you through the interview process, spend whatever time is necessary today to answer your questions and help discern if a role on our team is in everyone's best interests. We view hiring an associate in the same manner that a company considers spending millions of dollars for a piece of machinery or any other asset. Time, training, and education are investments in human capital much the same as investments in physical assets. As such, we are committed to the same rigorous analysis to determine what our return on investment will be for a new colleague."

Ryan listened intently to Tracy, and his eyes never left hers. In a sense, he was searching for even the slightest recognition, but he found none. Realizing he was holding his gaze longer than proper, he heard himself stammer, "Have we met before, Tracy?"

"I don't believe so," she answered in a brisk and seemingly genuine tone.

He realized that he needed a break to process what was going on in his head and as if on cue, Tracy said her goodbyes and left. As she turned to go, he thought he even recognized the same subtle scent of perfume she had worn when they were together. It was almost too much to bear.

Pat seemed to sense his need for a break as well. "Okay, Ryan. John Tedder, Tech Team IT lead is first up on the interview schedule. How about you take twenty minutes to familiarize yourself with John and his role, maybe freshen up or check on any business matters, and then we'll resume the program.

"Thank you, Pat."

Ryan headed straight to the men's room where he splashed cold water on his face. He then went into a stall to privately process what he'd just experienced. He needed to compose himself as best as possible. *What the hell is going on here? I could confront Tracy or even just walk out this minute, but I feel like I should just go along for now and see how this plays out.* He stared at his right hand for a few moments longer. He had touched Tracy's hand for the first time in over 15 years. He took a deep breath and headed back to the conference room.

As he entered the room, Pat asked, "Is everything okay Ryan?"

He weighed the sincerity of her concern and considered that it seemed authentic. If Tracy was playing with him, maybe Pat wasn't in on the game. He nodded, saying, "Yes, everything is fine. Maybe I'm a little jet-lagged on so few hours of sleep. The break and the coffee really helped. I'm ready to move on if you are."

"You bet Ryan," said Pat.

The rest of the day was a whirlwind of meetings, and he forced himself to focus on the task at hand. After each meeting, Pat gave him about fifteen minutes to make notes and read up on the next associate. He really appreciated Pat's professionalism and support of his situation. She was a genuine person and would be a trusted, valuable mentor should he join the firm. Based on what he was learning, he wanted in on this opportunity.

His future colleagues shared insights into the work he would be doing and the chances he'd have to learn, grow and network. Of course, they also discussed his potential financial payoff. These people made serious money. Mid-six-figure bonuses were practically a given with senior managers snagging much higher payouts. Partners, of course, split the profits or shared in the losses of the firm. While there were a few tough years in the late 80's, profits were now back to stratospheric levels. He guessed Tracy was pulling in millions. Just like she said she would.

His mind wandered during a break. As he stared out the window, he mused. *Maybe it is all an act. Maybe she knows exactly who I am, and she's brought me back to toy with me. Or she wants me on her team, and this is her way of signaling that what happened in the past is over and it would be all business. You don't get to her level without being able to pull off almost any deal.* He rubbed his eyes as he thought back to the little cottage in Lille. He remembered the time he thought he was teaching her card games, like poker. She seemed to catch on so easily and beat his hands more often than not.

He remembered how eagerly she seemed to listen as he explained the nuances of poker to her and how to keep your opponent guessing about your hand by disguising your emotions. Maybe she was enjoying letting him *think* he was tutoring her when she was actually schooling him. *And to think I thought it was just beginners luck.*

Tutor. The word echoed in his mind like a loud drum roll. French words and phrases started coming into his head, and he quickly shut it all out. *Stay focused, Ryan. Just a couple more meetings and I'll be on a plane back to LA.*

He had already decided there was no way he would stay to meet with Tracy tomorrow morning. First, he needed to get back to his office. He reminded himself that he already had a great job and budding career. Second, he was not emotionally ready to meet one-on-one with Tracy right now. If she was playing with him, he needed to draft a counter strategy, steel himself for what it would be like to work around her. Heck, to work for her. From her bio, he discovered that she was in fact married to a commercial banker, Bill Knapp, and they had two young daughters. Tracy certainly had been busy over the last fifteen years, and professionally she accomplished exactly what she had set out to do. "Make partner by forty," she had confided to him that summer, and so she was.

About the only thing that seemed clear to him now was that Pat and the rest of the staff were not in on Tracy's scam if that's what it was.

Chapter 21

Flight 1027 to LAX

The long plane ride back to LA gave Ryan plenty of time to reflect on the course of day's events. The interview process seemed to go well. Each person he met had certainly done their homework on his background, and they both peppered him with thoughtful questions as well as provided input and answers to Ryan's questions about working at the firm and serving their clients.

Unsolicited, each associate shared with him that they felt very fortunate to not only be working for Fontella & Scharf but thrilled to be on Tracy's team. The consensus was that in addition to being brilliant, she was also fair, supportive, straightforward, and creative. And in a company and industry filled with giant egos, Tracy was described as the very rare example of a "servant leader," always willing to help and work as hard or harder than anyone on her team. He heard how Tracy gave people the space and freedom to do their jobs with the appropriate checks and balances built into the system to ensure projects were on the right track and completed on time. You had to accept being challenged directly and continually produce strong results in this business because the stakes were high.

Who knows, maybe she did just bring me there to toy with me, and I won't even get an offer. Was she cruel hearted enough to bring me to New York to let me see what she had accomplished and hear about her seemingly perfect life? Or maybe her life isn't so perfect, and this was her sick way of getting a good look at me face to face and consider what it might be like to have me in her life again. Maybe she thinks I'm worthy of her affection now that I've grown up and making my own fame and fortune.

He thought back again to the moment Tracy walked into the conference room, and their eyes met. Not a flinch. *She must be one heck of an actor and a cold-hearted bitch to pull that off. What else could it be?*

Ryan knew this was the environment he was looking for again. Today, he felt the familiar and comfortable rush that came from striving to win at competitive sports. He thought back to conversations in Lille, at how excited Tracy had become when she opened up about her passion for business and her personal goals. He remembered how he felt somewhat intimidated by this diminutive girl with such bold ambition and at the same time highly aroused by her competitive spirit.

He had come to realize that being with Tracy felt like seeing himself in a mirror, maybe even deeper than that. It was like seeing your heart and soul inside someone else's body. He chuckled to himself and thought how that might make him seem like an egocentric narcissist, but he didn't think so. *What I felt for Tracy was real, and I thought it was real for her too. It just simply felt like we were perfectly matched.*

Sure, we didn't have much time together so who knows what the future might have been for us if we had stayed together. Would I have gone on to play for Stoke City and achieved the level of fame and financial rewards I was fortunate to earn? Probably not, and by the time I graduated, the US league didn't exist anymore. Wow, I remember telling Tracy I would try to work my way onto a spot with the NY Cosmos just to be near her. How naïve I must have sounded to a more experienced woman that maybe already had her sights set on earning millions.

His anger flared, and he clenched his fists. *Well, two can play that game. Go ahead, Tracy. Make me an offer. First, I'll get you to up the offer because I know I'm worth it in many ways. Then I'll toy with you until you break. I've yet to meet a chick I can't charm into MY bed on MY terms. You changed me, Tracy Ward. Just when I thought I had become a man with a heart full of love, you shut me out, and my heart went cold. Since then I've let no one in that deep. Well, I can do this. I can ready myself for this game, and I can win it. In fact, I'm looking forward to it and making a whole lot of money along the way.*

He finished his drink, his anger diffused for the moment. He shook his head to clear it. *This is too much to process! he decided.*

He turned his focus on his accomplishments from the past fifteen years—the years that didn't include Tracy Ward. He held out his hand and tapped a finger with each one. *Refocused my efforts on both my education and soccer after that summer in France—check. Earned my engineering degree—check. Won the NCAA Championship—check. Played for Stoke City in the English Premier League--check.* He smiled and sat up a bit taller in his seat. *Pretty damn good for a kid from sleepy, suburban LA!*

He thought about all the people he'd had the chance to meet during his time with the English Premier League. He'd created true friendships with some amazing, talented and very wealthy people. Those connections have proved helpful already, as they've provided contacts and helpful ideas to support his professional life. He wondered how many people his age could say they've been to the Le Mans auto race, or witnessed the incredible Formula One machines of the Monaco Grand Prix, or skied in the Swiss Alps with true royals and spent weekends partying on multimillion-dollar yachts anchored off the French Rivera? He let his mind wander back over the good times and wondered if he should pinch himself to be sure he wasn't dreaming it all.

I'm really glad I realized that I needed to prepare for the rest of my life by earning my MBA and getting serious about a career. Would I be the man I am had my life taken a different path?

He was startled out of his reverie by the flight attendant. "May I bring your dinner and refresh your drink Mr. Kupford?"

"Oh, yes, to both questions Ms. Chambers, and thank you."

The perfectly prepared medium rare steak and loaded baked potato combined with the gin and tonic on top of a long day all came together. He yawned and stretched, feeling the need to succumb to much-needed sleep. He hoped tomorrow would bring a clear head and a clearer picture of the direction he should take. He found a comfortable position and slept soundly for the rest of the flight. As the plane began its descent, he awoke refreshed. What was ahead of him in the coming days came into sharp relief. *Game time*, he said to himself as the plane touched down.

As soon as Ryan deplaned, he turned on his favorite new gadget, a Motorola StarTAC flip phone and scrolled through the missed calls. After seeing several work and friend numbers, he found what he was hoping for, a call from area code 212, New York. He navigated through the throng of people to find a quiet space to listen. Then he pushed the button to play and heard Pat Holiday's familiar voice.

"Hi, Ryan. Hope your flight was uneventful. It was a pleasure meeting you. I'm thrilled to inform you that we want you to join our team and, if the delivery service does its job, the envelope containing the offer letter should be at your door before you get home. Call me if you have any questions and we're looking forward to your signed acceptance."

Ryan replayed the message, then stood quietly for a few minutes to let the magnitude of what was happening sink in. These people were on their game, and he wanted in. Tracy might have her hand to play, but he could play too. *I need to be careful and not kid myself. This is no ordinary opponent. She is smart, well regarded, and powerful. Right now, I'm a newbie. I need to learn, figure out the system, contribute and gain acceptance. My career may be at stake but this opportunity and this game, if that's what's going on, are too good to pass up. And it all starts now.*

Chapter 22

Two years later. Offices of Fontella & Scharf, New York, New York.

"What's up, Tracy?" Ryan asked as he picked up the ringing phone flashing Tracy's extension.

"Hey Ryan," said Tracy. "I need you to set up a team meeting this afternoon at 1:30 to go over the Ronone project. We need everyone's sharpest ideas to flesh out our strategy, theorize possible roadblocks, challenges, and counteroffers that might come at us when we're in France Wednesday to close this deal."

"Consider it done Tracy."

With a soft chuckle in her voice, she replied, "Thank you, Ryan. I really appreciate your attentiveness and willingness to act. How long have you been on board with us now?"

"Two years."

"And what an amazing two years it's been in many ways," said Tracy. "You slipped right into Pat's role six months ago when she was tapped to head up the Industrial Group. It was a great promotional opportunity for Pat and though you had less seniority than others you clearly earned the senior manager role on our technology team. Most importantly, you've earned the respect of your peers and the partners while contributing immensely to the firm's success. On top of that, I believe your energy sparked my creativity to even higher levels, and on a personal note, well, the connection we have is nothing short of amazing. Thank you, Ryan."

"You're welcome, Tracy. The pleasure is truly all mine."

Later that day Tracy and Ryan were chauffeured to the airport and boarded an evening flight to Paris. They each changed into casual, comfortable traveling clothes and enjoyed a delicious meal and a fine French Bordeaux in their business class accommodations. They hashed over a few details of the pending deal and were asleep within two hours of takeoff.

Chapter 23

France

About an hour before landing in Paris, Tracy and Ryan awoke from their five-hour slumber. They had just enough time to freshen up, change back into their business clothes and enjoy a light breakfast of fresh fruit, yogurt, and a chocolate croissant.

"Did you sleep well Tracy?"

"Yes, I did Ryan, thanks for asking." "And you?"

"Like a baby. Business class on international flights keeps getting better with more comfortable seating, better food, and fantastic service. Really helps minimize jet lag. I'm ready to work!"

"Good," said Tracy. "I believe we have a challenge facing us over the next couple days to bring this deal to fruition with terms that will be acceptable to both parties. Negotiating to buy privately owned companies can present unique issues due to the personal nature of the situation."

Ryan nodded. "I've been looking forward to this session. Vincenzo Piegari is an icon in the telecom industry and quite a personality from what you've shared and what I've read about him."

"Yes, he is," answered Tracy.

It was widely known that Vincenzo Piegari ruled Ronone with an iron fist. He founded the telecom company over fifty years ago in a barn on the family farm and now controlled over thirty percent of the French and Italian airwaves. While impressive, Ronone's market share had stagnated recently because newer, more expensive technological equipment was emerging to process talk and data at much faster speeds. What they had, however, was a very loyal customer base that Fontella & Scharf's client, Swedish conglomerate SBB, wanted to capture through the acquisition of Ronone. Vincenzo likely understood that it would take SBB not only money but time to grow their market share as a startup in these local markets and they were anxious to move faster. SBB was flush with cash from a recent IPO, underwritten by Fontella & Scharf, and had promised their investors aggressive top-line growth rates along with profit goals. For that reason, SBB had its sights set on Ronone.

Tracy and Ryan had carried on their luggage and briefcases, so after they deplaned, they followed the signage straight to the arrivals hall at Charles de Gaulle. Typical in Europe and different than airports in the US, was the presence of armed soldiers, with eyes watching every movement and fingers close to the trigger of their rifles.

Ryan commented, "I find it a bit unnerving to see such a heavy military presence in so many places around Europe."

"Funny, I actually feel *safer* because of their presence. I wonder how long it will be until something happens in our country that will force us to acknowledge and deal with the growing global risks we all face from terrorists?"

"There's our driver," said Ryan, spotting a man holding up a sign bearing their names.

"Bonjour. I am Gabriel," he said, as he bowed slightly.

"Bonjour Gabriel," Tracy and Ryan answered in unison.

The black sedan weaved through the narrow, crowded streets of Paris to the private residence of Vincenzo Piegari, in the very heart of the bustling city.

Tracy knew something was amiss as soon as they were greeted at the door by a younger man instead of Vincenzo Piegari. "Buongiorno," he said in Italian. Then he transitioned to almost perfect English and continued, "You must be Ms. Knapp."

"Yes, good morning, Signore," and Tracy's voice trailed off in somewhat of a question. She was at a loss for she didn't recognize this younger man.

Without skipping a beat, Ryan chimed in "Buongiorno Giuseppe, come sta amico?"

With that Giuseppe's eyes lit up and he gave Ryan a big bear hug. Giuseppe continued in English, "Ryan, my friend, how are you? Could it be that you are working for Fontella & Scharf?"

"Si, si," said Ryan, smiling broadly.

At this point, Tracy felt a bit like the subordinate rather than the manager. However, she was both thankful and impressed that Ryan was on such friendly terms with this clearly important, yet role unknown, person. She was processing the situation as quickly as she could, but at this moment the facts were few.

Where was her old friend, Signore Piegari, with whom she had expected to negotiate this deal? And who was this young man, Giuseppe, that answered the door and seemed very much large and in charge? And how in the world did Ryan not only know this person but seemed to be considerably more than a casual acquaintance? Well, certainly that was a positive development in an otherwise awkward beginning to this critical meeting.

Ryan quickly and graciously completed the introductions. "Tracy Knapp, please meet Giuseppe Probello, an old and may I say close, friend?"

155

"So good to meet you, Ms. Knapp," said Giuseppe as he offered a warm handshake. "Yes, of course, Ryan. You are a dear friend and seeing you makes me realize it's been much too long since we've been together," said Giuseppe with a wink.

"Come in and let's talk over an espresso," said Giuseppe guiding them into the foyer.

He led them into a spacious office. Tracy's heels clicked on the impressive gray and white marble floor. He motioned them to sit around an eight-foot diameter conference table set with fresh fruit, sparkling and still bottled water, and coffee.

As soon as they were seated, and espresso poured, Giuseppe started the conversation. "First, Uncle Vincenzo sends his deepest apologies for his absence. He took ill yesterday, and while a full recovery is expected, the doctor forbids him to work right now."

"Ms. Knapp, for your records, please retain this power of attorney signed by my uncle authorizing me to conduct business up to and including consummating a deal, should we find ourselves in that position," said Giuseppe in a tone that indicated he was clearly not there to simply make conversation.

"Thank you, Giuseppe," said Tracy. "Please give my warmest greetings and wishes for a full and swift recovery to your uncle. He is an amazing man."

"Si, si, gratzia. My uncle is truly a great man, and I am happy to do so," said Giuseppe.

"Please though, before we talk business," said Giuseppe, "I want to learn from my friend, Ryan, how it is that he is here today. I think the last time we were together was maybe at Le Mans."

"Yes, that was it, Giuseppe," said Ryan. "What a fantastic race and fun time."

What neither man said but was running through each of their minds was not only the fast cars but the gorgeous women that accompanied their group and the parties that went well into the wee hours of the morning during the French Grand Prix Race weekend. Fast cars, beautiful women, and way too much champagne, yeah that about summed it up. Ryan, however, kept that to himself, as did Giuseppe. Of course, Tracy didn't need to hear their thoughts because the broad smiles on their faces as they both nodded their heads in agreement pretty much said it all.

Ryan continued, "When I realized my football days were over, I returned to the US, put my energy into earning an MBA and helped with skills training for the Stanford men's soccer team. It was a great way to stay in shape, help young guys and ease my transition out of the game. I hired into the finance group at what was then a fledgling software company and the next few years were a whirlwind. Head down, learn the business and support the growth as we acquired several targeted competitors and complementary businesses. The company was driving for double-digit organic growth in key proprietary software applications. It was a fantastic experience and quite lucrative. After the deals were done, it was back to monthly financials, budgets, quarterly reports, and that's when I realized I enjoyed the M&A aspect of my work more than the daily tactical responsibilities. I reached out to a few contacts and the next thing I knew I was on a plane to New York to meet with Tracy and her team at Fontella & Scharf. I knew right away that this was what I wanted and thankfully I offered what Tracy was looking for too."

At that, he smiled warmly at Tracy, lifted his espresso and said, "Grazie, Signora."

"Enough about me, Giuseppe," said Ryan. He continued, "please, tell us how is it that you came to be with us today? As I recall you were literally in the business of racing as the owner of Probello Sportivo, yes?" asked Ryan, tilting his head with a questioning look.

"Ah, you have a very solid memory, Ryan," said Giuseppe. "I was living the good and frankly fast life of an owner and executive in the European racing industry, maybe for too long. Then about two months ago, Uncle Vincenzo called and made me an offer I couldn't refuse for two reasons. First, he is family, my mother's older brother and second, I am engaged to be married to a wonderful, beautiful woman who frowns on the lifestyle I was living in the racing business." He smiled wryly at Ryan and added, "Capisce?"

Ryan laughed heartily and said, "Yes, I know exactly what you mean, my friend."

Ryan smiled and thought back to the first time he met Giuseppe. It was summer, and they had been introduced by mutual friends as they partied on a yacht along The Cote d'Azur, or as known in English, The French Riviera, somewhere south of Monaco. He and Giuseppe hit it off as they both enjoyed competitive sports, fine wine, and beautiful women. Giuseppe was a fan of English Premier Soccer and specifically a fan of Ryan at that time. Ryan recalled that Giuseppe peppered him with many questions about the league and the players. He was especially interested in how Ryan was able to bond so well with his European teammates and win warm support from the English fans, who were generally not so accepting of American players. After Monaco, they met up at several high profile events over the next few years. Ryan also remembered that invariably Giuseppe had a beautiful

158

woman or women at his side and frankly, so did Ryan back then. Of course, he knew better than to drift off into that conversation in the presence of Tracy, but there was no mistaking that both he and Giuseppe were conjuring up the same pleasant memories.

Tracy, ever the professional, sipped quietly on her espresso, listened to the two men chat about their shared experiences and considered how this development would affect the business at hand. Clearly, she would have taken the lead in all respects had Sr. Piegari been present. But now, Tracy reasoned, it would be preferable to allow Ryan to take the lead role in the meeting, especially if the negotiations became tense and needed a more personal approach. Tracy was very pleased with Ryan's work as an analyst, and as the newest senior manager on this team, she had allowed him to be more participative in client interactions over the past six months. He was quite helpful in the Zeta General IPO deal two months ago. In fact, it was then that Tracy saw something in Ryan that really set him apart from his peers and even some of the more senior team members. He was a lightning quick thinker with the ability to ask critical questions and astutely lasered in on what really mattered to the client. This was huge in their business. Just thinking back to that trip stirred warm feelings in Tracy. She knew then that Ryan was very good and very special.

Focus, Tracy reminded herself, *this is a huge deal for the firm, and I need to get the job done.* While she hadn't anticipated this change in who would be leading the negotiations for Ronone, she had successfully made on the fly adjustments numerous times in negotiations over the years. This was a wrinkle in the process, and she was already well on her way to formulating a strategy of how they would navigate this deal.

The proceedings indeed went smoothly, and it was clear from the start that Giuseppe was intelligent, knowledgeable about the business and understood the financial and commercial benefits this deal offered for his company. Without admitting it, she could sense that he recognized Ronone's long-term inability to fund the capital investments necessary to keep pace with rapidly changing technologies in telecom. These deals almost always came down to leverage, and as long as you keep personal feelings and emotions out of the process, you usually got the right deal done. Private companies like Ronone could present a special challenge because some owners were extremely concerned about the employees, especially key managers and protecting the jobs of colleagues who were largely treated like family. Vincenzo Piegari was also known as a magnanimous benefactor to the arts and a very generous contributor to many social causes in France, Italy and across Europe.

Tracy had begun to wonder if Vincenzo really had taken ill or if perhaps he simply preferred to hand over the reins to someone who could truly focus on the business of the deal. In addition to his reputation as a legendary visionary, he was a vocal critic of the parochialism he believed was holding Europe back from achieving its true potential. Many Europeans were hesitant to cross country borders in search of work, and in some cases, reluctant even to leave provincial birth towns in their native country. He saw that many Americans had no such trepidation and moved freely around their country, state to state in search of work and the hope of improving their quality of life. The need to lead by example was the root cause of Vincenzo's decision to relocate Ronone's headquarters to Paris from Naples. It was the eve of the dawn of the European Union, and Vincenzo believed his actions showed support for a more unified Europe and for Ronone to become a truly European player rather than simply a regional company.

Tracy was aware that Vincenzo had one child, a son, Angelo, now in his early 40s, who had carved his own successful career as a renowned heart surgeon. He was a resident visiting fellow at NYU's principal teaching hospital, Bellevue. It was through Tracy's board position at NYU that she first met Vincenzo Piegari a few years ago while attending the annual black-tie fundraising gala. She knew the elder Piegari and his wife, Maria, would be present at that event and arranged for her and Bill to be seated with them. While much of the conversation centered on the hospital and Dr. Angelo Piegari's breakthrough research work, Tracy was able to talk briefly with Vincenzo about his business and the strategic, personalized M&A work Fontella & Scharf provided to its clients.

Tracy knew that his privately owned company had a loyal customer base and she had considered how an acquisition by a larger, well-capitalized global partner could help Ronone leapfrog a myriad of local competitors and begin much-needed industry consolidation. The current market was fragmented among many service providers, and while that competition kept consumer prices low, most of the providers were cash starved and grossly undercapitalized. Individually, they lacked the resources for necessary infrastructure improvements, and the result was spotty and unreliable service to many customers. As the largest of these European regional carriers, and with a progressive visionary leader like Vincenzo Piegari at the helm, Tracy, and likely other M&A firm leaders, reasoned that Ronone would be an ideal springboard to begin the consolidation process. And right she was. She kept in contact with Vincenzo, and when the time was right for her client, Swedish powerhouse SBB, to strike, Tracy reached out personally to Vincenzo to begin discussions about joining forces. He was willing to talk and made it clear that his trust in Tracy was a key to his willingness to explore the possibilities.

SBB made it known that they wanted, in fact, required as a condition of the deal, some of the key Ronone leaders to remain through the transition period or longer depending on the evolving needs of the combined organization. Perhaps turning the ship over to Giuseppe, the next generation of leadership, would provide the perfect bridge SBB was looking for while allowing Sr. Piegari some degree of emotional distance from this undoubtedly personal situation.

Ryan sensed at once and correctly that Tracy was handing him the reins and he performed better than she could have imagined. Clearly, he had done his homework in fully understanding the two companies. He was prepared, sincere and convincing in his statements to Giuseppe about how the acquisition would help Ronone in the long-term. Occasionally, he discreetly glanced to Tracy in search of confirmation that he was proceeding according to plan and was rewarded each time with an equally discreet nod of approval.

Perhaps he sensed Tracy's appreciation for his work because he continued with confidence as negotiations heated up. Toward the end of the process, as they worked to settle a couple thorny issues with one of Giuseppe's key advisors, he seamlessly handed the lead to Tracy who expertly mitigated and resolved the situation.

Tracy had allotted two days for the meetings and expected arduous negotiations; however, the deal was consummated in time for them to share a late dinner that first evening.

Giuseppe announced, "I recommend we dine together at Arpege to celebrate the bright future of our new company."

Tracy knew the restaurant and considered how even this choice pointed to a fresh new direction. Chef and owner Alain Passard was known for his devotion to using local, direct from the farm, herbs, and vegetables in his culinary creations and had recently earned a coveted, third Michelin star although the restaurant was barely ten years old. Additionally, the Art Deco interior lifted the establishment's spirit as did its musically derived name, a tribute to Alain's other passion.

Dinner was delicious, the wine spectacular and conversation flowed easily.

"You speak French fluently, Tracy," said Giuseppe. "How is that so?"

"I studied French from high school through college and spent a summer as a student at the Universite Catholique de Lille almost twenty years ago," said Tracy. "During that summer I also tutored a group of young American soccer players who were attending a skills camp and, as it turns out, Ryan was among them. Unfortunately, I have no memory of that summer because, as I drove to the airport, I was involved in a serious car accident."

"Oh my," said Giuseppe. "Were you badly hurt?"

"Yes. I was in a coma for several weeks, broke my nose and arm. Thankfully, I made a full recovery, except for a form of amnesia that has left me with no knowledge of that summer and a couple months prior. It wasn't until Ryan was already on board that we made the connection that he had been a student in my class that summer."

"I'm glad you recovered from your physical injuries," said Giuseppe. "And now we can all appreciate just how small the world is becoming with the stories of how we know each other through our history!"

This was only the second occasion Ryan had ever heard Tracy bring this up, and it worried him a bit because by now he was aware that Tracy had no memory of that summer before the accident. No memory of their past relationship and what they had meant to each other. He recalled how horrible he felt when he learned about the tragedy that almost ended Tracy's life and had also extinguished the budding romance between the two young lovers.

While Tracy was certainly an accomplished leader and expert negotiator, he came to realize that what he initially thought was a cold, calculated plan to lure him into the company and flaunt her success or some other sordid plan, was purely coincidence. Sometimes, he allowed his mind to view it as perhaps a stroke of serendipitous fate bringing them together again.

He watched her talk animatedly with Giuseppe. *If only she knew what they had meant to each other, that I still harbor strong feelings for her, feelings I try hard to keep buried deep inside. If only she knew that sometimes it takes every ounce of self-control, I have to hold back the urge to bring her close, stroke her cheek, run my fingers through her hair, kiss her passionately and make love to her just like we did in Lille.* He shifted in his chair and took a sip of water. He knew Tracy was married and the mother of two adorable young girls. *How she can do that in addition to her unparalleled commitment to her work is nothing short of amazing.* She didn't share much about her personal life. No one in the firm really talked much about their personal lives, if they had one. Some people literally worked fifteen plus hour days, six or even seven days most weeks, which didn't leave much time for anything else.

Ryan's mind came back to the conversation just in time to hear Tracy and Giuseppe discussing the high-speed trains from Paris to Lille and figuring out how they might be able to squeeze in a quick visit.

"So, we could take the first train tomorrow to Lille and be back in plenty of time to catch our evening flight to New York?" Tracy asked.

"Absolutely," said Giuseppe. "I'll order a car to pick you up at the station in Lille and drive you wherever you would like to go."

"Grazie, Giuseppe," said Tracy. Turning to Ryan, she added, "Well, isn't this a pleasant surprise Ryan? You will get to see Lille again, and I'll get to experience it for the first time, again!"

Ryan's face didn't give away the sense of dread that he felt. Tracy seemed to be growing more excited about the prospect of visiting the city where she almost lost her life.

His mind was racing, trying to think a way out of going to Lille. As he searched for a plausible excuse, he heard Tracy say, "I'm excited to learn a bit more about the place I spent an entire summer of my life. Ryan, isn't Lille where the European scouts first showed interested in you?"

"Yes, it is," stammered Ryan. "It was a summer of firsts, and memorable in many ways." *Oh man. Why did I just say that?* he thought angrily.

"Do you think you'll remember enough to be an effective tour guide?" challenged Tracy. "Of course, it will all be new to me so wherever we go should be interesting."

He nodded and smiled. *This trip is really going to happen!* He silently ticked through the possible outcomes of a visit to Lille, but he knew Tracy well enough to know that nothing he could say would change her mind about making the visit. All he could do was hope that certain memories would remain buried, for Tracy's sake. For a fleeting moment, he allowed himself to fantasize possibilities of what might be if it all came back, and they could pick up where they left over fifteen years ago. The thought of really being together again made his pulse quicken and brought a sense of fullness to his heart that he hadn't expected. *Get a grip, dude,* he commanded himself.

The trio capped the evening with a leisurely walk down the Champs Elysee toward the iconic Arc de Triomphe, shining brightly in all its historic grandeur. It was a lovely late summer evening in Paris. The sky was clear and thankfully the humidity was low. Afterward, they walked a few short blocks to their hotel where they bid goodnight to Giuseppe.

Ryan and Tracy rode the elevator to their floor. As they stepped out, Tracy said, "Thank you for your work today Ryan. You were brilliant." Their eyes lingered on each other as they stood just outside the elevator.

Ryan felt his cheeks flush. Although he took pride in always being prepared and felt confident in his growing contributions, he knew this was huge. It was the first time he was truly the lead dog, and he nailed it. And Tracy knew it too. Today the student rose to the level of the teacher.

"Thank you for the compliment Tracy, and for your confidence to give me the number one seat at the table today. You have taught me more than I could ever have imagined and inspired me to be the best I can be. Sleep well."

"You're welcome, Ryan. You inspire me as well. Good night."

Chapter 24

Ryan's hotel room

Ryan collapsed into a heap on the oversized armchair, loosened his tie, unbuttoned his shirt, and kicked off his shoes. He reached over and grabbed a bottle of still water from the nightstand. He took a long drink. What a day this had been, capped off by a moment in the hallway that took every last ounce of energy he had to control the urge to reach out and take Tracy into his arms. He *was* proud of his work today, and he was equally as proud to have Tracy there to see it.

I thought I was doing well in keeping old feelings buried but, I think I'm still in love with her. I felt my heart stir today when she complimented me and looked into my eyes. Now it's aching to be with her again.

He took another long drink of water, leaned back in the armchair, and stared at the ceiling.

Ryan's stream of thoughts continued. *Fate brought us together in the first place, separated us in the most painful way imaginable and then brought us back together. At this point, only I fully understand the depth of our past relationship and corny as it sounds, my DNA passed to her and hers to me. Who really knows what the science of that does to two people? Over the past couple years, I've come to know and understand Tracy. I see how similar we are in many ways, and I feel an electricity between us, but does she?*

Since I joined the firm, our relationship has been strictly professional, and I've worked hard to keep it that way maybe as much out of fear as anything. At times, I think I've caught a look in her eyes that was more than just a good feeling for a job well done. Other times, her eyes have held my gaze a little longer, as if she saw something deeper. I've had to look away or risk losing control and perhaps allowing Tracy to see the unmistakable look of love in my eyes. Would it trigger her memories of us? Would she fall in love with me again? Or dismiss my feelings like a third grader with a crush on their teacher? Oh Tracy, if only you knew what we once meant to each other and the promises we made before we left Lille.

Ryan got up from the chair and undressed down to his boxers. He unzipped his luggage and retrieved only his toiletry bag then staggered to the sink in the bathroom. He wasn't drunk, just dog tired mentally and physically. He fished out his toothbrush and toothpaste, turned on the cold water then made a feeble attempt at giving his teeth a once over.

Without ever looking in the mirror he turned off the faucet, tapped the toothbrush on the bowl and left it on the vanity. He went back to his suitcase and mechanically took one of the other two lightly starched, neatly folded white dress shirts out of his suitcase and hung it up in the wardrobe. He reached back into the suitcase for a pair of gray slacks and hung the slacks next to his shirt. He looked around the room and retrieved his slightly rumpled suit jacket from the chair where he had dropped it. He gave it a shake then hung it in the wardrobe.

He picked up the phone, dialed the front desk and asked for a 4:30 AM wake up call. He stood there for a few minutes just staring at the phone, fighting the urge to dial Tracy's room. He thought about her alone in her room, just down the hall, maybe already sound asleep. Then he saw her in his mind lying in bed with him. He remembered how much he loved to stroke her soft curls while she slept and how she looked like a smiling angel, secure and happy in his embrace. He breathed in deeply, remembering her scent and felt transported back to the cottage in Lille.

He shook his head as he tried to clear the memories and conjured up thoughts of his girlfriend Cathy.

He turned out the light, pulled back the white duvet and top sheet and sat on the edge of the bed to collect his thoughts.

Cathy was sweet and by all accounts a real looker, voluptuous in all the right places. *We have good times together* he told himself. *She works hard as an administrative assistant and tries to be available when I can make time for her. I know I shouldn't expect her to understand the demands of my career but there's no way I can have a relationship with a woman that isn't on board with my needs. I have too much at stake in my career right now. Tracy understands that. I guess her husband understands that too because he changed jobs to support Tracy's career and their family. She seems happy with her life, although I remember that she said something last week about how lucky I was to be single and able to do whatever I wanted in my free time.*

He rubbed his hands through his hair and sighed.

Tracy's life does seem to be nonstop scheduled events. I could take her away from all of that. It would be just the two of us. She could quit her job and relax. I'm earning enough to support both of us, and I've got a great career ahead of me. I can just picture her waiting for me when I get home from work. She might be wearing one of my shirts or a sundress on a hot day. I can see her in the kitchen prepping a fresh salad for dinner. She would be happy to see me, and dinner could wait because I would want to hold her tight and make love to her first thing in the door.

He laid back on the luxurious bed and nestled into the soft feather pillows trying not to disturb his fantasy. He thought more about that recent conversation with Tracy and recalled that she had asked him about his quality of life in New York compared to LA. She inquired about his social life, and he had told her he'd made a few friends at the office and from his fitness club and that he was dating Cathy. She asked what type of work Cathy did and how she responded to changes in his work schedule.

He assumed it was simply a boss trying to show interest in the well-being of an employee, but he wondered, or maybe wished, that secretly she was interested in him, in his life. What if it was the competitive streak in her instinctively determining if another suitor was stalking her prey? *What if?*

He took a deep cleansing breath and exhaled slowly. He thought about the events of the day and indulged in acknowledging just how big of a day this was for *him*. He was the driving force behind closing this deal, and it felt great.

This was a good day for the firm; a good day for Tracy's team to seal this important deal and a defining day for him. Tracy communicated her appreciation for the way he stepped up and drove the deal to a successful completion today, and she assured him he would earn a substantial bonus for his work. Tomorrow would come, and with it, whatever direction fate would take them. Tonight, he owed it to himself to be happy and proud of his contributions to the firm. *Ryan Kupford, you are on your way to the big league and really big money*, he thought. The next thing he heard was his phone ringing with his 4:30AM wake-up call.

Chapter 25

The train to Lille, France

Tracy and Ryan arrived at the Gard du Nord station and boarded the TGV, Train a\ Grande Vitesse.

The train wasn't very crowded, so they had their pick of seating. They chose a row with seats that faced each other and settled in for the just over one-hour ride to Lille.

The train picked up speed quickly and the countryside became a blur.

"It's hard to believe that we're traveling well over one hundred miles per hour!" exclaimed Tracy.

"It sure is. I believe these high-speed trains reach around one-fifty."

Tracy took a sip of the espresso she had picked up at the hotel before they left. She held her cup out in front of her face. "Look at this, steady as a rock. Amazing. Of course, it makes sense that the train better be steady at these speeds."

Ryan laughed. "That's for sure. But I know where you're coming from. We're used to many US trains that shake, rattle, and roll."

"Did you sleep well Tracy?"

"Like a baby, Ryan. How about you?"

"Like a rock," lied Ryan.

He pretended to be calm though on the inside he was as anxious as a kitten.

"Hey Ryan," Tracy said, breaking his anxious musings, "Yesterday, I made an assumption that you haven't been back to Lille since college. Now I'm wondering if that's true because of your years playing professional soccer in Europe."

"I have been to other cities in France, but not Lille. By the way, I made a few notes this morning about places we should try to visit. Of course, I'm not sure if you've been to all of them but kind of the highlights of Lille, assuming things haven't changed too much."

He was trying to play the part of impassive tour guide. Ryan noted that Tracy didn't appear to display even the least amount of apprehension about the visit to Lille. Perhaps it was because, even after all these years, she still had absolutely no recollection of that summer. To her, this was all just exploring a new place, and he knew that Tracy thrived on learning new things. *Maybe it's just as well,* he thought. Right now he harbored enough fear for them both.

The sun was well above the horizon now and shining brightly in a cloudless sky. Farmlands surrounded them, having passed the city limits.

"The fields here are lush and green," said Tracy. "They must have had a lot of rain this summer."

"It is a beautiful country," agreed Ryan.

Ryan retrieved two chocolate croissants out of the white paper bag he had brought from the hotel. "Breakfast is served," he said.

Tracy's eyes lit up. "Thank you!" she said gratefully. "Mmm, croissants just taste better in France," she said as she savored the chocolate delicacy. She sat back and relaxed in her seat. "I feel quite calm this morning and largely have you to thank for that Ryan. Cheers to a job well done yesterday." She raised her coffee cup in a toast.

"Thanks! It was a pleasant surprise to find Giuseppe heading up Ronone. I knew he was a sharp guy from our past interactions, but I had no idea he had any affiliation with Ronone."

"Nor did I," said Tracy. "It was a stroke of good fortune that you and Giuseppe turned out to be old friends. I suppose that lends credence to our hiring practice of looking for candidates with global experience."

Tracy turned back to the window and gazed silently out at the countryside. Ryan scribbled notes on a pad, trying to appear occupied and avoid conversation about the day's journey.

Tracy broke the silence. "I left word for Jeremy to call the convent in Lille and let them know we would like to visit today. I don't remember any of the Sisters, although I send them an annual donation. My family learned that there were nuns by my side from the moment I was brought to the hospital until I was released to fly back to the States. I have only vague memories of hearing their constant prayers, soft chants, and songs, as well as having my hand held. It was comforting and made me feel secure at a time when I was confused, scared and heavily medicated."

"Oh," said Ryan. "I didn't have it on my list of places to visit. I've never been inside the convent building. We all tried to avoid the nuns around the university since they usually just told us to straighten up, slow down or suggested we should dress in something other than soccer shorts and tee shirts."

Tracy laughed at the thought of a ragtag group of soccer players and then shook her head, saying, "It's just hard to wrap my head around the fact that you were in that group of boys. I never asked you, was I a good tutor?"

"The best," said Ryan as he looked intently at Tracy. Then he looked away and added, "Of course it was just an hour class, and I think I missed a lot of them getting physical therapy or taking part in special training, so it's hard for me to really say much about it."

"Well I'm excited about this adventure," Tracy announced. "For years, I declined trips to France out of fear that my memory would be jostled. I realized I needed to overcome that anxiety for myself as well as for the sake of the business. France is too important a country to simply avoid. I've been here several times now, mostly in Paris. According to the postcards I sent to my parents, I've also since revisited a few of the parks and museums I toured that summer. My doctor thought those visits might trigger memories, but nothing looked familiar. I've come to accept that it's all likely buried in my mind forever. Catholics believe that everything happens for a reason, so we rely on our faith and put our trust in God. It's a tall order for a self-admitted control person. However, I believe that as important as I am as a single human being, I humbly exist at the fancy of Our Creator, and ultimately I work to do His will."

"I feel like this is where I'm supposed to shout 'Amen!'," said Ryan as he raised his arms up in the air.

"Sorry about that, Ryan," said Tracy. "I don't mean to sound preachy. Maybe it's me that needs the sermon. The older I get, the tougher it is to hold to the tenets and commandments of my religion. It's easy to stretch gray areas to fit actions I've taken for the good of the business, personal gains or lapses that suit a situation. Often, we tell ourselves and each other, 'it's just business' when we make decisions that adversely impact people or even capitalize on others' mistakes."

"I understand what you mean, Tracy. Although I don't actively practice a specific religion, I was raised a Christian, and I believe in God. Mostly I think people should be fair, honest and help others, especially kids down on their luck through no fault of their own."

They stared pensively at one another and let the conversation lapse. Tracy nodded and turned back to the window, while Ryan focused again on his pad of paper.

Neither spoke for the rest of the ride.

Chapter 26

Lille, France

The train eased into the station at Lille. Ryan mentally noted that it appeared nothing had changed.

As they stepped onto the platform, Ryan pointed to a black four-door luxury sedan.

"I'll bet that's our car over there."

"Well, by my watch, we have about three hours to see the sights, so let's get started," said Tracy as she headed toward the car.

"Bonjour, welcome to Lille," said the driver. "I'm Anthony. You must be Ms. Knapp and Mr. Kupford."

"Yes, thank you, Anthony," said Tracy. "We're excited to be here."

Anthony opened the car door and said, "I took the liberty of bringing a thermos of coffee, croissants and bottled water for your comfort."

Tracy smiled at Anthony. "That was very thoughtful of you. Thank you, Anthony."

Ryan leaned forward to speak to Anthony. "I have a short list of places we'd like to visit today. We're on sort of a trip down memory lane because we were both in Lille during college." He left it at that since he figured Tracy would prefer to keep private the accident and her memory issues.

She smiled at his act of discretion. Quietly, she said to Ryan, "Which reminds me, I do not want to visit the hospital."

"Understood."

Ryan directed the driver to the Citadel near the Deûle River area.

"Ah there's that tall white tower in the park," said Ryan. "It was always kind of a marker to look for if you got lost in the park or on the trails."

Tracy had picked up a sightseeing booklet at the Lille train station, and she found a reference to the iconic park. "It says here that the entire area was designed by Vauban and now considered one of his architectural gems. Vauban designed the pentagonal structure, and the buildings and grounds were originally a military installation built around 1670! Wow, that's a long time ago."

Tracy looked out the window and said, "Look, there's a paved trail winding along the river." She glanced at the guide book. "Ah, yes, the Deûle River. I'll bet I went bike riding here. My parents remember me telling them during a phone call that the nuns had given me a bicycle to use for the summer."

Ryan pretended to look at the scenery though he was mostly watching Tracy for any signs that she might be regaining memories.

Both were silent for a few minutes while the driver steered the car slowly through the grounds. Tracy broke the silence. "For a minute, I thought I remembered seeing the large white obelisk, but now I'm not so sure. As you know, there are many just like it all over Europe, typically erected to honor war heroes and victorious battles that saved towns from being overtaken or annihilated by an enemy. I've probably seen one very similar elsewhere," sighed Tracy.

"What did you do while you were in the park, Ryan?

"Well, I remember biking along the trails sometimes and mostly just hanging out here with my buddies."

"To me, it looks like a lovely place to throw down a blanket, read a book and have a picnic of bread, cheese, fruit, and wine," exclaimed Tracy.

That was precisely the picture in Ryan's mind only it was a real memory of doing just that with Tracy. The only part she left out was the two of them locked in a lover's embrace. He continued to look out the window and felt his cheeks flush. Ryan said to their driver, "Anthony, would you please turn the air conditioning up, it seems warm in here."

"Mais oui, monsieur," said Anthony.

Tracy sensed Ryan was holding back information. "Care to share your thoughts Ryan?" she asked as she leaned toward him.

He scrambled to think of something halfway plausible. "Just remembering some fun times the guys and I had coming over here and kicking the soccer ball around during our free time. At first, the local kids and their parents seemed hesitant to approach us, but eventually, they warmed up to us, and we even taught them some skills and tricks. I don't mean to sound like I'm bragging, but the kids loved to watch us juggle a soccer ball, and I was good at it. One time, I was on a roll, and as the number grew higher, it drew quite a crowd. I was so focused I had no idea how many people had gathered around me. When the ball finally hit the ground after nine hundred fifty-six consecutive juggles, I dropped to the grass exhausted and realized about one hundred people were clapping and shouting '*Bon travail.*' The game of soccer is truly universal, and the language barrier was almost nonexistent when we came out here and interacted with the locals."

Tracy laughed with delight at Ryan's story and seemed satisfied with his explanation. "That's a wonderful story, Ryan! What a great life lesson on finding common ground with people all over the world," said Tracy.

"It sure is, and I have fantastic memories, too. I agree that as an adult I see the experience through a broader lens and feel even more fortunate to have had the opportunity. It's an unexpected pleasure to be back here in Lille," said Ryan.

Ryan felt safe sharing that story because Tracy was not at the park that day. It was a difficult task, but he was trying to avoid pointing out events that might trigger memories.

She went back to peering intently and curiously out the car window.

Tracy lamented with a sigh, "I was hoping that being here would unleash some memories, at least the good ones. Unfortunately, it all looks new to me."

A few minutes later, she turned to Ryan and said, "I'm enjoying this opportunity to spend time with you Ryan and get to know you a little better. Our business is fast-paced, highly focused and leaves little time for anything other than work. We're all hyper-aware that time is money and we use it wisely because it is a finite commodity."

"I do, and I love it, Tracy," said Ryan. "Yesterday reminded me of big game days when all the practices, workouts, watching films and strategy sessions were put to the test. At that point, you and your teammates would dig as deep as you could to put everything you had into winning. Yeah, I felt that charge again yesterday, and it felt great."

Tracy smiled as she listened to Ryan and their eyes were locked on each other.

"Okay, my turn," said Ryan. "Penny for your thoughts, Tracy."

Tracy laughed and said, "That's fair. Listening to you reminded me of my first real win. It was about ten years ago when Michael Fontella took ill with an appendix attack during the final stages of negotiations on a huge deal. At Michael's direction, I was assigned to take the lead. Like you, I had prepared well, and after some tense last-minute back and forth, we won the deal for our client at a desirable price. At the time I was unaware that I was also making history for women in our firm as the first female to hold the lead role. I remember how proud Michael was of me and I'm excited to be in that same position with you right now. At the risk of sounding egotistical, I believe you and I are similar in many ways. You put tremendous time and effort into learning about the deals we're working on and what's meaningful to both parties. You're also a good listener, and you're intuitive. Yesterday you offered creative solutions to concerns raised by Giuseppe without diluting our clients offer." She hesitated, then smiled warmly and added, "I suppose it could be said that the student rose to the role of teacher yesterday."

Hearing those words echo in his mind was almost too much to bear for Ryan. "Thank you, Tracy," he stammered and turned to look out the window. He felt her eyes on him and wondered what was going through her mind.

The limo turned out of the park grounds and headed southeast. Tracy looked out the window at the street sign and announced, "Boulevard Vauban." Shaking her head, she added, "Can't say I remember it, other than what I read in the brochure today."

As she glanced at Ryan, it struck her that in some ways he was very much like her husband. Ryan was tall and athletic, affable with an outwardly calm demeanor under most circumstances. Ryan was a "man's man" and had developed strong relationships with male colleagues, while at the same time, he typically included female colleagues in lunch invitations and cocktail hours. Most importantly, he listened to women during business meetings and gave support to their points when in agreement. He also gave credit to female as well as male colleagues for their contributions.

She admired Ryan's intelligence and his sense of confidence. Ryan had a natural ability to put people at ease and communicated as effectively with rank and file employees as he did with top-level executives.

She particularly appreciated Ryan's understanding that even professional women wanted, deserved, and expected male colleagues and business associates to display common courtesies such as opening a door, offering a woman to exit an elevator first, and extending a helping hand to place a carry-on bag in the overhead bin of an airplane.

Ryan was also quite handsome and more than once she was thanked by women in the organization for hiring the most delicious "eye candy" they had ever had on the staff. While professionally Tracy glossed over this unacceptable banter and pointed out that for years women have railed against similar sexist epithets, there was no denying Ryan was easy on the eyes, and she found herself holding his gaze a little longer than other male colleagues. She also had to admit to herself that on a couple occasions when just the two of them were standing and talking together, she noticed Ryan's eyes drifted below her face in a way that might show sexual interest in someone. Normally, she would have felt insulted and as a manager been compelled to call him out on that behavior, even if unintentional. In this case, though, she realized she had no desire to object and rather enjoyed that he seemed to be appreciating her as a woman and he had seemed pleased with her silent but unmistakable look of approval.

Tracy wasn't blind to the hypocrisy of this behavior or the danger of moving down what could become a rapidly slippery slope. To this point, she convinced herself that she had control of her emotions and enjoyed the creative rush she knew she and many others derived from such encounters. While business was Tracy's major in college, philosophy, psychology, and the arts were her other passions, and she had filled her electives with heady courses in those subjects. She was particularly intrigued by the study of heightened creativity and performance of artists under the aura of an inspirational "muse." In Greek mythology, each of nine beautiful goddesses, Muses, preside over a different art or science and have a special power that can be tapped into by seeking help from that deity. Over time the term "taking a muse," came to mean engaging in a relationship, usually sexual, that helped inspire an artist's work and accelerate their creativity through increased levels of certain hormones and chemicals in the brain.

The paintings of Frida Kahlo and Diego Rivera are undoubtedly contemporary examples of the inspirational power generated by a sexual muse. For him, it took the form of four marriages and scores of lovers; for her, a volatile lifetime relationship with Rivera marked by divorce and remarriage to him while she too carried on many outside affairs with men and women. Their relationship was almost as legendary as their artwork, and the masterful Rivera recognized Frida's talent and encouraged her to paint. Somewhat sadly, wide acceptance of her style, classified by some as Neomexicanismo, new Mexican folk art, and monetary reward for her paintings, mostly came years after her death.

In the modern world, drugs such as LSD and cocaine, along with alcohol, also seemed to provide some artists, inventors and even business professionals with a creative boost while others appear to be in no need of such stimulus to give the world their gifts of song, art, accomplishment, or scientific breakthroughs.

Tracy reasoned that for many years her pure passion for business, her love for her family and her Christian faith were more than ample drivers of her motivation. Lately, though, Ryan's presence seemed to stimulate her, and she wondered if she had found her "muse." *Or could it be something more? I know that feelings can crop up between colleagues that work closely together. People look their best, generally act well-mannered and simply spend most of their waking hours together. Add in the stress-laden, testosterone-fueled atmosphere of a high stakes, fast growing firm like theirs, and you have a veritable Molotov cocktail of sexual tension ready to erupt at any given moment.* In some ways, Tracy had felt immune to these feelings over the years as she focused largely on her work, her family, and civic duties. *Maybe I'm not as impervious as I thought I was.* She shifted uncomfortably in her seat with this thought.

She felt a huge responsibility to be a role model for other professional women striving to climb ladders in the financial services sector. The path she forged to become Fontella & Scharf's first female partner was also creating a roadmap for women in her firm and across Wall Street as word of her success and acceptance spread through the male-dominated jungle of investment banks and M&A firms. While not yet at the midpoint of what she hoped would be a lengthy career, Tracy had been around long enough to see a wide array of questionable behavior between colleagues, most of which she had avoided to this point.

There were situations where females, some strikingly pretty and let's say equally well endowed, were hired into the firm in administrative or even management trainee roles and were swept up into office romances with associates, managers, and even partners. The credibility of aspiring female junior leaders was sometimes undermined by these sexual dalliances and occasionally created awkward working conditions. In some cases, the romances indeed turned into marriages and invariably off went the female to start over at another firm or out of paid work entirely, tending to babies and managing their new households.

Typically, the men's careers, as well as their reputations, were largely unscathed regardless of the circumstances and curiously, some seemed to enjoy a more elevated status among their peers as their conquests became public knowledge. Whatever the case, Tracy tried to avoid engaging in conversations about these personal situations or allowing these facts to impact her opinions of the affected parties. After all, she reasoned, we're running a business, so unless their behavior resulted in laws being broken or company policies deemed breached, the results of the work being generated were what mattered most.

The car hit a large bump and momentarily jarred her from her thoughts.

"Je suis désolé! I am sorry!" Anthony exclaimed.

Ryan and Tracy both laughed. "Ça va, it's okay," Tracy replied. She glanced at Ryan who seemed engrossed in his notes. She smiled and turned back toward the window and her thoughts.

Tracy also strove to see people as individuals, each to be afforded the same high levels of respect and trust right from the start. She perceived the openness that came with trust and respect as fundamental to fostering productive business relationships. She considered that if you were honest with yourself, you would recognize that you almost can't help "seeing" gender, race or religion. Her method for blocking out the obvious visual differences was to focus on the eyes of the other person during encounters and meetings. She also listened closely for sincerity or a lack of, in their words and the tone of their voice. Perhaps because of this, she believed that she had developed a heightened ability to assess whether someone was offering her and others the same level of personal respect. If she believed this quality was lacking in a candidate or a subordinate, she promptly eliminated them from the mix. The course of action sometimes became more complicated, delicate and stressful when the offender exhibiting this detrimental behavior was a peer, superior or client. Tracy sometimes felt frustrated about the precious resources, especially human energy, wasted by the need to politically manage through these situations. She also worried that it negatively affected the firm in addition to people whose careers were stifled or even derailed by such narrow-minded individuals.

One of her growing concerns was whether the pace of global social change necessary for women to succeed would rise as fast as the rate of international business alliances. Thus far, she had interacted almost exclusively with men in many foreign business dealings. Some were visibly uncomfortable with Tracy and the few other women who actively took part in meetings. They constantly looked to male colleagues, even subordinates, for affirmation of whatever statements "the woman" had made. Sometimes, there were no easy answers to these complex situations and Tracy reminded herself that even in the US there remained clubs and private golf courses that excluded women members through their by-laws and, in some cases, even as guests on the links or in the clubhouse. Recently, two Fontella & Scharf partners cut ties with their clubs over this very issue when they were taken to task by large corporate clients who expressed their unwillingness to work with firms associated with such clubs.

"The Universite is just ahead," said Anthony, startling Tracy out of her thoughts again.

As the car approached the main gate, Ryan felt his heart beat a little faster.

"Anthony, it would be great if you would pull into the courtyard to let us out, then return in about fifteen minutes," said Ryan.

"Oui, oui," Anthony said nodding.

"I'd like to say these tall, black wrought iron gates look familiar," said Tracy. "But again, I've probably seen hundreds of them in my lifetime."

Ryan led Tracy through the courtyard, lush with green foliage and the fragrant scent of summer flowers. Tracy lingered behind as she tried to search her mind for some memory of this place. Looking around she saw a simple wooden bench shaded by large trees and envisioned that perhaps she had sat there to read or study.

Ryan was already ahead at the entrance to the stately two-story red brick building. He stopped and said, "I believe your French class was in this building, Tracy."

He held the door open for her, and she waited just inside the entrance. Ryan entered and looked around. "In fact, I think your room was about halfway down this hall on the left," he said as he pointed toward the long corridor to their right.

The building was nearly devoid of students at this late summer date and fall semester still a few weeks away. The sound of their shoes on the marble floor echoed off the smooth interior walls and wood and glass doors.

Ryan approached one of the rooms and slowly opened the door.

"I'm not one hundred percent sure if this was your classroom, but it was in this area."

Tracy entered the room and took it all in as she slowly looked at the walls, tables, and classroom chairs. "Ryan, do you remember if you sat at tables like these or were there desks in the room back then?" she asked.

"I think there were desks, though I can't be certain. It's been a while," he answered as he tapped his temple.

Tracy walked to the teacher's desk and ran her hands over the wooden surface. She even sat down in the chair, although it was a newer style than what would have been in the room over fifteen years ago. As she sat in the chair, she looked out over the classroom as if trying to visualize how it would have been when she was teaching. She turned and looked at the full wall blackboard behind her. "Did we use the blackboard often?"

"You would write sentences in English on that side of the blackboard," he said, pointing to the left side. "And then we would translate them into French and write them out on this side of the board," he finished, pointing to the right side.

Tracy stared at the board a while longer. She shrugged and got up from the chair. She took a last look around the room and then briskly walked back into the hallway. Ryan closed the door behind them.

She walked to the end of the hallway, stopping to peer into classrooms along the way and looking at pictures and plaques on the walls. She stopped at the water cooler and took a drink. "Hmm, that seems familiar to me. I'm seeing myself getting a drink here on the way to or from class," said Tracy. "Oh, I don't know. It's not a clear vision, maybe I'm just conjuring up what would be a logical possibility and hoping it's real to jog my memory. How about you Ryan? Will you share your memories?"

Cautiously, Ryan stopped and looked around the hallway. He began, "Well, the whole team would generally head over from our apartments and, as a group, we were pretty loud. You know, young guys teasing each other maybe joking around about a cute girl one of the guys met up with or horsing around with each other. Looking back now, I guess it was a lot of stupid stuff, but we worked hard during practice, so we needed to blow off steam in our free time. I remember some days it took a few minutes to get all the rowdies calmed down and focused on the program. You made learning fun by bringing in posters of local events that we would interpret and gave us ideas of things we could do. I also remember that you brought menus from restaurants, programs and brochures from museums, towns, and historical places we might visit. It was all very helpful. Since we were earning college credit for the course, we had to participate." He paused as if searching for another errant memory. Then he shrugged. "I guess that's about it."

"Interesting," said Tracy. "Sounds like I was pretty creative and glad you and your teammates found the course helpful."

"Yeah, it really was. There's more to see in Lille, so we should go." Ryan turned away from Tracy to prevent her from seeing the emotion welling up in him. He took a deep breath and walked quickly to the front doors. His mind was full of vivid visions of Tracy standing in front of the class, laughing along with some of their adolescent jokes, showing amazing patience with even the slowest guys and trying, but thankfully failing, to keep her loving eyes from glancing his way after their relationship began. As for him, he remembered simply staring at Tracy. He was head over heels in love with her and wanted to be in her presence as often as possible.

"Well it's news to me if I've been in this building before," proclaimed Tracy when she reached the front doors. "Nothing looks or feels familiar to me. I suppose that's just as well. It's all in the past and has no bearing on my life today."

Ryan nodded and opened one of the doors. "Shall we head out?"

"Yes, let's drive through the town square and then head over to the convent to finish up our visit," said Tracy.

Anthony was waiting for them just outside the door. They settled back into the limo for the short drive through the town square and to the convent just a few blocks away.

"Lille is a charming city," said Tracy. Has it changed much from what you remember Ryan?"

"Some of the stores and restaurants look familiar. Of course, we were college students on a limited budget and the program provided team meals during the week. It was only on weekends that we had to fend for ourselves. The small delis were our favorite for sandwiches. Freshly sliced salami, cheese and bread that seemed to have come right out of the oven is what I lived on."

"That sounds delicious," said Tracy. "Let's stop and get a couple sandwiches to go for the train ride back!" She leaned forward.

"Anthony, will you please stop at a deli of your choice where we can pick up a couple sandwiches?"

"Mais oui, of course, Madame."

To Ryan's relief, Anthony pulled up in front of what appeared to be a newer establishment. They got out of the car and walked into the deli.

"Bonjour Madame et Monsieur," called out the proprietor.

"Bonjour," echoed Tracy and Ryan.

"I could just stand here all day and breathe in the smell of French bread and fresh deli meats. And just look at all these cheeses!" Tracy exclaimed.

Slowly, carefully they each made their choice, and the sandwiches were wrapped securely in white butcher paper. "Merci, au revoir," said the shopkeeper as Tracy and Ryan walked out.

"Hey, that's my old apartment building," said Ryan pointing to a building across the street from the store. "We had the unit on the third floor in that corner."

"Wow, I'm glad we stopped here Ryan. Would you like to go over and walk around the building if we can get in?" asked Tracy.

"No, thanks. It was just a basic two bedroom, one bath flat, definitely not an architectural gem," laughed Ryan. "Great memories of fun times though." Then he added, "I'm sorry, Tracy. This must be very hard for you."

"Oh, no worries. I'm fine. It's wonderful to see you enjoying this experience."

As they walked toward the car, which had moved to avoid getting a parking ticket, they passed a flower shop. Ryan stopped to admire the array of blooms. "Hey, what do you say we bring some flowers for the nuns?" he asked.

"I think that's a lovely idea, Ryan!" They made their selection, and Ryan paid the attractive young shopkeeper, who smiled shyly at him.

Back in the car, the aroma of the sandwiches filled every inch even though their treasures were securely sealed. "I can't wait to dig into my sandwich," said Tracy.

"Me too," agreed Ryan.

Chapter 27

The Convent, Lille, France

The car pulled into the gravel driveway through open tall, black wrought iron gates. The sign on the right indicated it was a one-way road and indeed it was in the form of a semicircle that led up to the front entrance.

"Jeremy messaged that we're good to visit the convent and tour the grounds. We're to ask for Sister Susana," said Tracy.

"Is that one of the nuns you sort of remember from the hospital?"

"No. Jeremy said she doesn't know me either because she arrived at the convent only about eight years ago."

"That's good." He immediately regretted his words.

"What do you mean by that?" asked Tracy, a bit taken aback.

"Ah, nothing, actually I just meant it's good that someone will be able to see us." He felt his face flush.

Tracy's eyes squinted a bit as she considered his answer. "Well, in any event, there is at least one sister still living in the convent who remembered me and knew about the accident," said Tracy. "Jeremy said her name is Sister Santina and she's well into her eighties. I'm excited to talk with her."

Ryan instinctively pulled on his shirt collar to loosen it a bit. "I interacted with a few of the nuns around the university, but I have no idea if Sister Santina was one of them," said Ryan. "I've never been in the convent, so I have no idea what to expect."

What he didn't say was that his main goal was to avoid being seen on the grounds when he visited Tracy, especially at night.

Anthony stopped the car at the front of the three-story gray stone building.

"There's a parking area just up the driveway. I'll wait there for you," said Anthony.

"Perfect," said Tracy. "We shouldn't be more than fifteen or twenty minutes, and then we'll head back to the train station."

Tracy and Ryan walked up the three wide cement stairs and were about to ring the doorbell when a young, energetic woman of the cloth opened the door and greeted them with a smile. "Bonjour Madame and Monsieur, entre vous s'il vous plait," she said as she gestured for them to enter the building.

"Bonjour et merci beaucoup," said Tracy, thanking the nun for her warm welcome.

"I'm Sister Susana," the nun offered in nearly perfect English. "I spoke with Jeremy on the telephone."

"Yes, thank you so much for allowing us to visit on such short notice," said Tracy. "This is my colleague, Mr. Kupford, who coincidentally was in Lille at the Universite de Catholique that same summer as a member of an American soccer team."

"Bonjour, Sister Susana," Ryan said as he presented her with the beautiful bouquet of flowers he'd hidden behind his back.

"Oh, merci, Monsieur Kupford et Madame Knapp, pour ces belles fleurs," said Sister Susana nestling her nose into the fragrant bouquet.

Tracy couldn't help but notice that the young Sister's cheeks blushed ever so slightly. *Even when he isn't trying, Ryan exudes a natural and somewhat disarming charm.*

Sister Susana escorted them through the small but spotless vestibule into a large, sparsely furnished yet again immaculate dining room where a thin, frail-looking nun was seated on a bench at a long wooden table. "Sister Santina, Mademoiselle Knapp et Monsieur Kupford have arrived," announced Sister Susana loudly, in her native language.

Sister Santina smiled at Tracy and said in French, "Come closer, my child, my eyes fail me these days."

"Mais oui, Sister Santina." Tracy obliged the elder nun and sat down right next to her on the bench. They searched each other's eyes, and Sister Santina reached out for Tracy's hands.

"Yes, I remember you, my dear," said Sister Santina. "Your brown eyes still sparkle brightly."

Tracy was hoping she too, might see a familiar face but instead she peered curiously into warm and caring eyes that were intently studying Tracy's face.

Sister Santina continued, "Sister Agnes was our Mother Superior while you were here, and she took a special interest in you. She passed over to eternal life with our Lord about five years ago, but until her death, she prayed for you and your well-being. After the accident, it was Sister Agnes who arranged for the Sisters to hold a vigil in your hospital room. Here at the convent, she called upon all to offer constant prayers of intercession to our Lord for your recovery. She was elated when you awoke from the coma, though somewhat sad that you had no memory of the close bond that had grown between the two of you. Of course, she respected your doctor's directive to avoid straining your mind with trying to remember forgotten events or even people. Your progress was nothing short of a miracle, and she only wanted the best for you, even if that meant you had no memories of your time with us."

"Oh, Sister Santina," sighed Tracy. "This is new information to me. I wish I had known and properly thanked each one of the dear and kind Sisters."

"Don't worry my child," said Sister Santina. "And of course, we are very grateful that you have remembered us every year with your generous gifts."

Tracy gently encircled her arms around the nun, and Sister Santina responded by embracing Tracy as well. Tracy released the nun slowly and said, "I do have vague memories of nuns in habit being present in my hospital room when I regained consciousness. It was comforting to have my hand held and hear their soft prayers and songs. Unfortunately, I still have no memories of any summer activities before the accident. I thought perhaps being here would unlock the vault in my mind," said Tracy.

Tracy sat up on the bench and craned her neck toward an open door. She took a deep sniff of air.

"Mmm, what is that delicious smell coming from the kitchen?" asked Tracy. Quickly, she answered her own question, "Poulet, roast chicken, I believe." She leaned back and looked slowly around the room.

"I see a room full of nuns, dressed in gray and black habits. Their heads are bowed, and their hands are clasped together to form a circle around the table." And then as if in a trance, Tracy began to recite the Hail Mary in perfect French. "Je vous salue, Marie, pleine de grace, le Seigneur est avec vous."

Sister Santina and Sister Susana joined her to finish the prayer.

"Tres bien, very good," said Sister Santina.

"The Hail Mary is my favorite prayer," said Tracy. "It's a foggy memory, but I recall being in this very room and reciting that prayer before meals. Would that have been your practice?"

"Oui," replied Sister Santina.

"And it is still the same today," chimed Sister Susana.

"Maybe it's the delicious smell of the chicken roasting in the oven that brought me back for this moment." And just as suddenly the vision drifted out of sight, and she was back to the present, seated beside a kind and caring stranger.

A ringing phone in the next room shattered the peaceful silence.

"Excusez-moi," said Sister Susana. "I must tend to administrative matters. It was very nice to meet you both. Thank you again for the beautiful flowers."

Ryan nodded and smiled.

"Thank you for allowing us to visit, Sister Susana," said Tracy. Sister Susana waved and then hurried to answer the persistent caller.

Just as Ryan was beginning to think they would get through this visit without any further frights, he heard Tracy ask,

"Sister Santina, would it be possible for me to see the cottage where I'm told I stayed?"

Ryan felt his heart start to pound. For a moment, he considered offering to wait in the car but knew that would seem odd, suspicious even.

"Of course, my dear," said Sister Santina. "My legs are not strong enough to walk with you today, but if you go through that door, the path will lead you to the cottage. It's now a reading room, although I doubt the furnishings have changed much given our vow of poverty." The nun folded her hands in prayer and bowed her head toward Tracy.

Sister Santina continued, "We make improvements to the house only for necessary maintenance or in support our mission work. The lone exception is our beautiful garden which gives us not only herbs and vegetables for cooking but a creative outlet for many of us who love to toil in the dirt, praying while we plant and prune. Even if you do not remember your time here, please take the time to stroll in the peaceful garden and consider offering a prayer for Sister Agnes at the Shrine of Our Lady."

"Thank you, Sister Santina. I will," said Tracy. She gave the nun a final embrace. "Goodbye, Sister Santina."

Tracy and Ryan left through the backdoor that Sister Santina had pointed to and walked down a narrow, winding footpath cut through the lush foliage. They came upon the Shrine dedicated to Mary, Mother of Jesus and, as instructed, Tracy knelt to pray for Sister Agnes. Her thoughts drifted back to the vague memory of kind and caring nuns at her bedside. Tracy silently asked her forgiveness for not realizing the depth of their relationship. She also prayed to Mary in gratitude for her many blessings, especially her family. She and Bill were extremely fortunate in worldly matters. And then, as she did many days, she prayed for strength, patience, wisdom, and grace. She was acutely aware that by her own choice, she worked under extremely stressful conditions and recognized that she was vulnerable to human transgressions. She was thankful that Bill had scaled back his career to support the needs of their growing family. But the girls needed their mother too, and as hard as Bill tried, Tracy realized that as Nicole and Jean grew older, they needed her more for emotional support as they navigated through the typical peer pressures of a young girl's social life. Silently she prayed, Please Mother Mary, help me make more time to be with my daughters and to listen to their needs with an understanding heart. She finished by making the sign of the cross and uttered a barely audible, "Amen."

She rose to her feet and walked quickly to catch up with Ryan, who had walked ahead to give her some privacy.

"Mmm, do you smell the herbs?" she asked.

"Sure do," said Ryan as he inhaled the pungent aroma. "I smell basil and maybe oregano."

Flowers, vegetables, and herbs grew from seemingly every patch of earth in the large garden. Magnificent pink, red, orange, and yellow blossoms delighted the eyes, springing forth on vines, trees, and flowers of all types.

"I feel like I want to just stand here for hours and breathe in the fresh scents of all the flowers and herbs," gushed Tracy. She closed her eyes and breathed in deeply and then exhaled slowly. As she stood there, a vision came to her.

"That was weird," she said, opening her eyes.

"What that's?" asked Ryan.

"I saw myself walking down this very same path, carrying my gray messenger bag. That's where I kept my books, folders, wallet, and passport. I still have it. I was told that after the crash, the delivery driver pulled me and my messenger bag from the wreck before the whole mess caught fire. My luggage, souvenirs, and camera all burned to ashes."

"Oh Tracy, I can't imagine what you've been through," Ryan said quietly.

Tracy was now walking in front of him and rounded a curve in the path. A simple wooden bench came into view nestled into an opening among flowering white hydrangea bushes. Tracy, feeling a bit unnerved, sat on the bench. She traced the worn wood slats with her fingers and closed her eyes. The faint scent of the showy blossoms teased her nose. Another vision arose. She was nestled on this very same bench reading a book. She tried but couldn't recall the subject of the reading material. What was coming into focus, however, was that she was now certain that these fragmented memories were real, not imagined.

"I definitely remember being here!" she stated triumphantly.

"You...do?" Ryan asked haltingly.

Tracy, ever perceptive, turned toward Ryan. She looked at him but said nothing. She turned and held her arms out wide. "I remember being in this beautiful place! Oh, I am so grateful for this shred of memory."

Ryan, attempting to sound calm as possible, glanced at his watch and said, "We should probably finish up here and get back to the car, so we make it to the train station on time."

Tracy sensed his anxiety, and it struck her that this nostalgia tour was really all about her.

Her voice sincere, "I'm sorry to be wasting your time here, Ryan. I'll be finished shortly."

"Oh Tracy, that's not it at all. I'm sorry if I sound like I'm in a hurry to leave. Maybe it's just jet lag catching up with me. You take all the time you need here. I'm glad that this visit has helped fill in some of the blanks for you. I can't imagine what it would be like to have no knowledge of a segment of my life."

"I was pretty angry at first. And then, it continued to bother me greatly for a few years but eventually through therapy and prayer, I was able to let go of it. It wasn't until yesterday when this opportunity came about that I felt tempted to consider the possibility of regaining any memory of that summer again. Right now, it's as if someone is opening and closing a photo album with pictures of me that I don't remember being taken," said Tracy. "At this moment, it's shut tightly again, and I can't seem to open it. It's frustrating. I feel like my mind is teasing me."

Ryan knew he needed to be strong for Tracy's sake. She did not and should never know how painful it was for him to be here, in this area of the convent grounds. While it was true that he had not set foot in the main house of the convent before today, he had come into the garden many times that summer through a back gate, to study with Tracy during the day and eventually, sneaking in after the nuns were sound asleep to spend nights with her in his arms. Being here was more difficult than he had thought possible. Feelings buried long ago surfaced, and it scared him. Over the years, memories of Tracy and their time together had dimmed. Days, weeks, and eventually months passed without her face coming to his mind. His broken heart mended as well. Slowly but surely, over time he found enjoyment in life again and in relationships with other women.

But ever since he had "found" Tracy, he realized that his heart still held feelings for her. And right now his heart was pounding. Over the past two years he had been careful not to look into her eyes too long for fear of showing how much he still longed for her. Thankfully, their work kept them busy, and their projects demanded extreme levels of focus and mental energy. Probably the most difficult situation he had experienced with Tracy to this point was an encounter during a recent party celebrating the consummation of one of the firms largest IPO's transactions. One by one the partners were giving accolades to key contributors among the ranks and let each say a few words. When Tracy singled out Ryan, he thanked his colleagues for their support and had to resist the urge to tell Tracy and the whole world that it was she who introduced him to this business and inspired him to stretch himself educationally and professionally so many years ago. In that proud moment of celebration, he fought the urge to pull her to him and tell her how much he still loved her. He wanted to remind her of a similar event that they witnessed together, long ago at a rooftop bar in Brussels, when they were young and falling in love. Instead, he held it all in and smiled through a tightly clenched jaw.

Tracy rose from the bench, took a last look at it and continued walking down the path as if drawn by a powerful force. She slowed her gait. She was breathing fast.

"What is coming over me?" she asked in a barely audible voice. And then there it was, a small brick structure, barely visible, overgrown with vines and wild pink roses.

The sight of the cottage brought it all back to Ryan. Beautiful memories of being with Tracy filled his mind and his heart. Fresh, strong emotions washed over him like ocean waves. He feared he would be sucked into the strong current and completely lose control of his senses. He commanded himself to be strong for Tracy. Thinking of her well-being was the only thought that kept him from giving in. He knew he was gone, but he could not let Tracy down. He sensed she would need him, and he was right.

They walked through the unlocked door into the cottage. It was just as Sister Santina described it; the cottage looked like a small library, though devoid of any visitors at the moment. One wall was filled with metal shelves lined with books, mostly religious titles. The small kitchen was equipped with the same single faded white porcelain sink atop a white wood cabinet. An old metal refrigerator, once white but now yellowed, hummed busily next to the sink. A gray metal file cabinet occupied the place where Ryan remembered an old white stove once stood. A small black microwave sat on top of the cabinet. The lone window in the kitchen was open and below it was the same small, round, metal mesh top table. Even the chairs were unchanged over almost two decades, metal frames with cushioned backs and seats, deep red as he recalled, now worn thin and faded to light pink, still tied in place yet sagging tiredly.

Tucked into a corner under identical windows on adjacent walls, was an old daybed with metal railings at the head and foot. The original white painted rails, fresh and pure as snow in his memory, were now faded and chipped. Three oversized, flower-patterned pillows were propped up against the wall to give the bed more of a wide sofa look, a sign of today's use.

Tracy stood frozen, just steps inside the doorway of the cottage as snippets of memories flooded her mind. "I see myself propped up on the daybed reading a book, although I don't recall the subject," she said.

Tracy walked over to the kitchen table, placed her hand on one of the chairs and looked around slowly. "She closed her eyes, and there she was, sitting at the little table with a young man, his head was down. They were playing cards, a pile of pennies on her side of the table." She hears herself announce, *"Royal Flush."* The boy tosses his cards on the table and shakes his head. *"Again?"* he says. But she senses that his anger is feigned because he laughs good-naturedly about the obvious loss.

"Ha, ha!" Tracy let out an audible laugh.

She looked at Ryan and saw a perplexed, though kind and somewhat concerned expression on his face as he remained silent. For his part, he studied Tracy's eyes and wondered what was going through her mind.

"I saw myself playing cards, with a *boy*," she announced. "I guess I made at least one friend that summer though I have no idea who he is."

She slowly ventured over to the daybed and sat down. She breathed in the scent of the Triomphe de Lille roses that peeked in through the open windows and felt overcome with emotion.

Ryan stood close by silently, like a sentinel watching over his charge, ready to act if needed. What he didn't know was what action he would take. His mind was incapable of playing out this scene. He would have to trust his instincts.

Tracy laid back on the daybed, closed her eyes and in an instant more memories flooded her mind. No longer were these single frames of vague pictures.

As if in a trance she began to speak, "It's raining and stormy. I see lightning, and I hear thunder. But I'm not afraid. I'm safe and secure in my cottage, in someone's loving arms, right here."

Her body was overcome with the powerful sense of longing for another human being. Her heart pulsed rapidly, her chest heaved as her breathing quickened and just as she thought she would faint from the intense emotion, she heard a voice saying the same words that filled her mind. Words that comforted her so long ago and now, here today in this room, in the very same voice with conviction and compassion, "Tracy, I'm here for you."

Tracy opened her eyes to meet Ryan's now familiar deep blue gaze and true to his promise, he was there for her. For what seemed an eternity, they held each other tightly. Ryan gently stroked Tracy's hair and neither had the strength nor felt the need to break the silence. Seventeen years melted away. In an instant, they were carried back to the summer of '81.

It took every ounce of strength she had to absorb the shock of the visions running through her mind and the pain that was piercing her heart. *Can this really be true? Is my mind playing tricks on me? Could it be jet lag or exhaustion after the events of the last few days?* Her rational mind was desperately seeking a logical reason for this illogical state of events. No, this was a reality she couldn't have imagined. She saw them just as they were, young lovers, completely absorbed in each other, the pure magical feeling of new love, her first true love. Her eyes were closed, but she saw the longing in his eyes, recalled his gentle touch on her skin and remembered the pleasure of their passions satisfied. Here in his embrace, she felt her body hunger for him once more. Then, her rational mind compelled her to ask again, *Can this really be true? Has this beautiful love been lying dormant in my heart all these years?* She knows now that what she remembers and feels is real.

Chapter 28

The train ride to Charles de Gaulle

They both remained silent during the train ride to the Charles de Gaulle airport. The sandwiches were left untouched in their wrappings. Tracy and Ryan were seated side by side. She allowed Ryan to put his arm around her as she drifted in and out of sleep, her head resting on his broad shoulder. She was emotionally spent and physically exhausted, yet she felt oddly at peace, in this safe-haven. When she awoke, her head was filled with amazing visions of a life, her life, that she had never known now becoming clear. Tracy searched her emerging memories as she tried to connect the circumstances of how they came to be together and wondered how they parted. Little by little, the visions came. She felt as if she was watching a movie for the very first time. It was a beautiful love story filled with innocence, hope, energy, playfulness, lust, passion, and a sense of adventure. She now recalled trips to amazing places, museums, churches, bike rides along the Deûle River and nights in his arms. The used train ticket she had found in her salvaged wallet now had a story to go along with it. A clear, vivid and heart-warming memory of sipping champagne with Ryan, huddled in a cozy corner of The Little Bar. Two carefree young lovers considering a future of limitless possibilities.

Her heart swelled with joyful exuberance, then just as quickly felt stricken with profound grief for this lost love and guilt since she is now a married mother.

Oddly, though perhaps mercifully, the old movie had no end. It simply faded on words so very similar to those that brought it to life this afternoon, "Tracy, baby, I'm here for you always." She clearly remembered a younger Ryan making this promise to her years ago on a warm, bright summer day. No doubt the accident that almost ended her life had cruelly ended this fledgling young love story, their love story. She now knew both rationally and emotionally that when she opened her eyes, she would see a man that she once loved deeply.

It was a love story that Ryan had lived through too, maybe was still living through. Part of her ached to know his feelings, his thoughts and at the same time, she feared knowing. *Ryan, my poor Ryan.* He had remained stoic and silent save for those few words.

And as selfish as she knew it was, she simply didn't have the strength to hear his story right now.

Her body's defense mechanisms seemed to direct her thinking and her physical actions. Emotionally, she was close to the breaking point. She felt confused and turned her mind to prayer as she often did to block out unwanted thoughts and to calm her mind. Prayer was her form of meditation. Prayer had helped her endure the physical pain after the accident and throughout rehabilitation. Prayer had guided her through the stresses of life that sometimes threatened to overwhelm her. *Please Lord, help me understand what is happening to me. Guide my free will to take the path that you have set for me. The path that serves your will.*

She dozed off for the rest of the ride.

As the train pulled to a stop at the airport station, Ryan retrieved their roller bags and briefcases from the overhead storage area. He started to pull both roller bags when he felt Tracy's hand on his. It felt like a bolt of electricity went through his body.

"Thank you, Ryan. I can manage my bags from here."

He slowly released the handle from his grip and just as slowly Tracy removed her hand from his. They both avoided looking into each other's eyes.

They walked slowly through the maze of hallways and followed the signs that led to the departures area. They looked up at the electronic flight information board and discovered that their return flight to LaGuardia had been canceled.

Tracy simply stared at the screen in a zombie-like trance.

"I'm sure they've made other arrangements for us," said Ryan. "Let's head over to the reservations desk."

"How may I help you?" asked the agent.

"Our flight to LaGuardia has been canceled," said Ryan. Ryan and Tracy handed their passports to the agent.

"Ah yes, our apologies," said the agent. "It's an equipment issue that requires the jet to be serviced by maintenance and expected to be completed tomorrow." He turned to face Tracy and said, "Ms. Knapp, we've rebooked you on our next flight into Newark which departs in one hour. Is that acceptable to you?"

"Yes, thank you," Tracy said flatly.

Then the agent addressed Ryan, "Unfortunately, Mr. Kupford, we have no more available seats on that flight, so we've rebooked you on the first flight out tomorrow morning. We have also reserved a complimentary room for you at the on-site airport hotel. Of course, you may choose to wait at the gate on standby in case a seat opens on Ms. Knapp's flight."

Ryan stood silent for a moment. He hesitated to leave Tracy alone right now though she seemed to be in a stable frame of mind. He also simply wanted to be with her. Tracy remained silent. Deciding she might want time alone, he finally said, "The morning flight will probably be fine." Turning to Tracy, he said, "This will give me time to finish up the Ronone paperwork. I'll have it emailed to you before you reach the office tomorrow."

"Sounds good. Thank you, Ryan." She spoke slowly with a weak smile. Her face was pale, and she looked as if a strong gust of wind could blow her over. She steadied herself with one hand on the counter and the other on the handle of her carry-on luggage.

"Just give me a moment to finish up the paperwork," said the agent.

"I should be giving this seat to you for your work on closing the deal yesterday," Tracy said looking up at Ryan.

As their eyes lingered on each other, she felt her mind and heart open to him more fully, and a pulse of energy seemed to radiate between them.

Ryan smiled broadly and warmly. "Tracy, you know I wouldn't let you trade flights with me," he said with a soft chuckle.

Tracy's head tilted ever so slightly, and she responded in a soft, appreciative voice, "I do."

"Here is your boarding pass and the hotel confirmation paperwork, Mr. Kupford," said the agent.

"Thank you," said Ryan as he put the paperwork into the pocket of his jacket.

They moved a few steps away from the counter and stopped. Ryan felt as if his feet were glued to the floor. His brain seemed to process a thousand thoughts simultaneously. *Does Tracy remember everything? Does she realize how deeply in love we were during that summer in Lille? Does she remember that we professed our love for each other and vowed to be together again? Does she, like me, now remember in vivid detail almost every moment we spent together that summer? When we held each other and made love all night long in her quiet little cottage?*

Then he wondered how these memories would affect her and their relationship. Though he had tried to bury his feelings for Tracy, he knew his feelings were still strong.

As tough as it had been, he was able to control himself when Tracy was unaware of their past. It was his secret then, and he'd kept it buried. Now, he felt torn between a sense of profound guilt for being an accomplice to Tracy regaining her memories and his growing excitement about what the future might bring. Then, just as quickly, he thought about their jobs, Cathy and Tracy's family.

He took a deep breath and exhaled slowly. Physically he felt like he could run a marathon, but emotionally, he was drained.

Ryan's eyes searched hers as if looking for some sign of what to do next. At that moment, Tracy felt both emotionally raw and physically aroused at a level she hadn't felt in a very long time. She stood, almost paralyzed, not knowing what to do or say next. Ryan's broke the silence. Speaking quickly so he wouldn't change his mind, he said, "Have a safe flight, Tracy. I'll see you soon."

"Ditto." Tracy's voice was hushed and tired. She bit her lower lip, trying to control her emotions. She couldn't meet his gaze.

Ryan nodded, turned, and strode quickly toward the airport hotel.

Tracy watched him walk down the corridor until he faded into the crowd. She looked again at the numbers on her boarding pass, squinted to focus on the signage and walked slowly in the direction of her assigned gate.

Chapter 29

Charles de Gaulle Airport Hotel

Ryan quickly settled into his hotel room. He undressed and took the extra shirt he had packed out of his suitcase and hung it in the closet next to his gray slacks and jacket. *Good thing I always bring an extra pair of underwear too,* he thought. He put his toiletry bag on the bathroom counter and grabbed a beer from the mini-fridge.

He called room service and ordered a cheeseburger and "pommes de frites," French fries, thinking he needed some comfort food. Shoving his emotions and thoughts of Tracy into the familiar compartment in his brain, he got to work on the Ronone report. Before he knew it, there was a knock on his door. He looked up, startled, his food order temporarily forgotten. *Could it be...?* He shook his head to clear it. *No, Tracy is on a plane back to New York.* He got up, mumbling to himself as he opened the door for the bellhop.

"Am I glad to see you," he said motioning for the tray to be set on the coffee table.

"Merci et bon soir," said the young man, smiling at the sizable tip Ryan had given him.

Ryan enjoyed that meal as much or more than the finest filet. *Maybe it's the over easy egg they put on the burgers that make them taste so good.*

He spent the next few hours finishing the report. He was about to hit the send button and hesitated. He leaned back in the chair and collected his thoughts. *Maybe I should add a personal note to Tracy*. His heart swelled with emotion, and he wanted to reassure her that he *would* be there for her. He also wanted to know if what he thought he felt from her when they parted at the airport was real or imagined.

His fingers hovered above the keyboard. In an instant he was back in Lille, lying on a blanket with Tracy under the shade of an ancient oak tree.

He guided his hands away from the keyboard and rested them on the desk as he stared at the screen. He took a deep breath and exhaled slowly. "Think this through Ryan," he said aloud. "Maybe it's better to give her time and let her make the next move, if there is one."

He looked at the email for about thirty seconds more and then hit the send button.

Chapter 30

Flight 2602 Paris to Newark

Tracy settled into her seat, thankful for the privacy afforded by her first class accommodations. When activated, the pod configuration created a veritable shroud that guaranteed almost complete and much-desired solitude.

"Bon soir, Madame Knapp," said the flight attendant.

"Good evening," answered Tracy in French.

"May I bring you something besides water to drink?" asked the flight attendant as she offered Tracy a choice of still or sparkling bottled water. Tracy chose still water and ordered a glass of red wine.

"Of course," said the flight attendant. She also handed Tracy the menu of dinner selections.

Tracy stared at the menu although it could have been a blank sheet of paper at that moment. Her mind was unsettled as she reviewed the life-changing events of the last twenty-four hours. How ironic that for years she prayed to be given the gift of her memories from that summer and now she wished to be granted the ability to press them back into that deep, dark space in her mind. Certainly, she had never wanted to recall the accident itself and had still been spared those terrible memories. What she was told of the details evoked a sense of sheer horror, and she dreaded the possibility that these memories someday would be unleashed on her brain like lightning bolts. Could she even survive such pain?

She didn't want to think about it. No, she had simply been curious about those lost months of her life.

She now remembered how she had so looked forward to the study abroad in France, and how, in the few phone calls she made to her parents from Lille, she had shared wonderful, happy experiences. She had never uttered a word about Ryan, so they were completely unaware of his existence. There were no pictures because her film went up in flames along with the car. A phrase her grandmother was fond of came to mind,

"Be careful what you wish for because you just might get it." *Well, I've got it all right. Frame by frame the action movie that was my life in Lille during the summer of 1981 is playing out in full vivid color in my mind. Visions of walking on paths in the lush green hillsides came into view. Sitting down to breakfast and dinner with the Sisters, enjoying simple yet delicious meals, flavor enhanced by the fresh herbs plucked daily from their garden.* In an instant, she was kneeling in a pew at morning Mass right beside dear Sister Agnes, her superior, her friend. Then saw herself alone, reading on that well-worn bench nestled in the trees on the convent grounds.

The Universite building she walked into earlier in the day like a stranger now welcomed her with the sounds of rowdy young men echoing through the hallway as they approached her classroom. The room was filled with old style desks, not tables. She then sees the tall, handsome young man with deep blue eyes and sandy blond hair walking into class, laughing with his friends as they enter. Before he even looks for a seat, he searches the room for her. She feels her heart beat faster in his presence and a warm rush of endorphins courses through her veins. She knows she is probably blushing as their eyes meet.

Then her thoughts turned to her cottage. Her private little space that she called home for three months. She smiled at the memory of finding the red seat cushions and chair backs at the thrift shop in town and how they added a desirable pop of color to the drab interior. The cottage that became their cozy love nest where a young man captured her mind and her heart—*A man to whom I surrendered my body willfully and completely. Oh Ryan, how could I have forgotten you?* She picked up the glass of water from her tray table and took a sip trying to quell the tears that threatened to fall.

"Here you go Madame," said the flight attendant as she set the glass of red wine on Tracy's tray. "Have you made your dinner choice?"

"Thank you, I'll have the chicken." As the flight attendant turned to the next passenger, Tracy took a sip of wine and thought, *I should just ask her to leave me the whole bottle.*

The flight took off without delay and dinner was served promptly after they reached cruising altitude.

She tried to clear her mind and enjoy her dinner. She turned her thoughts to her family. The girls would be at school, and Bill settled in at his office. Another typical day at the Knapp house. She breathed in deeply and could almost smell the fresh scent of her two little girls wrapped in towels straight out of the shower.

"May I pour another wine for you?" asked the flight attendant.

"Yes, please."

The flight attendant also noticed and refilled her empty water glass. Tracy ate about half of her meal and drained the wine glass. She got up from her seat, steadied herself and headed toward the bathroom. She spotted the flight attendant in the galley area and said, "I'm planning to sleep for a few hours now."

When Tracy returned to her seat, she was greeted by a clean space, a fresh pillow, and a blanket. She put on the ear phones, located a channel playing soft music and adjusted her eye mask to extinguish any light. She pressed the button to close her pod and settled back into the darkened space to sleep. She tried to calm her thoughts, but they continued to race. She attempted to pray the rosary, but her mind was unfocused. She sighed. She remembered how Dr. Nick, her physician, had warned her about the possibility of regaining some or all memories, good and bad. She moved around in her seat, searching for the most comfortable position. *I remember thinking that the situational roleplaying exercises seemed a waste of time. Now I know that I'm fortunate to have had some rational consideration of what it would be like as these memories flooded my mind. Even now though, my brain feels battered, bruised, and tired.* She sighed again.

Me, me, me, Tracy scolded herself. *What about Ryan? How could I have been so cruel? I feel like a monster, like someone I don't even know, yet it's me who lived this life, albeit until now, unknowingly.* Tears welled up in her eyes again, and this time Tracy let them fall silently in the darkness of her little cocoon.

Painful memories seared her mind, and it felt like daggers were piercing her heart. She tried to sort out the facts and solve the problem rationally, but the memories of Ryan and their times together that summer seemed to wash over her mind uncontrollably. What else was it her grandmother used to say when she was a little girl sharing thoughts that worried or scared her? "You are the gatekeeper of your mind Tracy. It's your choice to replace negative thoughts with positive images." *Oh, Grandma, I wish you were here to help me now. I feel incapable of pushing these thoughts out of my mind. Maybe it's because they're not negative thoughts. On the contrary, these are beautiful memories. Memories filled with laughter, happiness, and love that I really did experience and simply had no knowledge of until today.*

Today, the day I secretly wished for with all my heart for so many years. To know about those months sealed tightly in the bottle that was my mind. Well, the genie is out of the proverbial bottle, and his name is Ryan.

In her mind, she crafted provocative wishes she might ask him to grant her. She relaxed and smiled as she felt his touch, remembered the warmth of his body against hers and their shared passion.

Knowing what she now knew it was obvious that they were madly and deeply in love during their time together in Lille, brief though it was. Silently she wondered if he might still have feelings for her.

Then her thoughts turned to the reality of the situation.

Did he know about my accident when it happened? If so, then he knew I was the managing partner of the team when he came for the interview. If not.... Then she recalled the circumstances of his interview day, when she was unable to spend more than a few minutes with him because of an important client meeting. She remembered that during the post-interview meeting, Pat Holiday confided to Tracy about Ryan's honesty in not having read any of the materials sent to him because he had worked all weekend on an important last-minute assignment from his CFO. That turned out to be an important aspect in the decision to hire Ryan. It spoke of his willingness to do whatever it takes to get the job done, his understanding of weighing leverage in a situation and most importantly his character. Ryan proved to be honest, willing to take calculated risks, self-confident, yet not overly egotistical and open to seeking help, as he did from Pat that day.

She recalled the very moment she "met" Ryan in the conference room. There's no mistaking it now that his momentary look of shock was genuine. And to think she had answered "no" when he asked if they had met before. In the two years since he came on board, he had never once said anything that would indicate their past relationship. Even when it was "discovered" that he was one of the US soccer players in her French class in Lille, he acted surprised at the coincidence, saying he was very focused on the soccer aspect of the program and not the most engaged student. Yes, he thought he remembered her, but that was it. Initially, Tracy had peppered him with questions thinking he might tell her something that would spark her memory, but Ryan had offered little. Was he trying to keep those memories buried because they were unimportant to his life today or because he didn't want to hurt her? Tracy had downplayed the extent of the accident, saying only that she was involved in an unfortunate car crash on her way to the airport and had lost all memory of that summer.

His words and actions today seemed to say it all. Even now she could still feel his strong, caring arms around her and how he gently stroked her hair. *"I'm here for you Tracy,"* reverberated through her mind. And now she needed to face her own feelings.

I now remember that we were intimate physically and emotionally that summer. In the cottage today, I felt powerfully drawn to him again. Thoughts of interactions with Ryan at the office began to surface in her mind. Perhaps the appreciation she had developed for Ryan over the past two years was rooted in much more than simply shared traits or professional respect. She admitted that she had found herself growing physically attracted to Ryan as they worked more closely together. She thought about a recent conversation over lunch when she asked him how it was that a handsome, successful guy like him was still single. He initially joked that although he's dated many women, he supposed that he just hadn't yet found "the one." Then in a rare, serious tone, she recalled that he looked at her intently and confided that he once came very close to spending the rest of his life with someone only to have the relationship abruptly ended by circumstances out of either party's control. He didn't elaborate on the comment, and Tracy didn't pry. While she felt that their relationship had progressed beyond colleagues to a level of genuine friendship, she sensed he didn't want to talk about it, so she just let it go.

How could she have not known that the woman was *her* and her car accident was the tragic circumstance that shattered their young love? For two years she's worked with Ryan, spent time getting to know him and yet never realized until today what they meant to each other, maybe, what they still mean to each other.

Tracy began to question how she was able to fall in love with Bill when she should have known that hiding deep in her heart was love for Ryan. If what she and Ryan shared was true love, could the love she and Bill have for each other be real as well or was her heart tricked into a lie right from the start by her brain's inability to remember Ryan?

Can someone truly, romantically love more than one person at the same time? Tracy felt confused and conflicted.

She thought back to when she and Bill first met. She felt a physical attraction to him early on, although she put her feelings in check because he was on the other side of the deal being negotiated. Later, as they got to know and enjoy each other, their hearts opened, and she fell deeply in love with him. She still admired Bill for his good nature, athletic, handsome physique, kind spirit, sharp mind and, of course, being the amazing father of their two adorable young girls, Nicole and Jean.

Thoughts of her precious children ran through her mind, and maybe that was the one thing of which she was certain right then. She knew that the love of a mother for her children lies deep in most women's hearts. Though her work and other activities meant she had to be away from her daughters, she loved them more than anything on this earth and would protect them from harm.

With her mind a blur of thoughts, and her heart bursting with emotion, Tracy succumbed to sheer exhaustion.

As the plane cruised along smoothly, she fell into a deep and much-needed slumber. She saw the faces of her two little girls, Bill's broad smile and felt the warmth of Ryan's strong embrace. It will all work out she told herself. *Que sera, sera; whatever will be, will be.*

Chapter 31

Offices of Fontella & Scharf, New York, New York

Tracy knocked on Ryan's open office door. "Hey Ryan," Tracy said with a smile. Ryan put down the report he was reading to look up and visually drink in the woman in front of him with a long, appreciative look.

"Hey, Tracy. Come on in."

She sat down at the round glass conference table. He pushed his chair away from his desk, rose and stretched himself out. She took in the view of his elongated body as he reached his arms up toward the ceiling, moving his torso right and left to relieve the tension from sitting for a long time. Her eyes instinctively roved from head to mid-section and seated as she was, it was easy for her glance to land just below belt level. *Hmmm, very nice,* she thought to herself, but out loud she asked, "How is the Digital Dynamics analysis shaping up?"

Ryan came around from behind his desk and took a seat next to Tracy at the conference table.

"I'm just finishing up the strategic planning section. Do you have about fifteen minutes to go over the high points?"

"That's why I'm here," said Tracy.

"This is a match made in heaven, Tracy," Ryan gushed enthusiastically. "These two companies complement each other in many aspects, and the synergies that can be exploited are incredible. I've calculated that at least two hundred million in annual cost savings could be immediately realized by optimizing key operating assets, another three hundred million in one-time inventory reductions through consolidation and another eighty to a hundred million in annual savings by eliminating redundant back-office functions such as treasury, cost accounting, credit and human resources."

Tracy listened intently and said with a smile, "That's awesome, Ryan." She gazed admiringly at the aspiring junior executive and thought how wonderful it was to see him in this moment. The passion he had for his work was evident in the care he took to understand his client's needs and objectives before plunging into strategic planning. This was a valuable and somewhat rare quality in their business, where big egos could send bankers down a path with little regard for what the customer genuinely wanted.

Ryan was leveraging his undeniable intelligence, knowledge gained from his education and years of valuable business experience. Tracy couldn't be happier for him. And for them.

Ryan continued, "And on top of the increased cash flow resulting from the cost cuts and working capital reductions, I can see potential market share gains of at least fifteen points to be realized by marketing and cross-selling products through their existing sales channels. I've already sketched out the top product opportunities, the framework of a marketing plan and an overview of resources needed to train their sales staff. These actions will support their strategic goal of being number one in all the key markets they outlined to us. With the right execution, they could get it done in about twelve months. Of course, I'll define it as eighteen to twenty-four months in the white paper because it's better to under promise and over deliver." Ryan winked at Tracy and with a broad smile said, "I've been taught by the best."

Tracy nodded and couldn't help but feel appreciative of Ryan's compliment. She looked past him and saw the New York skyline and Statue of Liberty visible from his newly established window office on the sixty-third floor of the gleaming International Commercial Building. The move came with his recent promotion. How far they've come, from two kids laughing and dreaming in the warm sunshine on a grassy knoll in Lille, France, to this day when they're both accomplished executives, still rising to even higher career milestones.

Tracy was now Vice Chairman of the firm and the partner overseeing Ryan's Technology segment as well as the firm's Metals and Mining segment managed by Pat Holiday. Together, Tracy and Ryan had combined their talents to successfully complete numerous lucrative deals since the SBB/Ronone acquisition that forever changed their lives.

Sometimes it seemed like an eternity since the day they went to France, met Giuseppe Probello and took that fateful side trip to Lille.

Lille has now changed my life twice, thought Tracy as she returned her attention to Ryan's plans for the Digital Dynamics deal. "What do you think Tracy?" asked Ryan.

"Your plan is brilliant, Ryan. As usual, you've nailed this one down nicely. I like that you've worked through the cash flow improvement. This CEO may already be thinking about her next acquisition and trying to figure out how to pay for it. Knowing this deal will contribute significant free cash flow right away may well be the linchpin to sealing the deal."

"Thanks, Tracy. While the market share growth is important, I'll be sure to focus appropriately on the cash flow. Heck, with the pace of change going on in business lately, they may decide to flip the whole thing before these strategies are fully executed. Bottom line, it's about the money."

"Outstanding," said Tracy as she rose to leave Ryan's office. She paused in the doorway and turned back to face Ryan who was watching her leave. "How about an afternoon workout and dinner at Tavern on the Park?" she asked.

Afternoon workout was code for together time at the firm's Park Helmsley apartment.

Tracy continued, "It's a beautiful night, and Bill knows I'm staying in the city for an early morning meeting tomorrow."

"That's exactly what I was hoping you would ask, Tracy. How about 4:30?"

Their eyes locked, and Tracy lingered in the doorway. Without a word, Ryan came around the glass table and stood just inches from her. He breathed in her scent and knew that in a few short hours they would be together again.

Chapter 32

New York, New York

At 4:30, Ryan put the key in the door of suite 4612. Tracy was casually seated on the sofa sipping a chilled glass of Pinot Grigio and gazing out the huge floor-to-ceiling window.

She said, "This might be my favorite view of Central Park. What a magnificent ocean of greens and browns and the trees arching over the wide expanse of lush lawns. People walking, riding, skating, pushing strollers on the paths that meander through the park. Museums, cafes, ponds and even the zoo all co-exist peacefully in this oasis in the heart of the city that never sleeps."

"It is a gem," said Ryan.

On the coffee table sat a plate of fresh fruit, yogurt and almonds, a welcome sight after a long day and both having worked through lunch. She was already out of her "business blues," referring to their office attire of traditional blue suits. Women were starting to break out, and Tracy had added a few tailored dresses to her professional wardrobe, but the suit just wouldn't die.

This afternoon, she had donned a brightly colored satin robe. Ryan looked longingly at Tracy and surprised her with a bouquet of exotic pink and white Stargazer lilies.

"Oh Ryan, they're beautiful! Thank you."

Tracy rose from the sofa, retrieved a crystal vase from the cabinet and filled it with water. She quickly arranged the flowers and then poured a glass of wine for Ryan. He took off his gold-tone tie and started to loosen his cufflinks. She set the glass down on the gray and white marble counter and said, "Allow me." She removed his cuff links and started to unbutton his crisply starched white dress shirt. As she did, Ryan gently kissed her ear and said, "I remember when you gave me these for my birthday last year." He gazed at the exquisite, hand painted pieces of artwork now sitting on the table. "I've never seen such beautiful craftsmanship." At the center of each cufflink was a delicate white lily of the valley with green petals and stem. Then, locking eyes with Tracy, he said, "Of course, the best part is that every time I look at them, I think of you."

Ryan lifted Tracy's glass from the counter and gave it to her, then picked up his and offered a toast, "Cheers to my beautiful Lily of France and to another wonderful evening together." They gently tapped their fine crystal glasses together and took a long sip of the cold, delicious wine.

"Mmm," said Tracy. That hits the spot." Tracy tilted her head back, her long hair falling below her shoulders. She drew a deep breath and exhaled slowly, savoring this moment. "There's nothing better on a hot New York summer afternoon than a chilled glass of Pinot Grigio."

"Nothing?" asked Ryan playfully.

He set down their glasses and wrapped his arms around Tracy. Their hungry mouths found each other in a gentle but powerful kiss. As they explored each other, their passions grew. It's almost inexplicable but for them each time feels like the first time. Within minutes, they're locked in each other's arms in the cool satin sheets of the luxurious king-sized bed. Tracy loved the feel of Ryan's long fingers gently caressing her body. Just when she felt like she couldn't hold back, he entered her, and their bodies moved together in harmonious rhythm. Physically she was here with Ryan. In her mind, she was carried away to the lush green countryside of Lille and a simple bed in the rustic, charming cottage where she and Ryan made love for the first time so many years ago. From simple surroundings then, to the plush penthouse suite they enjoyed today.

If only it could be that simple. Ryan and Tracy snuggled together afterward, their hearts still beating wildly with each aware of the other's deep breathing after this act of extreme physical exertion. In the bliss of it all, Tracy felt the familiar pangs of guilt. She tried to chase the thoughts away, but they came back unbidden.

She is a married woman and the mother of two beautiful daughters. She is the weekend soccer mom and occasional creator of elaborate Halloween costumes for her precious young girls. A vision of Nicole and Jean each dressed as mermaids came to mind, and she smiled inwardly thinking back to the year they decided they each wanted to be mermaid princesses. The costumes, hand sewn by Tracy during weekends at their summer house in The Hamptons, barely made it through the day. The silk fabric was beautiful, rich, bright aqua blue with shimmering silver accents, but so delicate that it seemed to lose threads with every step they took. By the end of the day, the gold fins were almost completely shredded, and safety pins were all that was left holding the costumes together. The girls loved those costumes and looked and felt as beautiful as princesses that day. Sure, Tracy could easily have contracted a seamstress to custom make the outfits, but this was truly a labor of love. The girls had also enjoyed the whole process of going to the fabric store to choose the material then watched as the dresses took shape weekend after weekend over the course of the summer. Tracy worked on them when the girls played together and when the family wasn't boating, bike riding or playing badminton.

As she thought back to that Halloween, she saw herself walking hand-in-hand with Bill, a few paces behind their two trick or treaters. It was a joyful memory. How fun it was to watch Nicole teach her little sister the proper etiquette of the process. She could just hear her eldest daughter instructing, "You need to speak up and smile when you say, 'trick or treat,' Jean. That way they'll give you more candy, maybe even the big candy bars." Nicole was excited to tutor her eager and attentive little novice. It was hard not to chuckle when "twick or tweet" came out with Jean's smile, even more endearing as she was missing two front baby teeth that became stuck in an ear of corn just the weekend before. Without skipping a beat, Nicole beamed at her younger sister, "Perfect, Jean!"

At that moment, Tracy couldn't imagine enjoying being anywhere in the world other than right there, walking the streets of their community with Bill and her two little girls, greeting neighbors and spending time together as a family.

Yes, her love for Bill and the girls was true and deep. So how could she feel so fulfilled and calm, lying here with Ryan? She felt a wave of anxiety coming over her. As if he could read her mind, Ryan broke the silence, "I'm starving. Let's go to dinner and then take a walk in Central Park. There's a concert tonight, so if you would like to go, I'll ask the maître d', Zachary, to prepare wine and fruits to take along for dessert."

Tracy replaced thoughts of Bill and the girls with the scene at hand. "That sounds delightful Ryan." One look at Ryan assured her that she was where she should be right now, reason unknown. Work had been more stressful than ever lately with the economy in a downturn. The pressure was on all the partners to call in their chips with clients, and wherever possible bring valuable business into the firm to weather the storm. Ryan had been very helpful to her in this effort, and the ease with which they communicated was almost uncanny. But mostly, Tracy just couldn't resist bringing Ryan back into her life when she realized what they meant to each other in the past. Hiding the truth from Bill about regaining her memory was the hardest thing she had ever done. And the most deceitful since it spiraled into afternoons and evenings like this one.

Sometimes she wondered if Bill had any inkling of her secret double life with Ryan, but she quickly extinguished any such thoughts. Tracy's job required her to be strategic in planning, flawless in tactical execution, and, of course, discreet due to the nature of their business. Many of their clients were public companies, and even the slightest leak about a pending sale or acquisition could kill a deal or result in information hitting the street prematurely. This, more than anything, was the kiss of death for an investment bank or an investment banker. Clients had to have one hundred percent confidence that every member of the team understood, respected and took action to insure ironclad secrecy.

Well, that training sure paid off, and so here they were. At work and in most public settings, they looked and acted like colleagues. Tracy had made the Fontella & Scharf Board aware of their relationship, and the board had no problem with it so long as Tracy and Ryan kept it to themselves and acted professionally. This really wasn't surprising since sidebar relationships, even among colleagues, was common. She also believed the divorce rate among folks in the industry was higher than average. She didn't have any research to back up her opinion, but a quick tally of associates and acquaintances made her confident that the number was significant. Divorce wasn't what Tracy wanted anyway. She loved her life with Bill and the girls. *Her life with Bill and the girls*. The phrase seemed to come from her lips so naturally and so beautifully. She did not want to be the one to tear their family apart, but then, she had to consider that her actions had perhaps already broken their family unit in addition to her wedding vow of faithfulness to Bill.

No, it was hard to explain, but, in her heart and maybe her mind as well, she reasoned that because Ryan had come first, the real betrayal had been against *him*. Always the gentleman, Ryan had never uttered a cross word about Bill or exerted any pressure on Tracy to leave Bill. He seemed content with sharing her and was clear that he cherished their time together.

Well, tonight is not the night to solve that dilemma, she decided.

Tracy and Ryan took a quick shower in the luxurious six-head sauna and pleasured each other one more time before they changed into casual clothes.

"I'm starving!" exclaimed Ryan as closed the door to the apartment.

Their usual table was ready when they arrived. It was tucked discreetly in the back corner of the restaurant away from prying eyes. Even so, they were careful to control their affections in public. Tonight, like most nights, the conversation was largely business anyway, so anyone eavesdropping would likely think it was strictly a professional dinner.

As they finished their after-dinner coffees, Carla, their favorite server, presented a simple basket of fresh fruit, hard cheese, a Syrah with glasses safely wrapped in cloth napkins and a light blanket. "Thank you, Carla," said Ryan, "This is perfect."

"You're welcome, Mr. Kupford."

"Yes, it is perfect, Ryan," said Tracy, her eyes locked on Ryan's. "Thank you for your thoughtfulness."

With basket in hand, they strolled toward Central Park headed toward the lawn near the main Pavilion.

The sidewalks were teeming with people eager to enjoy the glorious evening after a stretch of unusually hot, wet weather. The temperature at 8:00 PM was a balmy and dry seventy-five degrees with the low predicted to be around seventy. The sun started its descent behind the tree line in the western sky, turning more orange and red as it dipped toward the horizon.

"I love how the setting sun alters the urban landscape," said Tracy. "Look how the glass facades change color and reflections bounce off the metal and polished stone surfaces. It reminds me of being in Arizona, looking out over the Grand Canyon at sunrise and sunset, watching the rock walls shift colors rapidly as reds, greens, hues of yellow and orange cascade and collide together. The grandeur of God's handiwork is on full display in its timeless beauty and strength."

"The Grand Canyon is a magnificent sight," agreed Ryan. "Being here in New York with all the noise and pollution, it's hard to believe that gift of nature is out there right now, evolving slowly, as it has for over seventy million years."

"I find both the urban and natural landscapes desirable; beautiful and incredible in their own ways. Just look around. We're amidst once unfathomable edifices of metal, glass, and concrete that also reach high into the sky. These majestic structures were imagined by some of the most creative architectural minds in the world and brought to life by armies of engineers and construction crews who toiled fearlessly hundreds, even thousands of feet above the ground. Like the Grand Canyon, New York is constantly changing, though at the pace of a nanosecond compared to the time it has taken for the Colorado River to carve out its present form. Look around at all these cranes," she said gesturing. "Progress in motion."

"The city that never sleeps," said Ryan.

"And neither does the global business world," said Tracy. "Cities are largely where business is transacted, where money is made and lost. And he or she who has the money has the power, so we toil most of our waking hours and invest our creative energy delivering value to our clients, to make money for our firm and ourselves."

"If I had a drink in my hand I would toast to that," said Ryan.

Tracy laughed and raised her hand to meet his in a mock toast. Their pace slowed as the sidewalk grew more congested.

"Of course, things can get complicated when we consider how money and power are used or abused and by whom," said Tracy. "From a positive perspective, whether in our own city of New York, localities around the US or the world over, we see and read about people that use their money and their power in productive and wonderful ways. Individual earnings support families, profits are used to invest in and grow businesses, employ more workers who, in turn, support their families and contribute productively to society. The payment of legally required corporate and personal taxes support the activities, principles, and ideals of our great country. Adhering to our laws and ordinances fosters healthy competition and protects the interests of our citizens. If we disagree with laws or elected officials, we have the right to make changes through our vote, by voicing our opinions and directing our money to activities aimed at driving desired changes. And of course, contributions to charitable causes bring help and hope to many."

They stopped to wait for a light.

"Then again," said Ryan, "there are those who choose to use their money and power in very dark ways or cheat the system to gain unlawful advantages. Remember the Bigsby acquisition last year?"

Tracy nodded.

"That was my first encounter with what turned out to be a serious case of malfeasance." He continued, "I'll never forget discovering those fees, in the millions, stated as payments to two consulting firms for research work, supposedly related to a sale in the prior year. I couldn't find any consulting companies with those names anywhere in the world, so I came to you for advice. You reviewed my findings and agreed that the issue called for further investigation. The forensic accountants went to work and found a trail that ended with an FCPA concern. Thankfully for our client, that division wasn't an integral part of the acquisition so cutting it from the deal worked out just fine. The life lesson for me came about six months later when I read about a few folks getting arrested and charged with crimes related to that situation. As it turned out, the executives of the parent holding company had no idea there had been questionable payoffs to foreign officials to land a big contract. Our investigation brought it to light, so they dug deeper and figured it out."

"I remember that situation vividly," said Tracy. "We all understand and accept that the calls get tougher as responsibilities grow. Also, situations have turned more complex as business has become global. It's not just US laws to consider. We must ask more questions about local ordinances and seek interpretations from legal folks. The US Foreign Corrupt Practices Act is just one of any number of laws we need to understand and be on alert for possible signs of infraction. On a personal level, I value my freedom almost more than anything in this world, which means staying on the right side of the law."

"It was tough in the moment," said Ryan. "Our client was pushing to move quickly, and no one wants to bring bad news to the boss. I weighed the facts and believed it was the right thing to do. Sure, I thought about wasted resources and the needless concern I might cause if things were above board but, in the end, the facts and my gut came to the same conclusion."

"Your analysis and instincts were spot on," said Tracy. "And as it turned out, your work and actions on that situation supported the firm's decision to promote you to the next level."

As they entered the park, the temperature dropped slightly as the trees overhead shaded the sidewalk all day. The crowd had thinned, but Tracy and Ryan, deep in conversation, hadn't noticed.

Tracy looked over at Ryan and smiled. "Your story reminds me of advice given to me by one of my early bosses. He insisted on imposing a 'twenty-four-hour rule' when he wanted time to think something over. Occasionally, it felt frustrating to wait for a decision because my tendency, like yours, is to process information quickly. But I'm a better leader for adopting his approach.

Asking more questions and thinking through certain situations can often be the better route."

"Learning and accepting that our greatest strengths also manifest as our greatest weaknesses is one of life's most important, and humbling lessons," said Ryan.

"Yes, closely related is being open-minded to learn about blind spots we all have and then changing our behavior to become more effective," added Tracy.

As they entered the expansive lawn, Tracy said, "Wow, looks like an ocean of people tonight!" They stopped to survey the terrain.

Ryan strained to see open spots. He pointed to the left toward the stage. "I see a spot over there that looks perfect for our blanket."

"I'm glad I'm with someone who can see over most of the crowd!" Tracy said as she laughed.

After spreading their blanket on the grass, they looked around to see if they recognized anyone. They settled on the blanket, satisfied that they were anonymous in a sea of strangers. Ryan dug into the basket and brought out the Syrah. He expertly uncorked the bottle and poured a glass for each of them. He then unpacked the cheese and arranged it on one of the small, white Melmac plates. He reached into the basket once more and pulled out the bunch of grapes. He pulled one off and held it near Tracy's mouth.

"Does this remind you of anywhere you've been before?" he teased.

"I'm happy to say yes, Ryan," she replied with a wistful smile. "We're in Lille on a blanket near the Deûle River." She closed her eyes, opened her mouth, and took the offered grape from his fingers, kissing them as he gently released the fruit to her waiting lips.

They sat quietly as they waited for the concert to begin. As usual, Tracy's thoughts drifted back to business and issues currently facing her firm and the financial industry at large.

Recently, a competitor had become snagged in an odd litigation and already spent huge sums of time, money and resources defending their actions on a deal that had been completed almost two years ago. The firm was being sued by their client for what they claimed to be gross incompetence in the deal valuation because the acquired company failed to generate profit expectations. The details were scarce as the case worked its way through the court system. However, the mere existence of the case had the industry abuzz as unprecedented on multiple fronts, the most concerning of which was that the client's contract included a standard arbitration clause as the vehicle to resolve any disputes. The client had argued that the investment firm was grossly incompetent and as such the contract, including arbitration clause, should be nullified. The investment bank contended that the client simply botched the integration of the acquisition. Legal briefs to abort the proceedings had already been submitted. This just added to an already complex and stressful business environment.

Somedays she felt like her *only* job was managing risk. Business leaders and workers at all levels made hundreds of daily decisions, sometimes in a split second, based on their training, education, understanding of laws, business guidelines, experiences, and judgment. In addition, organizational structure, hierarchy, past practices and perhaps most importantly, the culture of an organization were all critical factors that affected a person's judgment.

It was difficult to balance the desire to give workers the power to make decisions with the need to establish appropriate controls and checks in the business system.

The pace at which business operated was increasing. Faster, more powerful computers churned through reams of data and transmitted information at lightspeed. Global business expansion brought whole new cadres of laws or lack thereof, monetary, and political considerations and cultural differences into the picture. Behaviors that were accepted or legal in some countries were vice versa in others or perhaps gray and as such open to interpretation. The number of women in leadership roles of US companies had been growing over the past decade. This occurred not only as a result of legal rulings but seemingly also through the acceptance of executives as bottom line improvements were acknowledged as attributable to increased diversity of staff. Women were now being educated at universities at rates nearing men in many disciplines, and it seemed logical that this would support an equal opportunity to work their way up the proverbial ladders.

Somewhat alarmingly, though perhaps unsurprising, global expansion seemed to bring new barriers to women in the world business arena. One of those was the outright refusal by men in some cultures to interact with women. Closely related, and perhaps to some, a solution to that concern, was the sheer number of talented and increasingly US-educated international males available for hire in the market. Work had become more virtual and could be performed anywhere in the world. Even if these males didn't fill legislative or corporate diversity requirements, they offered the appearance of inclusivity. In reality, these hires only added to the hurdles women faced as they sought to advance their careers, especially in US multinational corporations. Women simply wanted the opportunity to be hired, judged, and promoted based on their knowledge, abilities, performance, and contributions.

Ryan turned toward Tracy as he heard her take a deep breath then let it out slowly. "You okay?" he asked.

"I'll be fine," she answered. "Just a lot of balls in the air right now, at work and at home."

The 10-piece jazz band, almost an orchestra, took to the stage and the concert began. Tracy and Ryan leaned back and relaxed under the clear sky. For the next ninety minutes, they were lost in the beautiful music.

To their delight, they were treated to an amazing fireworks display after the concert.

They decided to walk back to the apartment and, as usual, the conversation turned to business. "The biggest challenge for me as a manager now is to let my associates develop strategies and potential answers to problems rather than doing it myself," Ryan admitted.

"It's a tough transition for many leaders," said Tracy. "We tend to hire folks who are doers since they fare well in our environment, while an effective leader recognizes how much more productive a team will be if each member grows and contributes."

"I'm thankful that the firm invests heavily in leadership development training," said Ryan. "The programs I've attended have helped me build my skill set and knowledge base of effective tools and tactics. The key for me now is to step up at parsing through issues that don't seem to yield clear-cut answers even with strong cases built from facts and reams of data."

"Ryan, you're doing just fine. You're intelligent, knowledgeable, and experienced at a higher level today than yesterday *and* there will always be more to learn tomorrow.

It's important to remember what we both gleaned from sports about failure being a learning tool. The key is to analyze gaps, ask tough questions of yourself, team members, clients, peers, even superiors, and mentors, and then make changes to drive success. Ryan, you possess the valuable inner confidence to stand up to others, including me when you believe you are right. You have helped me grow and see things through your thorough analysis that I might otherwise have missed. Rare is the person who can operate from a healthy sense of self without being overtaken by ego."

Tracy continued, "With that said, sometimes, it's the ability to effectively communicate the *why behind the what* to win agreement of an idea. It's perhaps most difficult for some of the brightest people who process data so rapidly that an idea or answer can seem almost intuitive to them while someone else maybe just nods along or doesn't make the connections. It's that *how do you not see this* feeling when you know the answer, and yet depending on the situation, it may be necessary to painstakingly present the facts and your reasoning to others. This may be useful when looking for buy-in, perhaps for a process change from subordinates, or absolutely critical when you need approval from superiors or clients to go ahead with a project. Are you with me?"

Ryan was contemplative and after a few moments of silence said "Yes, I'm with you one hundred percent, Tracy. I value and appreciate your insights. I've earned and been given, an opportunity to contribute to the firm in a larger role, and I will do whatever it takes to be valuable to our clients, to secure the future of our firm and provide the lifestyle I want for myself and possibly someday my family." He stopped and looked intently at Tracy as he said those last words. Tracy held his gaze, her heart full of love and her body burning with desire. As they resumed their walk, she wondered, *Would this, could this new, yet old love last? Will Ryan remain satisfied with our arrangement or want more of me and my life than I'm presently willing to give? And will it be enough for me?*

Chapter 33

Park Helmsley, later that same evening

After they made love again, Ryan lay awake and lingered in the envelope of comfort that surrounded him. His mind drifted back to the events that led up to the first time he and Tracy made love after the fateful trip to France.

Several months had gone by, and neither of them had spoken about what happened in Lille. Ryan wanted to talk it over with Tracy, but she had tried very hard to keep it "business as usual."

He sensed that Tracy was studying him when they were together, and he had noticed a change in her demeanor around him. She smiled warmly, and her eyes sparkled with excitement. He felt her gaze trained on him after meetings. Secretly, he had hoped they would be together again. He longed for her, ached for her in the most primal way. He had wondered if he should approach her. Maybe she just needed time to end her marriage and start a new life with him. A familiar scene played out in his mind. Tracy would be in the kitchen when he walked in the door after work, maybe chopping salad and vegetables. Steaks seasoned perfectly would sit ready for him to work his magic on the grill. He visualized himself coming up behind her, holding her close, the fresh scent of her hair right at his chin level. She would turn and welcome him with a smile and a deep, long kiss. Dinner could wait. What he hungered for was Tracy. Any time, any place, and the kitchen with a fire crackling in the fireplace was as cozy a spot as one could want. He played this out in his mind many times, too many times and realized he needed to block out these thoughts or risk driving himself crazy.

He prided himself on his rational abilities, though he knew from personality profile tests and his own experiences, that his normal tendency was to go with his intuition and that his instincts were most often, correct. He had to recognize, however, that a life with Tracy might never happen. She was, after all, a married woman with two young daughters and he was around her enough to see that she doted on them. He recalled that, on occasion, her assistant would discreetly interrupt a meeting when one of her girls was seeking to talk with her. Tracy would calmly excuse herself to take the call and return, typically with a residual smile that showed her joy at talking, even briefly, with her children. He knew he would welcome Tracy and her daughters into his home, he loved her that much. *Was this just a pipe dream? Has snow ever fallen in New York City in July? Maybe not, but I felt that we had a chance. Thank goodness work was hectic and weeks flew by as I tried to follow her lead.*

Ryan's technology segment was booming with the explosion of the Internet. Early adopters were creating mega-companies on a single application, and large corporations were willing to pay unheard of and seemingly illogical valuations for fledgling startups.

A few months after the Ronone acquisition was completed, Ryan and Tracy were deep into another deal, and their client was a Swedish entity based in Varmland, just North of Stockholm. They were courting an American startup that had written valuable code related to emerging internet search engine technology. This powerful new tool used complicated algorithms to alter the visibility of an advertiser to a user. The negotiations were set to take place at a resort in the far North of Sweden, deserted at a time of year when daylight lasted less than four hours. While not ideal for the weather it offered complete secrecy. After a grueling two days, they came to terms, and the deal was done.

Dinner that evening was a chance for associates of both companies and their M&A representatives to kick back and enjoy the moment. The Swedes were consummate hosts, and song sheets were passed around encouraging the whole group to join in on traditional Swedish folk songs, like Helan Gar, as they downed their first of many shots of Aquavit.

After dinner, their hosts announced that they had a special surprise in store for the group and they were bused to a private jet.

After they boarded the plane, the CEO, Erik Karlsson, took over the intercom. He said, "We are flying north to the city of Kiruna where a caravan of trucks will take us to the town of Jukkasjarvi, about two hundred kilometers north of the Arctic Circle. Each spring for the past few years, huge ice blocks are farmed from The Torne River, stored over the summer and then hauled out in late fall to create the engineering and architectural wonder that is the ICEHOTEL."

The reaction of the folks on the plane ranged from, "Wow!" to "What the heck is the Ice Hotel?"

Erik continued, "The craftspeople that cut, form and finish the blocks are as much or more artists as they are laborers, toiling in below freezing temperatures to create this magnificent and amazingly comfortable lodging space at minus five degrees Celsius, about twenty-five degrees Fahrenheit for our American friends."

With that, the entire plane erupted in applause and chatter. They quieted after a few minutes and he continued.

"Upon our arrival, each of you will receive a special parka, gloves, socks, and boots to endure the below freezing temperatures. The hotel will give full instructions. I assure you it is quite safe and an experience you will remember forever," said Erik.

The short flight was smooth. The normally black sky was bright with millions of stars that sparkled and the northern lights flowed mysteriously in incandescent shades of green, pink and yellow.

When the plane landed, the group boarded the vehicles for the ride over the frozen tundra toward the town of Jukkasjarvi. The ICEHOTEL came into view and was a sight to behold as it glistened in the soft light.

Upon arrival, each member was outfitted with cold gear and then escorted into a bar where champagne flowed freely as they sipped from glasses made of, what else, ice. This was as surreal an experience as any of the Americans could remember and that was saying a lot since it was a well-traveled group.

At the end of the evening, Ryan and Tracy left the bar together and headed toward their rooms.

"This is incredible," said Ryan.

"It sure is," echoed Tracy. "I have no idea how one actually sleeps in this environment, but they said just nestle into the blankets, and you'll sleep like a baby."

"Here's my room," announced Tracy.

Ryan lingered as she opened her door, then she turned to him.

"Thank you, Tracy, for opening up this world to me."

Tracy looked into Ryan's eyes and in a voice just above a whisper said, "I'm thankful to you for opening up my mind to a world I didn't know existed." She removed the glove from her right hand, reached up and gently stroked his cheek. He didn't resist her touch. She hesitated, and then in that same whisper asked, "Would you like to come in?"

He nodded and followed her into her room. She closed the door behind them and turned to find Ryan's open arms awaiting her. Although they started the night in layers of clothes, each was carefully shed to make love under the warmth of the leather animal skins. As they laid together in the quiet of their icy surroundings, silent and cold as a tomb, he considered that their lives were forever changed again. Time would yield the answer to whether the changes would be for better or for worse. But right there and then, everything felt right in his world.

These thoughts comforted him tonight and he fell into a deep and restful sleep.

Chapter 34

Early the next morning at The Helmsley

Well before dawn Tracy awakened but dared not disturb Ryan, his arm draped over her side and nestled up against her back. Her mind wandered to the recent Saturday when she introduced Ryan to her daughters. It was a risky move, and she knew it. But then again, she was amazed at how well the day turned out.

It all started on a Friday afternoon when the workload at the office was light and Ryan poked his head around her partially closed office door.

"Hey Tracy, I heard it's going to be a gorgeous weekend. Are you heading up to your house in The Hamptons?"

"Hey, come in. Have a seat, Ryan. No, we're not going this weekend. Bill is out of town deep sea fishing with his buddies somewhere off the New England Coast. I'm bringing the girls to the city for the weekend. We'll probably walk or bike ride in Central Park, maybe take in a movie and eat too much pizza and ice cream! Nicole and Jean love being here. They seem to thrive on the energy that emanates from it. They enjoy riding the subway and are intrigued by the throngs of people. I'm glad they've been exposed to the diversity of our population almost since birth, so they'll grow up with all of this as normal," said Tracy as she waved her hand toward the full wall of windows in her corner office overlooking a huge swath of the bustling city below.

"That sounds like fun. I'll bet the girls are also excited to have you to themselves for the whole weekend," said Ryan.

Tracy nodded. "Yes, they are. And I'm just as excited to be with them. I've been away quite a few nights this month, but I'm lucky to have great help at home." She consciously held back saying that a big part of that help was her husband.

Ryan said, "I read that the Central Park Zoo is having a big event Saturday to celebrate the birth of two sea lions. I was thinking about going myself to check out the little guys."

"Are you going with Cathy?" Tracy asked.

"No, she's out of town with her sister, so I planned to go solo. I'd feel a lot more comfortable going with a couple kids in tow," he said almost finishing as a question.

Tracy looked at him and bit her lip as she pondered his obvious invitation to join them. "You have kid experience?"

He smiled. "You bet! I have so many nieces and nephews that being the fun Uncle Ryan is easy for me."

Tracy hesitated for a minute more as she considered what this might look like, although she was equally curious to see what it would feel like to have Ryan spend time with her and her daughters. "Uncle Ryan....Okay, I think we can make this work," Tracy decided. For a moment, they sat smiling at one another like two schoolkids.

Ryan stood. "All right. Then I guess we'll meet..." his voice trailed off.

"Let's meet at the zoo entrance at 2:00. That will give me plenty of time to bring the girls in on the train, get them settled in the apartment, and grab some lunch first."

"That sounds great. I'll see you and the girls then."

After Ryan left, Tracy turned her office chair to look out the windows. She smiled. *We're going to have so much fun together tomorrow.* She felt a pang of guilt thinking that and she pictured Bill's smiling face. She shook her head to clear the image. *It's just a day at the zoo; Ryan will be discreet; it's no big deal.* She massaged her left temple. *Oh, who am I kidding? It could be a very big deal.*

Her thoughts were interrupted by a beep on her office phone. "Tracy?" Jeremy asked.

"Yes?"

"It's your husband on the line."

Central Park Zoo

Ryan was waiting for them at the zoo entrance with two cheerful sunflowers in hand, one for each of the girls. He knelt to greet them and presented each with a flower.

The girls blushed with delight and chorused in unison, "Thank you Mr. Kupford!"

"You're welcome Nicole, Jean. You can call me Ryan. Is that okay with you Mom?" he rose looking at Tracy.

"I suppose that will be fine," said Tracy with a smile.

To be considered in such an adult way really lit them up, and they warmed to him immediately. It seemed they went out of their way to call him by name, "Oh Ryan, look at the sea lions," implored Nicole. Then little Jean chimed "Ryan, come see the monkeys playing tag in the trees."

Tracy was amazed at Ryan's ease with the girls. At work, he was intense, perhaps even a bit impatient with colleagues who didn't keep pace. Today she saw a side of Ryan that Tracy had yet to experience. It warmed her heart to see him interact so well with her daughters.

She recognized that he was, in some ways, a lot like Bill, so maybe she shouldn't be surprised at how easily he got along with them.

As they walked around the zoo, Tracy's thoughts wandered to Bill. He was everything and more a father should be to his children. He was their tennis instructor, fitness coach, chess teacher, and homework partner. He was also there to mend a skinned knee, sooth away a nightmare and listen to his children when they needed an ear, especially when Tracy was busy working.

Bill confided to Tracy that he sometimes had to dig deep inside himself to figure out how to deal with certain situations, particularly emotional matters. He also relied on Tracy to share her motherly instincts with him. He appreciated and respected Tracy's willingness to be accessible to her family.

Tracy thought back to a conversation she and Bill had last weekend as they sat on their deck at the Hampton's house, watching the girls play on their enormous personal playground. Bill complimented Tracy on how she managed to, from his perspective, seamlessly transition from being the fast-paced, rational, fact-driven executive to a caring, warm and patient mother. He admitted that early on he assumed women must simply be wired more effectively to handle this juxtaposition of responsibilities. Tracy assured him that wasn't all there was to it. She confided that it was sometimes mentally exhausting and stressful. She said she felt some level of maternal instinct in situations, but struggled greatly with the physical, mental, and emotional work required to rapidly shift gears between the duties of executive and mom. Tracy realized that there were few if any, role models for women in her situation to turn to for advice or even look to as examples. The few successful females she knew were either unmarried or married with no children. Her own mother was a stay at home mom until Tracy was in high school. Later, her mom worked in an administrative role for an insurance company, largely to save for impending college expenses, although her mom had expressed enjoyment for the work, the office friendships, and mental stimulation.

Life was quite simple in the Ward household during Tracy's growing up years. Dad was college educated but not overly career driven. He worked diligently in his local government job and devoted most of his free time to his family. His diversions were reading and "tickling the ivories." He was a gifted musician who could play multiple instruments by the time he was an adult. But he was also a role model for lifelong learning by demonstrating what could be accomplished through focus, discipline, and hours of practice. Music also provided much needed extra income in the early years of her parent's marriage as his band played mostly contemporary tunes at neighborhood weddings and parties.

Her childhood seemed like a distant memory, sometimes as if it belonged to someone else. Almost every aspect of her life was so different now. The world she, Bill and their children lived was in sharp contrast to her upbringing, especially from a financial perspective. Geographically, their home in Rye was less than twenty-five miles from the borough where she grew up, but there was absolutely no resemblance to the crowded, middle class, though neatly kept, row houses and multi-story apartments that stood block after block in her old neighborhood.

Her estate in Rye was on almost five acres of beautifully wooded property and boasted a stocked fishing pond for Bill, an in-ground pool, cabana and an outdoor kitchen space with a brick oven, full stainless-steel grill, and appliances. They had all the trappings of financial success and certainly enjoyed and appreciated their home. But living that kind of life had repercussions. Every move she made up the career ladder decreased the time she was able to spend with her family. While this was not surprising to her, reality had a way of bringing the trade-offs front and center.

Buying the house in The Hamptons was a conscious effort to force togetherness. It was Bill's idea, and initially, Tracy was averse to adding yet another layer of complexity to their lives. But he convinced her that it would be a place where they could be together as a family without the distractions of their Rye home. They opted for a cozy four bedroom cottage nestled in the trees with beachfront property. Out here, there were no nannies, house-keepers or gardeners constantly traipsing through their home. Sure, they had hired help to clean the house and keep up the beautiful flower gardens, but that work was done when they weren't around. When the Knapp family was in the house, it was family time. Board games and scary stories by the fire pit ruled the evenings, with an occasional round of Ghost in the Graveyard after dark.

Yet with all going smoothly in her idyllic life, here she was walking around the Central Park Zoo with her daughters and Ryan, not Bill. She tried to tell herself that there was no danger in introducing Ryan to the girls, that he would remain just "Ryan" to them. Or would he? As she watched him with Nicole and Jean, she envisioned him tucking the girls into bed before joining her in their bed. Her body ached with desire at the thought of what would come next. The physical attraction that drew them together in Lille, France was as strong standing here today, almost two decades later.

Recently though, Tracy's feelings had grown beyond pure physical desire. As she came to know Ryan professionally and personally, she realized that his intelligence, ambition, and drive were as intoxicating as his physical attributes. Perhaps she had been drawn to him for those qualities right from the start, although the physical connection was so strong, she just didn't see it. She realized that she eagerly looked forward to whatever project would be the next opportunity to bring the two of them together. She now craved his mind as much, maybe more than his body.

The girls were growing tired, and Tracy realized that dinner time was fast approaching.

"Is Ryan coming to dinner with us, Mommy?" asked Nicole.

"Well, I..."

Tracy was interrupted by a chorus of "Please, Mommy!" from her girls.

"If he wants to..." Tracy started to say.

Nicole and Jean each grabbed one of Ryan's hands. "Please come!" they asked sweetly.

Ryan laughed. "I would be honored to dine with you!" he said with a slight bow.

The girls shrieked with laughter.

He added, "In fact, I know of a diner not far from here that has really yummy ice cream sundaes for dessert." He looked over at Tracy, who nodded. "But you have to eat your dinner first."

The girls willingly agreed to the deal.

The day that started at the zoo ended with dinner and ice cream sundaes complete with all the trimmings.

As they left the restaurant, they were greeted by guitar music coming from a nearby street performer. "Please Mommy can we stay and listen to him play?" pleaded Nicole.

Clearly, the girls had inherited their grandfather's love of music, and both already showed promise on the piano.

"Okay, just one song," said Tracy. Tracy was amazed at the high level of talent of many of the artists that played on street corners, in the subways and around the parks and bridges. While some appeared to be earning their livelihood, others seemed to simply play for the sheer enjoyment it brought them and their audience. Perhaps this was an opportunity to express their true passion or even a way to relieve their stress. Whatever the case, it was part of New York life and in cities, towns and venues all over the world.

When the song was over, Tracy hailed a cab to take them back to the hotel.

"It was nice to meet you, Ryan," said Nicole as she stretched out her hand.

Ryan shook her hand and said, "It was nice to meet you, too, Nicole."

Little Jean gave a tug on Ryan's pants. "What about me?"

Ryan scooped her up and gave her a hug saying, "It was nice to meet you, too, Jean."

Jean's smile said it all. She then gave Ryan a kiss on the cheek.

"Time for you girls to go to sleep now," said Ryan as the cab pulled up to the curb.

"Good night, Tracy."

"Good night, Ryan."

Tracy and the girls got situated in the cab as Ryan closed the door. He waved from the sidewalk, and the girls excitedly returned the wave. As the cab pulled away, Tracy glanced back to see Ryan watching them. The cab then turned a corner, and he was gone.

Chapter 35

Later that evening, The Helmsley Hotel

The girls were exhausted from their busy day, although the sugar from their sundaes provided just enough energy to get them through bath time. Freshly washed and comfortable in their pajamas, they climbed into the king-size bed and snuggled under the feather comforter with Tracy, eager for a bedtime story. It had been Jean's turn to choose the book. She had carefully packed it in her suitcase, shielding it from her mom and sister until this very moment. Her eyes sparkled, and she had the smile of one who was bursting to tell an exciting secret. First, though, it was time for prayers.

The girls folded their hands and began saying the universal Christian children's prayer aloud, "Now I lay me down to sleep. I pray the Lord my soul to keep. And if I die before I wake, I pray the Lord my soul to take. God bless Mommy and Daddy, who is away on a trip." They continued listing family and friends and ended by thanking their mommy for a wonderful day. "And God bless Ryan," chimed Jean. "I like him."

"Me too," said Nicole. "He's really nice."

"Yes, he is," echoed Tracy. She lingered on the vision of Ryan's warm smile.

Then it was time for the unveiling of the story. Jean slowly drew the book out from under the covers to reveal, *Goodnight Moon*. "I love that story!" said Nicole approvingly.

"It's one of my favorites too," said Tracy.

Jean was clearly proud that she had chosen something everyone liked. She handed the book to Tracy.

Tracy began to read, and within minutes the girls were fast asleep, one on either side of her. She reached over and put the book on the nightstand. She settled back into her spot and stroked their hair. It was amazing how all that energy was reduced to quiet, rhythmic breathing and the angelic features of sleeping children who truly haven't a care in the world. Of course, they were young and had almost no idea how fortunate they were. These lucky little girls were safe, secure with two parents and an extended family that loved them dearly. They also possessed amazing resources to provide for them.

Being here with her little girls brought thoughts of her childhood. While the economic circumstances of her family's household were vastly different than Tracy's situation today, the love, support, and respect she received from her parents gave her everything she needed and almost everything she wanted. Sometimes, Tracy worried that Nicole and Jean, through no fault of their own, would be completely spoiled. She and Bill often talked about this topic, and it was a stress point in their relationship. Bill had a hard time saying "no" to his little girls. Occasionally, she would come home to find their latest "had to have" toy or gadget tossed carelessly into the toy bin after it lost its initial luster. She felt strongly that this could drift easily into unhealthy selfishness and cloud her children's sense of value and charity as that money could be put to better use.

Tracy imagined this would get worse as they grew, especially knowing that their circle of friends would mostly be kids just like them, wealthy and privileged. They lacked nothing and had hired help to cook their meals, clean their home and maintain the grounds. Tracy and Bill each credited some of their own drive and ambition, prized qualities for business people, to their modest upbringings. Would their children somehow inherit these characteristics, maybe acquire them through playing sports as well as striving for top grades? Or might they turn out like some of the soft, whiny people they knew who exuded a distinct air of entitlement? Some were "trust fund babies," and while they rarely made it in firms such as hers, Bill encountered them at the bank. His commercial work entailed interaction with high net worth clients and he confided to Tracy that it disgusted him to hear some of the spoiled offspring complain about restrictions their parents or other relatives set on fund withdrawals.

Personal bankers for these families, he reasoned, might be better served to hold psychology degrees as they tried to deal effectively with the emotions and occasional raw displays of wrath by parents, children and even grandchildren in tangled financial matters. In some, you could sense that the dependent had slipped into a state of gluttony as they clearly gorged themselves on not only food and drink but spent lavishly on clothes, cars, boats or other adult toys. They were loath to work at all and drifted into a state of sloth, finding no purpose in toiling for pay, volunteering or contributing to society in any meaningful way other than spending money they had no part in earning. Of course, a vibrant economy is helpful to society, and Tracy and Bill felt strongly that their wealth was being used in positive ways. Their household employees were paid fair wages, they purchased goods and services, dined out, and contributed to select charities. She supposed that like most things, the problem was in the excess.

Maybe because of her modest upbringing, greed wasn't an issue for Tracy. She felt she could live happily without the mansions and many of the material accoutrements their incomes afforded them. Likewise, jealousy seemed to have little hold on her. She was happy to see and help others succeed and didn't gauge her lifestyle or possessions against others. Granted, she was a successful high achiever and had been blessed with generally healthy, happy children, so perhaps she had not been unduly tested in this area.

Pride was a different story. Tracy knew she could be headstrong, perhaps borderline ego-driven. With this blind spot acknowledged, she tried to manage it to her advantage. She operated in a rough and tumble, male-dominated environment. To succeed, she had to present her views clearly and confidently. While she encouraged input from colleagues, she readily took responsibility to develop and execute actions. It was at some of those most challenging times that she would force herself to take a step back and honestly consider her true motives to decide what was best for the business.

Big wins could prove problematic as well. They ignited ego like fuel on a fire and unleashed a near-primal euphoria that felt almost as good as your best sex. In this hyper-competitive environment, where losers might be professionally or financially destroyed, winners were held to the absolute highest esteem and earned obscene sums of money for their achievements. Tracy dug deep into her education and religious upbringing to understand the perils this might bring if unchecked. She discovered an analogy from ancient Rome. She considered that the lavish celebrations thrown by her firm and others upon completion of important deals were akin to the public parades hosted by Roman leaders celebrating the return of victorious warriors. Like the Roman soldiers, the

264

egos of triumphant business people were prone to swell, some to the point of extreme. In Roman times, legend has it that a lowly peasant was assigned to continually whisper, "You are dust, you are dirt" into the ear of the victor parading in his chariot. This was done to remind him of his mortality and, perhaps more important- ly, his morality. Trading one's passion for glory can happen almost without notice and may lead to a dark, empty place. She embraced this wisdom as relevant today and knew that for her, the essence of reason, of truth, came from her family and her faith in Jesus.

She saw it in the innocent faces of her children, felt it in the loving arms of her husband, learned it in the example set by her parents, earned it in the trust of her closest friends, colleagues, and associates. And when you opened your heart, you might also hear it in the voice of a homeless person on the street corner, refugees fleeing persecution, the sick, disabled or disadvantaged struggling near or far. *True wisdom comes from honest, unselfish love, God's love. Too often our hearts lie still, guarded from truth, from love, by choice. Our choice.*

She felt herself adrift in that state where you know you're dreaming, but not able to fully awaken. The dream beckoned her back. She was in her pew at St. Peter's. Father Michael was reading the gospel, 1 John 3:20, "God is greater than our hearts and knows everything." She hears him explain the meaning in his homily. "Our hearts can fail us. When we feel conflicted we trust in His commandments."

Her thought stream turned to Ryan and she felt compelled to consider their relationship through a lens tinted with the morality of her Catholic faith.

Love thy neighbor as thyself, she heard herself murmur.

265

Silently she continued, Ryan is my neighbor.

A vision of her own face, somber-looking with eyes downcast appeared, reflected in a mirror and asked, "Do you love me?"

She stared at herself in silence. Her thoughts turned to times she had failed to live in the ways of the Lord and the many occasions she sorrowfully, shamefully confessed her transgressions during the sacrament of Penance and Reconciliation. Try, fail, try, fail, try... Again, Father Michael's voice filled her head, "God's love isn't something we earn. He bought it for us through His death on the cross and gifts it to us freely as His children. His *suffering* redeemed us, *freed* us to know *we are loved.*"

The face in the mirror broke into a smile, her eyes now bright and joyful.

Even in my darkest hour, through my most grievous faults, I am loved. I can love myself and others in the ways of the Lord. What path should I take?

Proverbs 3:5 filled her mind, "Trust in the Lord. Do not rely on your own understanding."

Suddenly, she felt someone lightly touch her shoulder. She opened her eyes, expecting to see Nicole or Jean. "Ms. Knapp," said a flight attendant, "I'm sorry to disturb you, but the captain has indicated we'll soon begin our descent into New York. I've brought you a warm, moist towel."

Tracy struggled to focus on the woman's kind, smiling face and to comprehend the words being spoken. She robotically took the damp towel and began to wipe her eyes to remove the crustiness that had formed while she slept. Next, she wiped her hands, then deposited the soiled towel into the open bag held by the flight attendant.

"May I offer you coffee and a light snack of fruit, yogurt, and a pastry or a baguette with meat?"

Tracy groggily nodded her head and said, "Fruit, please and cream in the coffee."

Tracy blinked at her surroundings. She was definitely not in the Helmsley with her daughters. She shifted in her seat, awakening further. Reality was slowly returning. *I'm still on the plane home from my trip to France with Ryan.* So where is Ryan? She looked around and did not see him. She thought back to the airport in France and remembered their parting in the terminal. *That's right, he was booked on a later flight.*

The flight attendant returned with her breakfast. "Here you go Ms. Knapp. Let me know if you need anything else."

Tracy rubbed her eyes again and looked out the window. The events of the past two days and distant memories of Lille floated through her mind and she felt oddly at peace with it all. She sipped her coffee and nibbled at the fresh fruit as she considered what she would do in the coming days.

Remembering the look in Ryan's eyes when they said goodbye at the Charles de Gaulle airport, Tracy knew it was her turn to be strong. She almost couldn't imagine how Ryan had kept all this inside over the past two years since he joined the firm.

It was crazy. What were the odds of singling out Ryan's resume from the dozen or so that had made it all the way to her desk as they sought a new team member? Then again, choosing Ryan might have been driven by my subconscious mind. Fate can be kind or cruel, perhaps, in this case, it's both.

The gravity of the situation was almost overwhelming. Maybe it was a defense mechanism that kicked in, but Tracy felt herself fighting the urge to laugh. *You can't make this stuff up*, she thought. Ryan Kupford was my first true love. I know that now and am forever changed by it.

The pilot announced their final descent into Liberty Airport, and the flight attendant cleared her plate. Mercifully, she left the coffee cup, and Tracy tried to sip her way back to full consciousness.

Tracy looked out the window again. The sun was making its daily trek to the west and the early evening sky was royal blue, like the famous domes of Santorini and the shade associated with Mother Mary's veil. This color always seemed to have a calming effect on Tracy, and instinctively her breathing slowed. She prayed silently that God would continue to grant her wisdom and strength to discern the path that serves His Word and radiates His love.

She watched the buildings grow larger, the streets and landscapes come into focus as the plane approached the runway. She felt the plane touch down as the back wheels contacted with the runway. The nose of the plane followed suit and the plane taxied toward their gate.

It was too soon to think far into the future, but Tracy knew she would need to prepare herself mentally and emotionally for her next interaction with Ryan.

Before that though, it was home to her family, Bill, Nicole, and Jean. She knew she would share everything with Bill. Not tonight, but soon. She would have their nanny care for the girls, and she and Bill would go to their house in The Hamptons for a weekend alone. She was sure they would both need time to let this sink in. *Hmm, she thought to herself, while we're there maybe we can think about planning a real vacation, sans kids. A night here and there is nice, but I feel like we've drifted apart.*

Chapter 36

Fontella & Scharf

Ryan's flight arrived back in the US late-morning the next day. He was tired, and a bit jet-lagged after staying up late to finish the Ronone report and sleeping fitfully on the plane. Nevertheless, he decided to make a quick stop at his apartment to shower and then head to the office. He was anxious to see Tracy, to talk with her about yesterday and, more importantly, about the future. He wanted, no needed, to know what she was thinking, how she was feeling. He arrived at the office just before the end of the lunch hour, so there were few people around. He deposited his briefcase on his desk and headed to Tracy's office without calling ahead. As he rounded the corner, he saw that she wasn't there. Perhaps she had gone to lunch, or maybe she didn't come to the office today. His heart beat faster as he began to worry that she might have become ill after yesterday's events.

He had no way of knowing that she was just returning from the noon Mass at St. Peter's Church.

He turned around quickly, intending to ask others if they had seen Tracy today. He almost knocked her over as she came around the corner toward her office.

He was more startled than she and he froze.

"Good afternoon, Ryan," she said flatly, through a strained smile. "Thank you for completing the Ronone report. I've already reviewed and submitted it to file. It was well done."

He noticed that she was avoiding eye contact with him. "Thank you, Tracy," he stammered.

They stood in awkward silence for what seemed an eternity. He had to restrain himself from reaching out to hold her in his arms, to stroke her hair and tell her how much he still loved her. He wanted to reassure her that everything would be okay, that he would figure it all out and take care of her.

He heard her take a deep breath and exhale slowly. "Thank you for being there for me yesterday. I don't know what I would have done without you." She continued to look at the floor as she spoke.

He understood then that it would be business as usual, like it was before their fateful trip. While his heart sank at this realization, he had tried to prepare himself for this possibility. He felt like he knew what he had seen in Tracy's eyes in the cottage in Lille, but he also realized that she had built a life of her own over the past seventeen years. That life didn't include him. He longed to be alone with her and to talk with her. He wanted to know her true feelings. Or did he? He was conflicted and unsure of what to say or do next. He realized she was fighting her emotions.

As tough as this was for him, he worried that it was even more difficult for Tracy because it was all new to her. He had years to process the loss of her love and move on with his life. Even the two years since he joined Fontella & Scharf and came to understand what had happened to Tracy had given him time to adjust. His heart ached, truly ached, for her. He could see the pain she was in.

She finally looked up at him and said, "Thank you again for taking the lead with Giuseppe and helping drive the Ronone deal to a successful conclusion."

"You're welcome, Tracy. Thank you for teaching me so much over the past two years and having the confidence to hand me the reins."

"The pleasure has been all mine. You're bright, talented and very well suited for this crazy business."

Ryan knew what he needed to do before he even turned to leave. He would reach out to his contacts and find a new job at a new firm. He held no animosity for Tracy. A heart full of love has no room for hate. He just knew that he couldn't, maybe shouldn't, be this close to her, for both of their sakes.

Chapter 37

Three months later. A trendy tavern in New York.

Ryan's going away party was much like any other over-the-top investment firm shindig. Too much alcohol, iced cold jumbo shrimp, raw oysters, caviar, and bite-sized chunks of the best filet along with expensive cigars to be smoked, chewed, or simply tossed to the side.

At the end of the night, it was just Tracy and Ryan seated at the bar drinking espresso and reminiscing about Ryan's time at the firm. They knew they could and likely would run across each other's path as competitors in the future. They also knew that when that happened, they would each respect the other as honest, smart, and creative. If nothing else, fun challenges could lie ahead when they spar across the table.

"To old times," Ryan said holding up his cup.

"To old times," Tracy repeated as they carefully touched their cups. "And to new adventures," she added with a smile.

He took a sip from his cup, searching her eyes for a clue about her last statement. "Anything in particular you want to share with me?" he asked.

"Remember that foundation I mentioned to you years ago?"

He is momentarily speechless, thinking to himself, 'Yes, I remember. Just like I recall almost every word you ever spoke to me.' It strikes him that this is the clearest sign yet that she remembers much more than she has ever acknowledged in the months since they returned from France. He swallows his thoughts and says out loud to Tracy, "I do remember that your intention was to form a foundation to benefit young girls, right?"

"Yes, exactly! Well, Bill and I are in the early stages of forming an organization aimed at helping pre-teen and teenage girls find and keep their voice as they navigate what are perhaps their most pivotal years. At some point my goal is to work full time with our foundation."

"Good for you Tracy! Young people need positive role models, especially professional women."

"Thank you, Ryan. It's refreshing to invest my time and creative energy into a cause that stirs my heart."

Tracy paused and reached into her purse. "I have something for you." She handed him a small, square box wrapped in shiny white paper.

"What's this?" he asked as he took the gift from Tracy.

"Just a little something for old times," she answered.

After unwrapping and opening it, he peered in to see a black velvet box. He looked at Tracy with a quizzical expression. He pulled it out and slowly opened it. Inside, nestled in the folds of satin, were two intricately painted mosaic design cufflinks, trimmed in twenty-four-carat gold. In the center of each was a delicate white lily of the valley with green petals and stem. Ryan stared at them, studying the magnificent craftsmanship. He blinked several times, struck by the intensity of his emotions. "My Lily of France," he whispered.

"Do you like them?" Tracy asked, looking concerned.

He nodded as he turned to look at her. For the longest time, their eyes were locked with no words needing to be spoken.

Ryan cleared his throat and broke the silence. "Joe," he called out and as if on cue, the bartender handed Ryan a slender oblong box, dressed in creamy white satin and finished with a shimmering gold bow.

"This is for you," Ryan said in a hushed, gravelly voice.

Tracy untied the bow, slid the wrapping off the box, and slowly opened it. As she pulled back the soft tissue, she saw the most beautiful silk scarf she had ever seen. She drew it out carefully and examined the exquisite piece of artwork. The background was sky blue with a billowy light gray cloud pattern and in the center of the scarf was a large yet delicate, sprig of white lilies of the valley with lush green petals and stems. Tracy knew it was no use to try holding back the tears welling up in her eyes. Ryan readily offered his handkerchief. Tracy breathed a heavy sigh, composed herself and said, "Thank you, Ryan, for everything. You are a good and amazing man."

Six months later

Tracy was in her office late in the evening, working on another blockbuster deal when her phone rang. It was Ryan. Six months had passed since they parted at the bar, and they hadn't talked or seen each other since. He had, however, been on her mind.

"Hi Ryan," she said with a smile.

"Hey Tracy, burning the midnight oil?"

"Yes, I am," Tracy answered. "And it's a project you would love!"

He chuckled softly and teased her by saying, "Check, and too bad I'm not there to help you because you'd be done with it by now."

"Checkmate," she responded with a full laugh.

"I also have exciting news to share with you, Tracy. Cathy and I got married two weeks ago. We jetted off to Martha's Vineyard with our immediate families for the weekend and tied the knot during an outdoor ceremony overlooking the ocean."

"Ryan, that's such wonderful news!" Tracy exclaimed. "I'm so happy for both of you."

They talked for half an hour. It was as if they'd never parted.

While they talked, Tracy had turned her chair to look out the windows and, as she often did, propped her feet up on an open file drawer. The conversation had begun to wind down, and her gaze fell on a family picture on the credenza that had been taken last fall at a favorite local pumpkin farm. The four of them were in front of a twenty-foot high pyramid of giant orange pumpkins. Behind that was a cloudless blue sky.

"It's been great talking with you, Tracy. I'm glad you're well."

"You too, Ryan. I'm also happy to hear that you're enjoying your new job *and* that we haven't had to go up against each other, yet."

"It'll happen one day. I look forward to sparring with you," he said with a laugh. "Good night, Tracy. Take care."

"Good night, Ryan. You take care, too. And congrats again on your marriage!"

Tracy fixed her gaze on the picture of her smiling family, as she remembered how much fun they had that day. She heard a click, and the phone line went dead. Her eyes drifted upward above the bright lights of the city. In a voice that was just a whisper, she breathed, "Je t'aime."

About the Author

THERESA BRISKO is a Christian wife, mother, grand-mother, and long-time metals industry executive who resides in Chesterfield, Missouri. She has often found story telling to be a compelling and enjoyable medium for learning and communicating.

In this her first novel, she has worked to craft a fantastical story of love set in real and imagined places near and far while drawing from her own experiences, emotions and faith.

Theresa credits the lingering spirit of Ernest Hemingway and a cabana near a pool in Key West as added inspiration for much of her creative work.